Weaving Through The Years

Linda Sawley

Linric Publishing

Published in July 2012 by Linric Publishing
18 Victoria Lodge
READ, Lancs
BB12 7SZ

Classification: Historical Fiction

ISBN 978–0-9557258–5-2

Cover design by Graham Nightingale

Proof reading by Edward Habiak

Digitally Printed by
Sherwood Print Finishing
Sherwood Business Centre
Sherwood Road
Daybrook
Nottingham
Notts
NG5 6AY

Dedicated to all my regular readers.
Without you, there would be no point in writing.
I am still trying very hard to get famous so that you can flog my books on eBay!

With grateful thanks to Carolyne Entwistle and Richard Bell for your good advice and help.

Other books by Linda Sawley

Non-fiction

Everyone Else's Children
(1998, autobiography)

Fiction (Adult)

A Ring in Time (2002)
The Key (2004)
Changes (2005)
The Survivor (2007)
Anna (2010)

Children's Fiction

Joshua and the Horrible History Project
(2011)

This book is a piece of pure fiction but it has been inspired by my Great Grandmother Margaret Clarkson and her brother James Sutcliffe, who in 1911, opened a weaving mill in Burnley, Lancashire. (It was not on Staples and TK Maxx car park, though!)
They did have a family vault and were members at Haggate Baptist and other Baptist Chapels in Burnley, as their faith was an integral part of who they were, as it is for me today.
But the date of Margaret and Richard Clarkson's wedding has been crossed out in the Family Bible.
I leave you to draw your own conclusions!

June 2012

Carrie Greenwood drove her old Fiesta towards the back of the car park shared by TK Maxx and Staples in Burnley town centre. She pulled up on to the drive of a Victorian detached house that was incongruously sat at the back of the car park: alone amongst the parking bays. It had a small garden surrounded by a white painted fence and was situated under the lee of the canal bank of the famous straight mile of the Leeds and Liverpool canal.

Jumping out of the car, Carrie collected a casserole dish from off the back seat and hurried into her great grandfather's house. Opening the door, she shouted her greeting, to let him know who was walking in.

'Hiya GreatGramps, meals on wheels calling,' she quipped. There was no response, but that was not unusual. Walking into the living room, Carrie put the casserole dish down and leaned over to kiss her great grandfather's head. He raised his hand in greeting, not wasting his breath by unnecessary talk.

'How are you today?' Carrie asked. Jake Greenwood waved his hand from side to side to denote that he was 'so so'.

'Not too good, then?' asked Carrie.

Jake Greenwood removed his oxygen mask. 'Had better days,' he said slowly.

'Oh, is there anything I can do?' He shook his head.

Carrie continued, 'I've brought you a casserole. Do you want me to warm some of it up now and leave the rest in the fridge for tomorrow?' This time Jake nodded. 'Won't be a sec, then,' and Carrie disappeared into the kitchen to halve the casserole and put one half in the microwave, the other in the fridge.

Going back in to the lounge whilst it was heating through, Carrie plumped up Jake's V-pillow to make him more comfortable, despite Jake tutting whilst she was doing it.

'Now GreatGramps, stop fussing. You know you'll feel better when I've finished with you.' Jake smiled. It was true. He loved his great granddaughter passionately. Carrie continued

chastising him. 'You shouldn't have smoked Capstan Full Strength for forty years and then you wouldn't have been in this state.' Jake scowled.

'No Uni?' Jake asked her, wanting to change the too familiar subject.

'No, I've finished now. Just waiting for the graduation ceremony in July. I wish you could come. I'd feel so proud if you were there. I'm so grateful that you helped me financially throughout the course. I think I'm the only student who didn't have a student loan and isn't in debt. But I'm in your debt. I can never thank you enough.'

'Rubbish. Nothing. Only one great granddaughter,' Jake said using his words conservatively.

'Well, as long as you know I'm grateful,' said Carrie, giving him a hug. Jake just nodded.

'Getting summer job again?' he asked after a while.

'No, I don't start my job at St Peter's Primary School until September, so I'm going to research the family tree. It's probably the only time I'll have chance to do something like that. I've really got into it since watching 'Who Do You Think You Are?' on TV. I love that programme. They always say that you need to ask older members of the family for any information, so can you write things down for me?'

Jake nodded. 'Family Bible, up in attics,' he gasped.

'Wow, can I get it? Where is it?'

'Second attic, in cupboard, under window.' Carrie needed no second telling. She was up the stairs in a trice and rooting around in the cupboard under the window. She soon found a large dusty tome and hurried downstairs with it.

'Is this it?' she asked excitedly.

'No,' quipped Jake, 'that's my diary, whadya think?' but Carrie was reverently handling the Bible and didn't respond to the quip.

'So is this yours, GreatGramps?'

Jake shook his head. 'No, my grandma's.'

'Wow, so that's my great great great grandma, or something like that, isn't it?' Jake nodded.

'And can I borrow it? I mean, take it home with me?' Jake nodded.

'Oh thank you GreatGramps. All I know about her is that she started the cotton mill in Burnley with her brother. She must have been an amazing woman.' Carrie put the book down and reached over to hug Jake.

'Give over girl,' he gasped, 'let a fellow . . . get his breath.'

'Sorry. I'll leave you now. You're looking tired. I'll get your lunch and then leave you in peace.' Carrie brought the lunch in on Jake's special tray and made him comfortable. 'Aunty Gillian or Aunty Elaine is coming tonight to check up on you. OK?' Jake nodded and started eating his meal, waving as Carrie rushed out of the door with the Family Bible. He let out a sigh. Much as he loved Carrie, she did tire him out at times. But then it didn't take much these days. After his meal, Jake soon dozed off in the chair.

Chapter 1

1875

The last of the mourners drifted slowly through the door, quietly closing it behind them. It had been a good funeral, and it was kind of them to come back to the house but Mary Butler was glad that they had all gone. She was bone weary. Sitting in her chair, she looked at her two fatherless children and worried for their future. What was to become of her little family she thought to herself?

'Shall I lock up, mam?' asked eleven-year-old William, 'now I'm the man of the house, sort of.' Mary bit back a tear. What a burden for an eleven-year-old.

'Yes son, that'd be grand,' Mary replied, trying to keep the sadness out of her voice. 'And where's our Grace?'

'Gone to her room, mam, said she had to sort some stuff out.'

'Shout her down, will you William, that's a good lad?'

'Aye, mam.' William went to the door of the kitchen and shouted for his sister.

Fourteen-year-old Grace soon came downstairs: her eyes red from crying. 'Did you want me, mam?'

'Yes, I thought we'd all have a brew. Will you make one for us?' Grace nodded; glad of some task to do to keep her mind occupied. Having brewed up, the family all sat down together, not speaking, but all thinking their separate thoughts. Eventually, Mary broke the silence.

'Things are going to have to change round here. I don't know how long they'll let us stay in the house, now your father's gone.'

'What do you mean?' asked William aghast. 'It's our house isn't it?'

'No,' replied his mother gently, 'it's a tied house. Tied to the job. Your father's job.'

'But where will we go? Surely they won't throw us out straightaway?' asked Grace in horror.

'I don't know right at this moment, but the Lord will provide.'

‘And what if he doesn’t?’ snapped Grace, but Mary didn’t respond immediately, simply sat slumped in her chair, by the fire. She gathered her thoughts together, and then turned to her daughter.

‘Now then, our Grace, don't be disrespectful to the Lord,’ she said. ‘I can still work and you two will have to leave school. When I was your age, I’d been working years, and there was no schooling for us in them days.’

They were fortunate, living in the village of Briercliffe; the local Baptist chapel had a day school for the children, and they were able to stay at the school far longer than many of the children down in Burnley nearby.

William and Grace looked horrified at the news. They both liked attending the school and were able students. But they knew that many of their friends had had to go and work in the mill much younger than them because of the lack of money in the family. Grace was the oldest girl in the school and often helped as a pupil teacher.

‘Couldn’t I stay on and help at the school?’ asked Grace, but Mary shook her head.

‘I’ve already asked about that, love,’ replied Mary, ‘they couldn’t pay you anything and I need you to be earning. Sorry. Is that what you would have liked to do? Be a teacher?’

‘Not really, but I do like helping the little ones. I wouldn't like to be a teacher forever. I’d get too cross with those who wouldn’t work,’ she admitted.

Mary laughed. ‘I think you are right there, Grace. You don't suffer fools gladly, do you? What would you like to do if money didn’t matter?’

Grace thought about it and said, ‘I’d like to work with figures and organising people somehow. I’m not sure how to put it into words really.’

‘Well, I can understand that, you’ve always been good at sums,’ replied her mother, ‘but I’m afraid you’re going to have to go in the mill. I can’t see any other way of us having enough money otherwise.’

‘But where will we live, mam?’ asked William in horror.

‘We’ll have to rent a tiny cottage in the village. That’s if the mill master will take all three of us on.’

‘But mam,’ interrupted Grace, ‘your chest isn’t good. Won’t the mill make it worse? Dad always said he didn’t want you going back in the mill.’

‘That’s true, but what can we do? I never expected your dad to die so young. He was such a strong fit man and yet he just succumbed to that pneumonia so quickly,’ said Mary, her eyes filling up again.

‘Ah mam, don't cry, William and me will help you, won’t we William? We’ll both go and see the foreman at the mill tomorrow instead of going to school.’

‘Thanks Grace, and you too, William. Now I think it’s time you both went to bed. We’ve a lot of sorting out to do tomorrow.’ For once, the children didn’t argue, and after kissing their mother goodnight, they went upstairs.

‘And don't forget to say your prayers,’ she shouted up after them. ‘Pray that the Lord will provide for us.’

‘Yes, mam,’ they both chorused in reply, with little conviction. Their world had come to an abrupt end and neither could know what would happen. It was sad children that tried to sleep that night.

Mary was up early next morning and had the porridge cooking when the children came downstairs. Grace had an old skirt and jumper on rather than her school clothes.

‘I’ll not wear my school clothes to go to the mill, mam. Do I look all right in this skirt and jumper?’

Mary nodded sadly, sorry that her children’s dreams had been smashed, but also grieving herself for the loss of her husband.

‘Have your porridge and then we’ll go and see the mill foreman,’ their mother replied. Following their breakfast, the trio set off further up the village to the mill. With a heavy heart, Mary led the way in to the mill yard.

‘Hello Mary,’ said the foreman, ‘what can I do for you? I was going to pop down and see you later today?’

‘Oh? What for?’ asked Mary.

'Just to see how you were doing and to say I was sorry to hear about your Jack. Sad do. He'll be greatly missed.'

Mary nodded, unable to trust herself to speak, so the foreman continued. 'We will be needing the house back, Mary. There's no rush, the end of the week will do, but we need it for the new tackler.'

Mary nodded again but Grace jumped in quickly to answer for her mother. 'Couldn't you give us a little longer? We only buried my dad yesterday!'

'Fraid not, Miss, life has to go on. The new man will be starting on Monday.'

'Well, have you any jobs then, seeing we have to get out of our house so quickly?' Grace asked rudely.

'I could take the young ones on, but I've no job for you, Mary. It's well known that you've a weak chest. Your lungs would never stand it all day in the weaving sheds.'

'But the children won't earn enough for us to be able to rent anywhere else,' gasped Mary, 'what will we do?'

'Fraid that's not my problem, Mary. How old are the children?'

'I'm fourteen and our William's eleven,' replied Grace, 'and we can both read and write.'

'Reading and writing won't be much use to you in the mill. Most of the kids their age have been in the mill for years. Don't know why you let them stay on at school so long, Mary.'

'Because Jack and I wanted them to have a better start in life; didn't want them to be forced to go in to the mill,' said Mary proudly.

'Didn't get you anywhere, though, did it?' answered the foreman unkindly.

Mary bridled. 'Can you give them a job or not?'

'All right,' replied the foreman, 'but I don't want them giving themselves airs and graces because they've been to school longer than the others.'

'We won't,' replied Grace coldly, 'we'll work hard, like our dad always did.'

'That's all right then. Start on Monday. Three shillings for the girl and two shillings for the boy.'

Mary quietly thanked the man; it didn't do to antagonise the man who had the only chance of giving work in the village.
'They'll be there on Monday. Six o'clock?'
'Yes,' said the foreman, as he turned away.
'Come on mam, let's get home, away from that horrible man.'
'Nay lass, we need to see if we can find some lodgings first. We'll go to Mr Crowther's. He'll know if there's any houses to rent.' The three trudged slowly back down the hill, until they came to a large house, set back off the road. Mary knocked on the door. The door opened and an elderly servant asked them their business.
'Does Mr Crowther have any houses to rent?' asked Mary.
'I'll find out for you. Wait there.' The servant left them standing at the closed door for several minutes. Eventually she came back. 'There's a two up two down on Jubilee Street and a three bed-roomed on George Street.'
'How much?' asked Mary.
'Two bed-roomed is three and ten pence and three bed-roomed is four and tuppence a week in advance.'
'Thank you,' said Mary sadly, as she turned to walk away.
'Well, do you want one or not?' asked the servant.
'We can't afford them. We've no wage-earner. Thank you for your time. Come on you two,' she said to the children. On arriving home, the three of them sat glumly silent.
'Now what we going to do?' asked Grace eventually.
'We'll have to see if anybody has rooms to rent. We can't afford a full house. We might have to share a bedroom,' Mary replied. There was a stony silence. Both children had been used to having their own bedroom; the tackler's house being a three bed-roomed one.
'I'll go round and ask in the village,' said William, wanting to get away from the gloomy atmosphere, and ran out of the door before they could stop him.
'Well, it looks like the Lord isn't going to provide for us then, Mam,' said Grace.
'The Lord looks after those who help themselves and speaking like that won't help anything,' retorted Mary sharply.

Well I'm going upstairs,' replied Grace and left Mary to her own thoughts. When William came home, he'd only found one house that was prepared to take them in. It was on the street next to the mill and they could have one room for two and six a week, with a share of the kitchen, by arrangement.

'Good,' said Mary trying to be positive, 'where was it?'

'It was Mrs Shapcott, from chapel,' replied William.

'She's a goodly soul, is Mrs Shapcott. We'll be better off there than any of Mr Crowther's houses. And there'll be enough money left to buy food, so that can't be bad,' said Mary, trying to encourage the children. The children said nothing, but Mary could tell by their faces that they were not impressed at only having one room to share, however kindly Mrs Shapcott was. After packing the children off to bed, Mary sat for a long time in the dark, worried about the future, especially for her children.

A knock on the door wakened her out of her reverie, and straightening her hair, she hurried to the door. It was Mr Ormerod, one of the elders at the chapel; a tall elderly man with greying hair. He was a solicitor who had a practice in nearby Burnley.

'Come in, Mr Ormerod. How are you?'

'More importantly, how are you, Mary?'

'Not good, if I'm honest. But what can you expect?'

'I've heard from the minister that you have to leave this house by the end of the week. Have you found anywhere to stay yet?'

'Not really, I believe Mrs Shapcott from chapel could put us up, but I haven't been to see her about it. I can't seem to get myself going at the moment. Although I've got the children jobs at the mill. They wouldn't take me because of my weak chest.'

'I've felt so burdened by your predicament since Jack died, but the mill-owner wouldn't help when I went to see him. He wouldn't let you stay in the cottage.' Mary stood in silence as the realisation of what Mr Ormerod had just said sunk in. He had actually been to see the mill-owner on her behalf without saying anything to her. Not that he got anywhere with him though, miserable beggar. Still, it was typical of Mr Ormerod: quietly helping others without saying a word. He was a true gentleman and certainly lived up to his Christian faith, thought Mary. But being a quiet soul by nature, unlike Grace, she simply murmured her thanks.

'Well, I've got a proposition for you. I'm not sure what you'll think about it but I don't need an answer tonight; just think about it. Do you know Mr Haynes at Hillview House, down Lane Bottoms?'

'Not personally. I know who he is. Hasn't he got a shop in Burnley centre?'

'Yes, he has an ironmongers. He goes to St Peter's church in Burnley too. That's why you'll not really know him. We all know each other at chapel, don't we?' he said smiling. Mary nodded. 'Well, his housekeeper is leaving and he needs a live-in housekeeper. It'll be just light cleaning and preparing meals. He has a woman from Lane Bottoms to do his heavy cleaning work. Being a bachelor, he just needs looking after.'

'But what about the children? I can't leave them anywhere, not just after what's happened to their dad.'

'I hope you won't be offended, but I've taken the liberty of telling him about you and your circumstances, and he's willing to take you and the children if it helps. Don't give me an answer now. Think about it overnight and I'll call round tomorrow, on my way home from the office. I'll say goodnight then Mary. See you tomorrow.'

Mary saw him out and then collapsed into her chair by the sinking fire. What a turn up for the books! Wait 'till she told Grace about this. This would show her. The Lord did provide after all.

Chapter Two

Mary woke with a sense of purpose that she hadn't had since her husband had become ill. Once she had got the children off to school, she went through the house, cleaning and polishing it, ready for the next occupants. There was no need to think long and hard about the job offer; it was an answer to prayer, and would be much better than living in rooms in another woman's house, however kindly she might be.

Gathering her husband's clothes into a sack, she took them up to the chapel. They had a room where old clothes were kept, so that anyone in need could help themselves, or give a few pennies, if they could afford it. Mary breathed in the lingering scent of her husband on his clothes for one last time, and then sadly left them and walked away quickly.

Deciding she had better go and see Mrs Shapcott and explain what had happened, Mary spent an hour with the lovely lady before going home again. The day passed quickly and Mary was excited when Mr Ormerod knocked on the door.

'Good evening Mary. How are you? Have you thought about my proposition?'

'Yes, and I'd love to take the position, please.'

'Ha ha, I thought you might. Can you go to Hillview House now? Mr Haynes is at home and will see you tonight.'

'Certainly, I'll go right away. I'll just get the children, they're playing out. Thank you so much Mr Ormerod, it was so kind of you to think of me.'

'Think nothing of it. Mr Haynes was telling me about his dilemma in the café at lunchtime on the day I heard about your Jack. It took me a day or two to realise that it would be a good job for you. Especially as you're in a tied cottage. Let me know how you get on. I'm sure you will like Mr Haynes.'

'Thank you, I'm sure I will.' As Mr Ormerod left, Mary shouted for the children, telling them to get their hands and faces washed, hair combed and best coats on. Quick.

The children moaned until they saw the look on their mother's face and did her bidding. It was only as they walked up the hill, then back down the next hill towards Hillview House that she told them what was happening. The children were full of questions. 'Will we live there?' 'What's Mr Haynes like?' 'Can we stay at school?' 'Can we have a dog?' The last question being from William.

'Shush! I haven't got the job yet,' said Mary, 'he might not like me. Look, we're here now.' Mary told the children to stay by the gates and wait for her coming out. 'Now behave yourself and don't speak unless you're spoken to. Understand?'

'Yes, mam,' replied the children dutifully for once. The house was tucked away from the main road, so Mary reached up and opened the large iron gates that were all that showed of the house from the main road. As she walked up the long curving drive, her steps slowed as she admired the large banks of rhododendrons on either side of the drive. They were fully in bloom and a riot of colour. Going round the last corner, Mary gasped as the house came into view. She had never been so near it before, having seen only the roof and chimney from the upstairs windows of the chapel. The house was built in the local stone and the drive widened out into a large circle at the front door.

Mary stopped and gazed up at the house. There was a fine large porch that would keep the guests dry as they were handed from their carriages. There were two large bay windows either side of the enormous oak door, with smaller windows alongside them. Above these four windows were five more, one tall narrow one directly over the door. This window flamed with light as the evening sun caught the coloured glass in it. Above the five windows were another row of five smaller windows, under the eaves of the house. Mary stared in amazement, but was quickly brought to her senses when the front door started to open.

'Hello, you must be Mary Butler. Do come in,' boomed a deep resonant voice. 'Arthur Ormerod said you were coming tonight.' He led the way into a large hallway that was as big as Mary's house. Mary looked around her eagerly. At the far side of the hall was a large staircase, which divided into two, halfway up. Above the divide was another coloured glass window, which mirrored the one at the front of the house. Mr Haynes was leading her into the front room. Front room? thought Mary, and there was me, planning to go in the back door. Mr Haynes motioned her to sit down in a deep armchair, whilst he went over to the enormous marble fireplace and grasped a velvet pull chord. After a few minutes a very heavily pregnant young woman walked slowly into the room.

'Ah Annie, could you get us a cup of tea, please?' The young woman stared at Mary, but bobbed politely and said 'Yessir' to Mr Haynes, lumbering slowly out of the room again. Mary was embarrassed at putting the young lady to any trouble, but Mr Haynes brushed her fears aside.

'Annie'll be so glad to see you. She was worried that I wouldn't be fixed up before the baby came. She was newly widowed when she came to work for me and didn't know that she was expecting the baby, but she is going to live with her parents over Trawden way as soon as possible.'

Slightly relieved, Mary then felt sorry for the young woman who appeared to be in a worse state than Mary was herself. Mr Haynes started telling Mary about the duties that she would undertake as housekeeper and explained that outside help came in to do the heavy cleaning. Mary was amazed that her duties would be only to make meals, oversee the outside help and assist where necessary, ensuring the smooth running of the house.

'When do you think you could start?' asked Mr Haynes earnestly, 'that is if you don't think the position will be too onerous for you.' Mary gazed at her benefactor. She didn't know what onerous meant but she said that she could start immediately. Just then, Annie re-entered the room and Mr Haynes told her that Mary had accepted the job. Annie beamed at Mary as she handed her a cup of tea in delicate china.

'Begging yer pardon, missus, I'm ever so grateful ter yer fer coming. I can't wait ter go ter mi home town an' mi family. I only moved o'er 'ere wi' mi husband.' She patted her large tummy, "I don't think this 'un is goin' ter wait much longer, either.' Mary wished her God speed and a safe delivery as she left the room.

'Now back to business,' said Mr Haynes as Annie left the room. 'I believe that you have two children, do tell me about them.'

Mary gulped. 'Well, there's our Grace, she's fourteen and our William is eleven.'

'William? Same name as me,' Mr Haynes interrupted. 'Sorry, do go on, that was rude of me to interrupt.'

'That's all right. They both go to the chapel school and are doing right well with their lessons, especially our Grace, a real head for sums, she has. Wasted in a girl, really. If she'd been a lad she could've got somewhere. Now our William, he's a right softie for a lad. He's always bringing home birds what've been hurt and making them better. He's not soft, mind, he can fight with the best of them, but usually he's fighting 'cos some kid has got picked on by the bigger children. Always sticking up for the little ones, he is. Eh, I'm right sorry. Here's me gabbling on like I don't know what. What ever must you be thinking about me?'

Mr Haynes smiled and said, 'That's all right, Mary, what you are telling me is very interesting and useful. I'll look forward to meeting them.'

Mary thanked him and assured him that the children would be well behaved when they came to live in the house.

'Oh I know that,' said Mr Haynes. Mary looked mystified.

'I asked Mr Ormerod about them. I must admit, I was a little wary of taking them in but he assured me that they were well behaved. Now, from what you've told me I am looking forward to meeting them. When can you start?'

'Well,' pondered Mary, 'the mill owner wants me out of the house as quick as I can.'

'Why not move in straight away then,' said Mr Haynes. 'For the next week, you could get Annie to show you the ropes, and then she could leave. What do you think to that?'

Mary shyly thanked him and agreed with the plan. 'I'll get Jed from the chapel to give me a hand to flit tomorrow,' she added. Just as Mary was getting up to leave, Annie knocked on the door and announced that Mr. James had just arrived, and was fastening his horse up in the stable. Mr Haynes' face lit up with pleasure as he explained that this was his nephew. His brother-in-law Matthew had died from a seizure and James lived with his widowed mother Jenny, in Briercliffe. He ran the family food store belonging to his father's family, which was near to Mr Haynes' shop in Burnley centre.

'Stay and meet my nephew,' suggested Mr Haynes.

'Well, I don't rightly know,' started Mary, but she was too late. The door flew open and a lively young man bounded into the room.

'Hello uncle,' he bellowed, 'and who's this?' he said, looking at Mary.

'James. Meet my new housekeeper, Mrs Mary Butler.'

'Pleased to meet you, Sir,' stuttered Mary, standing up.

'And I'm very pleased to meet you, too, Mrs Butler. My uncle is in need of someone to look after him. I hope you'll be very happy here.'

'Thank you, Sir,' replied Mary curtsying.

'And we'll have none of that curtsying here, Mrs Butler,' replied Mr Haynes, 'We're not royalty, you know.' Seeing that Mary was looking nonplussed, Mr Haynes suggested that she should go home. 'I'll look forward to you arriving tomorrow,' he added. Mary left the room and let herself out. She almost skipped down the drive back to the gates where the children were.

'Mam, mam, a posh bloke came past and waved at us from his horse, but we didn't speak to him, like you said,' burst out William.

'Oh, that's Mr Haynes' nephew, you could've spoken to him. I hope you weren't rude? I don't want you starting us off on a bad note.'

'No mam, we waved and smiled back,' replied William.

'How did you get on, mam?' asked Grace.

'I got the position. I start tomorrow.'

'Tomorrow?' asked Grace, 'that's quick.'

'I'm going now so that the young lass who's there can show me the ropes. She wants to leave as soon as possible. But I'm sleeping there as well, so I can give this cottage back to the mill.'

'What about us?' shrieked William. 'Where will we go?'

'You are coming with me, you daft lummock.'

'When are we moving then, mam?' asked Grace.

'Tomorrow morning, if I can get Jed Hardcastle to move me.'

'Have you asked him, mam?' asked William.

'Well, not exactly,' she replied, 'it's all been a bit of a rush, really.'

'I'll nip down now and ask him, shall I?' asked William.

'Oh yes, that's a good idea, thanks. What would I do without you? You've an old head on young shoulders, that you have.'

'And I'll call at Betty's corner shop to get some boxes to put our belongings in as well, shall I?' asked Grace.

'Oh yes, we'll be needing some, won't we?' replied her mother.

William and Grace ran on ahead to do the errands and Grace soon came back with eight large boxes, and William returned to say that Mr Hardcastle was available with his cart tomorrow morning.

'You two get to bed and I'll start the packing now.'

'No mum, we'll take a box each and pack some stuff tonight, that way we'll have less to pack tomorrow.'

'Right lass. Good idea. What time's Jed coming then?'

'About eleven.'

'Grand. We should be ready by then.'

'I'll not go to school, I'll stay and help you,' offered Grace, 'after all, I won't be going for much longer, and so a day off won't harm.'

'You're a born organiser, that you are,' beamed Mary proudly. 'Now off you go and start packing.' The two children went upstairs into their tiny bedrooms and Grace made sure that William kept to the task in hand rather than playing with his toys.

Their few belongings were soon packed and Grace went downstairs to tell her mam where they were up to. She found her mother sat with a teapot in her hands, quietly weeping.

'Mam, what's the matter?' asked Grace gently.

'I was just thinking about things,' she replied, whilst wiping her tears on her sleeve.

'Just thinking what things?'

'About when we got wed and came to this house. This teapot was the first thing your dad bought me.'

'Oh mam,' said Grace whilst hugging her, 'you'll be all right up at Mr Haynes'. It's a new start for all of us.'

'Yes, I suppose so. But it's hard leaving this house, all the same.'

'I know mam, but it'll be better than worrying about living in one room with hardly any money.'

'Aye, you're right, Grace. What am I thinking about? You get to bed now and I'll get on with packing.' Grace waited until she saw that her mother had recovered and had actually started to pack before she went upstairs to bed. Grace knew that she would have to be very strong to help her mother make this move to a new job. Even though her mother hadn't mentioned what would happen to her and William when they lived at the big house, Grace quietly decided that she would still go to work at the mill. It was time to show that she was grown up and could help her mother. It was time to show she was a young woman and not a baby anymore.

With quiet resolve, but hope for the future, Grace got into bed, and after saying her prayers, blew the candle out, and was soon asleep.

Chapter 3

Next morning, the house was astir early. Even William wanted to do his bit to help with the move. All the boxes were piled at the front door ready for Jed arriving with his cart. Mary slipped out to see the mill foreman to ask if they wanted to buy her few bits of furniture that she wouldn't need at Hillview House. After a heated argument, Mary got a decent price for her belongings, helped by the fact that the next tackler was a bachelor who had no furniture whatsoever.

As soon as Jed arrived, the cart was quickly loaded and they set off slowly up the hill, then more quickly down the hill to Hillview House.

'My, you've landed yourself all right, Mary,' laughed Jed as they walked up the drive to the house.

'We certainly have. God is very good to us,' replied Mary.

'Shall I go round to the back?' asked Jed. Mary deliberated. She would expect to go round the back of a big house, but she had gone in the front door yesterday. But before she could decide, Annie opened the door, with a beaming smile on her face.

'Welcome, Mrs Butler. I'm right glad ter see thee. Come on in. I'll tek yer things and show yer to yer rooms.'

'No you won't,' said Jed asserting himself, 'not in your condition, if you forgive me for mentioning it.' Poor Jed blushed at mentioning such indelicacies.

'That's all right Mister, come on in. I'll be glad of help. And you can't help missing my condition after all,' she replied laughing, placing her hand lovingly over her large bump.

Jed went back to unload the cart and avoided Annie after that. He took the boxes up the wide staircase, past the first floor, and up the smaller staircase on to the second floor where the family were to sleep.

'There are five bedrooms up here,' said Annie. 'I've got this first un but yer can take yer pick of the others. And the room at the end is a water closet. Saves going out to the privy doesn't it?' she laughed. Grace and William looked stunned. They'd never been in a house with an inside water closet before.

Annie opened the second bedroom and suggested that Mary have this one. The room was far larger than Mary's living room at home. It had a comfortable looking double bed, with a clean cotton bedspread on it. There was a large mirror on the wall and a painting of a woodland scene on the other wall. Besides a wardrobe, there was a small chest of drawers, with a water jug and stand upon it. The window was large and had pretty flowered curtains.

'This is lovely,' said Mary, 'it doesn't look like a bachelor's home.'

'No,' replied Annie, 'that's his sister's influence. She only died two years ago did Miss Hilda. She liked nice things. I don't think Mr Haynes bothers really. As long as he gets his food on time.'

'What's he like to work for?' asked Mary.

'Grand. If it wasn't for my condition, I would've stayed, but I need t' be back with mi family now. I'm so grateful to yer fer coming so quick.'

'Shall we see the children's bedroom?' asked Mary.

'Of course, we can chat about th' job all night. I've already made a casserole fer the tea, so there's nobbut much ter do tonight any road.'

They walked into the next bedroom, which was pretty similar to the other one.

'I thought this could be the young lady's room,' suggested Annie. Grace swelled with pride to be called a young lady and looked round the room eagerly. It was just as big as her mother's room, but had only a single bed. There was a large wardrobe and a chest of drawers, with a similar mirror and picture on the walls. William had already gone to search the next room and he was equally pleased to have his own room: a mirror image of Grace's. Annie went back downstairs to make everyone a cup of tea, whilst the family put their belongings away. Meeting back in the kitchen, they all had a drink, then Annie said she would show them all round the house, so that they could get their bearings.

Downstairs, there were three large reception rooms and a dining room at the front of the house, with a study, kitchen, larder and pantry at the back of the house. Everything was clean as a new pin and had the latest modern appliances in the kitchen: even running water and a heater to give hot water. The rest of the rooms were beautifully and expensively furnished. Grace secretly admired them although Mary was actually overawed by the front rooms.

'Why don't the childer go out ter explore th' garden?' suggested Annie.

'Good idea,' said Mary, but Grace objected.

'I need to go into the school and tell them I won't be coming back.'

'There's no rush, Grace. Things might change now we're living here. Perhaps we can afford for you to stay on at school a little longer.'

'I don't want to, mam; I want to go out to work. I want to make my own way in the world now. I'm almost fifteen don't forget. I'm not a baby like William.'

'Here, I'm not a baby,' cried William.

'No, you're not,' replied Mary, trying to keep the peace. 'You go and explore and tell us about the garden and I'll sort Grace out.'

'I don't need sorting out,' declared Grace crossly. 'I'm going down to the school, whether you like it or not,' and stalked towards the door.

'Less of your cheek, little madam. You're not too old for a slap. Who do you think you are talking to?' replied Mary. Grace hung her head in shame.

'Sorry mam. Didn't mean to be rude. But I need to go and sort myself out. I won't be long,' and off she went.

Mary and Annie just looked at each other then laughed.

'I can see yer going to have fun with that 'un,' giggled Annie.

'Oh, she's a good girl really. She's a lot like her dad. Flares up quick but soon calms down afterwards and is all apologies. And she was a proper daddy's girl. Not that my Jack didn't love William as well. He did. But girls and their dads; there's something special, isn't there?'

Annie nodded, but Mary realised that tears were brimming at her lids.

'Eh, I'm sorry love,' said Mary, 'I weren't thinking. You've lost your child's father, like my children have lost theirs.'

'At least your husband saw 'is children. Mine won't, but I'm lucky, I've gorra special dad myself and he'll more than make up for the little 'un not 'aving a father.'

'Are you going to live with your parents?'

'Yes,' said Annie, 'I'm the youngest in the family so all t'others have left home now. I'll be all right. Better than some. If it hadn't bin fer my parents, it would've bin workhouse fer me. Here, now let's stop all this maudlin talk. Let me show yer the bedrooms.'

The two women went back up the stairs and Mary was amazed at the luxury of the bedrooms on the first floor. The first one they went in was an obviously masculine room, with solid furniture, dark coloured drapes, leather picture frames and leather covered toiletries set on the square unfussy dressing table.

The next bedroom was a complete contrast. It was chintzy, feminine and frills everywhere, with lots of small cushions piled on to the bed. A faint perfume of lavender hung in the air.

'This was Miss Hilda's room,' said Annie.

'I thought as much,' replied Mary. The other two large bedrooms were all as sumptuously dressed, but with less character than the first two. In the last bedroom, it was set up as a child's room, with lots of expensive toys scattered around.

'Has there been a child living here?' asked Mary, quite surprised.

'No,' replied Annie, 'it's Mr James' room. He used ter like staying here wi' his aunt and uncle when he were a little boy. But d'you know? He still stays in this room if he sleeps now, even though he's grown up. Sez it's got happy memories.'

The final room on the first floor was a bathing room. Mary was open-mouthed as she glanced round this room. She'd never seen anything like it. There was a large bath enclosed by a wooden hood, with shiny taps, a toilet closet, and a large sink.

'I've sometimes used this when I've got caught short,' said Annie giggling, 'y'know what it's like when yer expecting? Comes when it wants. But only when Mr Haynes were out, mind. I wouldn't have dared when he were in.'

The two women left the room and went downstairs and Annie told Mary about the routine of the house and the sort of meals that Mr Haynes liked to be served. Mrs Croft, the cleaner would be in next morning so Mary would learn more about the housework routine. Mary made notes of all that Annie was telling her. She was happy that the work wasn't too much for her, and she could be happy here. And bedsides all her food and lodging, she was going to get a wage. Yes, God was good to her.

* * * * *

Grace stomped all the way back up the hill, then down the hill to the school. She was still in a bad mood. Why did her father have to die? Why did she have to have change in her life? Why did she have to give up school? It wasn't fair. But then she stopped suddenly. She didn't have to give up school. Her mam said that she could carry on if she wanted now that there were living in Mr Haynes' house.

Sitting on a bench, Grace thought long and hard about her life. No, she wanted to move on. To be honest, she was getting bored at the school now anyway. If she went in to the mill, she would get to be treated like an adult, and make some money for herself. She could even buy some new clothes, instead of hand-me-downs like she often had to wear. With new resolve, Grace got up and went to the school, which was just below the brow of the hill; the chapel standing as a stark outline on the top of the hill.

Going in to the school, Grace swallowed and knocked on the classroom door before going in. Forty pairs of eyes turned to look up at her briefly, then back down to their slates.

'Good Morning Mr Hilton. I've come to tell you that I won't be returning to school anymore. I'm going to work in the mill. I start on Monday, but my brother will be continuing for the time being.'

'Well, I'm sorry to hear that, Grace, but I understand that because of your sad circumstances, things will have to change. I was sorry to hear about your father.'

'Thank you, and now I must go,' replied Grace with as much dignity as she could muster, as tears were threatening to destroy her new-found maturity. Running out of the schoolroom, Grace rubbed her face with her none too clean handkerchief. She hurried out of the playground and then walked more slowly towards the mill.

On arriving at the mill, she looked for the foreman and explained that only herself would be coming to work on Monday, as her brother was staying at school.

'That's all right, lass. I heard about your mother's good fortune. It solves more than one problem, doesn't it, her getting that new job?'

'Yes, it does,' replied Grace primly. 'We are very grateful.'

'Right then, I'll see you at six o'clock sharp on Monday. We don't stand any lateness here, Grace,' he said sternly. Grace nodded and hurried out of the mill yard. As she walked back to Hillview House, Grace felt a calmness about her life. This was the start of her adult life. She couldn't wait.

Early July 2012

Jake sat in his chair, glad that he'd made an important decision. The solicitor had just left, but he wouldn't tell the family about it yet. Let them find out after he'd gone; that was the best way, and then there could be no arguments. He smiled quietly to himself as he thought of the ructions that might happen after his funeral, but he didn't care. He was doing what he wanted to do, like he'd done all his life. It was just his body was letting him down now and he was stuck in this dratted chair. But never mind; it won't be for much longer now. Surely this old body won't hold out for much longer?

Reaching for the remote control, Jake flipped through the channels of daytime TV but wasn't too impressed at what he found. All repeats. What a waste of money. Might as well have a sleep, he thought drowsily but he was barely asleep before a noise wakened him.

'Hiya GreatGramps. How are you?'

'Okay,' he nodded, grinning at Carrie.

'I've brought you the photos from my Graduation Ceremony. Look, here's one of me and mum and Granny Watson. And one of Marc and me, oh and this is the three girls I shared the house with. That's Eleanor, that's Catriona and that's Amanda,' she said pointing at each friend in turn.

Jake looked at the photos and smiled at each one.

'I had them printed from my camera for you. I know it's hard for you to see the photos on my phone or camera. This set of photos is for you.

'Thanks. Proud.'

'Thanks GreatGramps. I'm quite proud of myself. When I was messing around in school in Year 10, I never thought I'd become a teacher, did you?'

Jake shook his head. 'Dad proud.'

'Yes, he would have been. It's funny but I missed him on the Graduation Day, even though he never knew that I'd got in at university. Didn't even know I'd got any GCSE's even.'

'Bad when grandson dies before you. Should've been me.'

'No GreatGramps, don't talk like that,' cried Carrie, 'where would I be without you? You've helped me so much.' She started to hug him but it provoked one of his coughing fits, so she went and got him a drink of water instead.

When Jake had calmed down and got his breath back, Jake asked if there was anything else new.

'Well, I've decided to get my own place and leave home,' said Carrie tentatively.

'Come and live here with me,' said Jake.

'I'd love to but er, well, er, . .' Carrie looked a little uneasy, 'I was going to move in with Marc,' she said, blushing furiously at the same time.

'That's OK, he come too.'

'Really? You wouldn't mind? I thought you'd object to me living in sin as you call it.'

'Like Marc. Nice man. Look after you.'

'Are you sure you don't mind? That would be great actually, 'cos it's so near St Peter's school. I wouldn't need to get up 'til half eight every morning!' she laughed.

'Happy. Plenty room. Have someone around.'

'Great. I'll text Marc now and see what he thinks.' Carrie flipped her phone out and quickly sent a message to Marc. The reply came back just as quickly. 'He'd love to come and live here with you, GreatGramps. Thanks. Now about our rent, we'll have to sort out a fair price to give you.'

'No rent. Just come.'

'I don't think Marc will like that.'

'Tough. My house. I say what goes.'

'Well thanks anyway. I'll not hug you again – don't want to start you coughing! But we're very grateful.'

'How you getting on . . . family tree?'

'Great. Didn't Grace have a lot of children?'

'Yes, but didn't all survive.'

'I know, it was so sad in those days. But I've noticed that the front page has been defaced. The actual year of her wedding has been scratched out – you can't read it. I wonder how that happened?'

Jake said nothing, but just shrugged his shoulders.

'Can we decorate our bedroom how we like it GreatGramps? We can share a bedroom, can't we?'

Jake chuckled. 'Isn't that point of moving in together?'

Carrie blushed, 'Yes, but I didn't want to upset you.'

'You can have other sitting room across hall. Make it yours.'

'But we'd sit with you most of the time.'

'Get too tired. Need quiet too.'

All right, if you're sure? Now I think I'll go down to B & Q and get some colour swatches. Are you bothered which room we use?'

'No, take pick. Plenty choice.'

'Right, I'll leave you in peace. Bye GreatGramps, love you.'

Jake nodded as she left, thankful that he could concentrate on his nap in peace. A good days work, all in all, he thought. Sorted my will out and told Carrie and Marc to come and live with me. Tomorrow, I must start writing down as much of the family history as I can remember, but not today, too tired. Yes, a good days work, he thought as he drifted off.

Chapter 4

1879

Grace walked slowly upwards from the mill, glad to be out in the fresh air again. She took deep breaths as she walked up the hill, glorying in the view from the top, down in to Nelson on one side and over to Worsthorne on the other. Eventually arriving at Hillview House, she slipped up the stairs to her room and then went to get some water to have a good wash. She always liked to strip off after a day's shift, as if she could wash the cotton dust from her.

Grace remembered her first morning. Her mother had found her some of her own old clothes from when she'd been a weaver and with a little alteration, they were a perfect fit and suitable for the job that she was to do. Fortunately Mary and Grace were the same slim build, and of similar medium height.

Mary had bought her some almost new clogs from the cobblers – the sort that every weaver wore in the shed. Grace already had a scarf, so she tied her fair hair up in a twist and put the scarf on. Arriving promptly before six o'clock, she'd been taken straight into the weaving shed by the foreman.

'You'll be working alongside Martha this week, to learn the ropes, before you get your own looms.'

Grace nodded in reply: her lungs trying to get used to the white mist that was swirling about everywhere in the mill making her cough. 'Hope you're not going to have a weak chest like your mother,' he grunted. Grace didn't bother to reply, but continued following him deeper into the mill. Grace thought that she was used to the mill environment, as she had often taken her dad's bait to the mill at breakfast time. Although she had never gone right inside before, the noise had been obvious in the entrance where she had waited for her dad. But now it was deafening. The noise seemed to overtake her mind and thoughts and reverberate through her chest. Could she stand this noise and white mist all day long? Grace thought to herself. But it was too late. She'd burned her bridges. Her mam said she could have stayed on at school for longer, but she had decided to be stubborn and make her own decision.

After a few minutes walk, the foreman stopped abruptly.

'Martha, this is Grace Butler. Jack Butler's lass,' shouted the foreman. 'She's a bit old to be starting, been wasting time at school, so she'd better pick it up quick or else she'll be out. Can't afford timewasters here.' With that, he marched off back the way they had come. Grace stood staring at Martha, wondering what to say, but Martha spoke anyway.

'Take no notice of yon foreman, he's all mouth,' Martha said kindly, and Grace smiled politely. She hadn't caught a word Martha had said, as she was very soft spoken.

'I'm sorry, I didn't hear what you said,' replied Grace.

'That's all right lass. We mostly lip-read in this weaving shed. You can't hear yourself think for all the racket. You'll pick it up quickly. Just watch my lips when I speak.'

Grace smiled politely again, unsure of about half of the conversation.

'Now watch me. I've got eight looms to look after. So you're up and down all day, checking up on them. If you get snagged, the tackler will come and sort you out, but in your turn. Sometimes he's quick, but sometimes he has a lot snagged at the same time and you just have to wait. Which is annoying 'cos you're on piecework and time stopped is money lost,' mouthed Martha. Grace nodded, her head already aching from trying to read what Martha's lips were saying.

Martha was a small plump woman but she could move surprisingly fast up and down the aisles between the looms. Grace carefully watched her as she handled the yarn and kept the looms running. The morning dragged on interminably but Grace kept her wits about her and studied what Martha was saying or doing. Suddenly a loud whistle reverberated through the weaving shed and all the machines stopped. The silence was wonderful and healing and Grace stood for a while, just savouring the silence.

Getting a dig in the ribs broke her reverie and Martha was telling her to follow her to the bait room. Clutching the parcel that her mam had given her that morning, Grace followed Martha into a small room that was vastly overcrowded for the number of bodies that were squashed in, trying to get some space to sit and eat. Even though the noise had stopped, everyone still spoke silently and people lip-read what each other was saying.

After eating her meal, Grace asked about the toilet facilities and Martha showed her to a row of long drop toilets outside the back of the weaving shed. They were primitive and smelly but Grace had no option. She realised how much living at Mr Haynes' house had spoilt her. The life of luxury had made her fastidious. And life at Mr Haynes' was luxurious. They had comfortable beds, with plentiful clean linen and towels. There was always good food on the table, and she didn't even have to make it, beyond helping her mother occasionally at the weekend when she wasn't working. Mr Haynes had even installed a bathing room up on the top floor, in the fifth bedroom, which no one occupied.

The only housework Grace was expected to do was to keep her own room tidy. Even then, Mrs Croft came in and 'bottomed' it every week, but that worked as a stimulus for Grace to keep it tidy in readiness for the weekly clean. Mrs Croft changed the beds as well at this time, so Grace had a very easy, comfortable home life.

After Grace had been to the toilet, she had a short walk in the mill yard, just glad to be out in the fresh air, but then the whistle blew again and the drive belts engaged to start the looms up again. The afternoon hurried by and at six o' clock, the final whistle blew for the ending of the day.

The mill hours were from six in the morning until six at night each day, Monday to Friday, whatever the time of year, because there was gas light in the mill, so that they could continue working when it was dark outside. The days rushed by and Grace soon got used to life in the weaving shed and made friends amongst the younger women that worked around her. And quite quickly, she got proficient at lip-reading! It was a case of needs must but she soon mastered it.

The mill finished at 2pm on Saturdays, and Grace loved to go down to Burnley to the market and do some shopping, or sometimes, she would go a long walk with William over the hills round about. She especially loved the walk down into Worsthorne, a small village, where she could buy a drink before she attempted the steep climb back up to Hillview House. Usually on Saturdays she spent her time with her friend from the mill, Katie Halstead. Katie and Grace had been friends from schooldays, although Katie had had to go into the mill a long time before Grace.

Sundays were spent up at the chapel. The family would attend the morning service, then hurry back down the hill to Hillview House to make Mr Haynes' dinner, then Grace and William would go back to the chapel to Sunday School, where Grace helped with the little ones, and then back again with their mam for evening service.

Mary Butler was much healthier and happier living at Hillview House. The work was easy and she had Mrs Croft for companionship most days. Mr Haynes was an easy boss to work for, and Mary never let a day pass when she didn't thank God for His goodness to her, in finding her this job.

Young William, too, loved his life at Hillview House. He was able to play out around the house, not just in the spacious garden but also on the hills, where he could observe the animal life around. Mr Haynes soon let him look after his horse and cart and taught him how to ride the horse and steer the cart. Often William would go for a ride after school on the other horse. Mr Haynes always kept two horses, so that one could rest each day. If Mary couldn't find William, she knew to look in the stable and was sure to find him there, if not in the garden.

William's best friend was a girl called Jessie Marsden from school. She lived in one of the cottages at Lane Bottoms near to Hillview House. They first got friendly when Jessie was being bullied by one of the older boys and William had stood up against the bully, even though he was a lot older and bigger. Since then they had been inseparable and tramped the hills together, watching wild life and caring for injured animals. Some of the bigger boys used to tease William for playing with girls, but William didn't let it bother him. He didn't seem to want to have a rough and tumble with the other boys.

Mr Haynes wanted William to try for the Boy's Grammar School down in Burnley, just near the parish church, but William would have none of it. William had been able to stay on at school until he was nearly fourteen, like Grace. He wasn't as sharp as Grace with his schoolwork, unless it was something to do with nature, then he outshone everyone else. Mr Haynes had tried to get him interested in accounting and book-keeping but he preferred to be outside playing. But Mr Haynes had found a kindred spirit in Grace. The sums came easily to her and she quickly absorbed the rules of book-keeping, and often did Mr Haynes' books for him.

'If you were a boy, I'd find you a place in my office,' laughed Mr Haynes.

'Why can't you? If I can do the work just as good as a boy, why shouldn't I get to do the work?' asked Grace perplexed.

'You know the answer to that, Grace. It's just not a girl's world. Girls can't work in offices or businesses.'

'But they can work in a mill or a mine or in service. It's not fair,' moaned Grace. 'Sometimes, I wish I'd been born a boy!'

But Mr Haynes had only laughed. He was very good with the children, and for that, Mary Butler was glad. He often taught them games and invited them all into his study or his lounge after meals. Sometimes, he would even come into the kitchen and have his tea with them all in the kitchen. Said it was less lonely than eating in his fine dining room.

On the first Christmas Day that the Butlers lived at Hillview House, he had insisted that they all ate together in the dining room, even though his nephew James and his sister Jenny Brown came as well. Although on Boxing Day, Mr Haynes had gone to stay with James and Jenny for the day, leaving the Butlers at home on their own. Grace had enjoyed herself that day. She told her mother that she felt like the lady of the house. They all had a long lie in and then mooched around the house in their nightclothes, rather than get dressed. Christmas had fallen on a weekend that first year, so the mill was shut for two days. Normally, the weavers only got Christmas Day off and were back to work on Boxing Day.

Grace was cross with William that he wouldn't take up the offer of a place at Mr Haynes' office. She would have loved the chance, but William was adamant. He wanted to go in to the mill, like his dad and Grace. And so, the day dawned when William got ready to go to work for the first time.

Chapter 5

It had been a difficult day. It was William's first day at the mill and things had gone from bad to worse. Grace's thoughts turned to the day when she had first gone to work in the mill. Her grief for her father had been so raw at the time, but she'd felt that she wanted to help her mother by going out to work. And now William was insisting on working in the mill, with a little of that same stubbornness that so characterised Grace.

The mill foreman had decided that William could train as a tackler but he had to work with a weaver first. He was assigned to Arthur Jones, a rough looking, loud-mouthed individual. Arthur started on to William from the first minute they met.

'Huh, what sort of mother's boy are you then? Not good enough to be a weaver like the rest of us. Being trained straight up as a tackler, are you? Nobody else got the chance first. Why you? There's lots of weavers as would welcome the chance to train as a tackler.'

'I didn't ask to train to be a tackler,' replied William, but this just seemed to inflame Arthur more.

'Did you hear that, Alf? He didn't ask to be a tackler. No, I bet he didn't. Bet his sister's been sucking up to that foreman, letting him have his way with her, to get her brother a soft job,' he sneered.

'Don't you speak about my sister like that. She's not that sort of girl,' shouted William in reply.

'Oh yes, and what are you going do about it, pipsqueak? Think you're a big man now do you, just 'cos you're going to be a tackler. Well, let me tell you. I rule this area of the weaving shed and what I say goes. If I want to make your life hell, then hell it will be. Do you hear me?' Arthur's voice was getting louder and he accompanied each word with a finger thrusted into William's chest, getting harder with each thrust.

Grace just happened to be passing whilst this was going on and shouted out without thinking.

'Leave my brother alone, you bully!' she screamed, easily heard over the sound of the looms.

'Oh, big sister come to save him, has she? What a lily-livered lad he is. He won't last two minutes in this weaving shed. I'll make sure of it. And as for you girl, you're in trouble now. Nobody crosses Big Arthur and gets away with it. '

'I'm not afraid of bullies. You're all mouth, Arthur Jones.'

'All mouth am I? Well, let's see what you are now?' Arthur replied and smacked Grace hard across the mouth, knocking her to the floor. Grace lay where she fell, stunned by the force of the blow. William dived on top of Arthur and pummelled him mercilessly, although Arthur managed to land a few blows on William as well.

Suddenly, the foreman dragged William and Arthur apart. The weavers realised that the power had been turned off on their looms. The shed was silent.

'I'll have no fighting in my shed,' roared the foreman. 'What's going on?'

Arthur, William and Grace all spoke out together.

'Silence. One at a time. You, Grace. Get up of the floor and Peter, tell me what happened.'

'I only came to it later,' replied Peter, one of the other weavers.

'Well, tell me what you saw.'

'I just saw Grace on the floor and William attacking Arthur,' replied Peter.

'Yes, the little swine, he attacked me for nothing,' shouted Arthur.

'Silence, Jones. I'll come to you later. Now who saw it from the beginning?' But nobody spoke. Arthur Jones was a vengeful man and nobody was going to tell tales on him.

'I'm waiting to hear what happened,' repeated the foreman. 'Your looms will be turned off until I get an answer, so it's you who'll be losing money when your wages come on Saturday.' An awkward silence remained. Eventually, an old lady spoke out.

'I saw what happened. I'm not frightened of Arthur Jones. I'll tell the truth.'

'At last, thank you Matty. Now let's hear it,' replied the foreman.

Matty swallowed. 'Well, Arthur were teasing the lad, like, and then the lad shouted back and then Arthur called the lad's sister names, and the lad shouted back, then Grace appeared and shouted at Arthur and he smacked her across the mouth, so the lad jumped on Arthur.'

'Well, it sounds as though you're all as bad as each other. I won't have fighting in my shed. All three of you will get half a days pay docked from your wages this week. Now get back to work.'

'But he started it,' whinged Grace, 'and look at my lip,' but she was silenced by the foreman.

'I said get back to work or I'll dock you a full days pay. I've made my judgement. Turn the looms back on.' He stalked off, leaving all the workers staring after him.

'He's always been well in with the foreman has Arthur Jones,' muttered Matty, 'now come and get that mouth sorted out, Grace.' Matty and Grace went to the sink that was in the bait room and bathed Grace's lip. It was swollen and painful, but at least no teeth had been knocked out. 'You look a right bonny mess, that you do. He's an evil man is Arthur Jones, but you have to be wary with him. He won't like it that he's to lose any pay. Be careful, Grace. He might want to get his own back on you. I'm an old woman; he wouldn't harm me.'

'I'm not frightened of him,' replied Grace.

'Well, you should be. He can cause a lot of trouble – for you and your brother – so you'd better watch out for him. Now get back to your own looms.'

Grace walked back to her own area of the weaving shed and started her looms again. Katie stared open-mouthed at Grace, but Grace shook her head. She would tell her what happened when it was break time. They'd already lost money this week and couldn't afford to lose any more.

When they were walking home, William and Grace decided that they would tell their mother an edited version of what happened when they got home, but it was no use. As soon as Mary saw Grace's mouth, she was ready to go to the mill and see the foreman, but William and Grace pleaded with her not to. It would only make things worse for them both. Eventually she calmed down, but threatened that if anything else happened like this, she would stop them working at the mill.

Grace hoped not. Although it had been an inauspicious start for William, she loved working at the mill. Even though it was hard work, and there were bullies working within the mill, most of the time, she loved the work and the friendships that she had made.

William was soon moved to work with another weaver and then eventually attached to an experienced tackler called Richard. He found he had a natural aptitude for tackling and was glad that he wasn't a weaver, even though Grace loved it.

He was even more pleased when Jessie came to work in the mill as well, as they still had a close friendship, which had continued since childhood. But William couldn't keep his mouth shut and often stuck up for workers who weren't getting a good deal. Although he was a good worker himself, he wasn't well liked by the management, as he was seen as a troublemaker, when all he wanted to do was ease troubles for people.

And often William would be missing when the weavers wanted him, but they knew he could always be found in the mill yard, talking to the horses that belonged to the mill. William knew all the horses by name and was very jealous of the man whose job was to care for the horses. Once, William had asked if he could learn the job, but the same family of Wilkinson's had cared for the mill horses ever since the mill had opened, so there was no chance of a job for William there.

Both Grace and William learned not to go anywhere near Arthur Jones, as he still seemed to have it in for the siblings. At least Arthur never came to their chapel; he was more of a public house man, so their social life was happy and trouble free. The workforce either went to the public house or to the chapel and nobody seemed to go to both. It was like two distinct social lives. But at least it meant that they didn't bump into Arthur Jones in their free time.

Grace was in the chapel choir and loved singing. Hers was a beautiful soprano voice that was a blessing to many at the chapel. She often sang solos at the chapel concerts or in the services. Her favourites were the Wesley hymns, but she also loved 'To God Be The Glory' by Fanny Crosby, and was touched by the story of the blind author of the hymn. Katie was in the alto section of the choir, so they would often grimace at each other and 'talk' across the opposite sides of the chapel. Being able to lip-read was an advantage, outside work as well!

Katie loved to come and spend time at Hillview House and thought that Grace was very lucky to live there. Grace was just glad that her mother was happy and they all had a good place to live, but she never took advantage of living there.

One Sunday, when they were waiting for the service to start, Katie mouthed across to Grace, 'Have you seen the new bloke just come in church?' as she turned her head to the back of the chapel. Grace followed the direction of her head and saw a tall slim fair-haired man, talking to one of the church elders. He was wearing a smart winter coat and clutching a hat in his hands. Eventually, the church elder led him down into the chapel and sat him down next to Billy Walters.

Now, Grace could see his face as well, and liked what she saw. He was a handsome looking man, with a high forehead, a strong jaw line and generous looking lips, which were covered by a neatly trimmed moustache and beard.

Just at that moment, her gaze was disturbed by the minister starting the service. As she moved to look at the minister, she noticed Katie laughing at her.

'Did you see enough of him, then?' she mouthed. Grace grinned but didn't reply as they were starting the first hymn. But she found it very hard not to keep looking at the young man during the service. I wonder who he is? she pondered, and if he is visiting or come to stay? It was her turn to do the tea rota after the service, so perhaps he would want a drink and she could get to know him then.

Grace couldn't get to the tea urn quick enough, trying to push Mrs Williams out of the way and saying she would serve today. But Mrs Williams wasn't having any of it.

'I always serve the tea urn, girl. What's the matter with you today? You're not always so keen to serve people. Last time it was your turn, I had to come and find you,' replied a grumpy Mrs Williams.

'Sorry. It's my new resolution, to be more helpful,' wheedled Grace hopefully, smiling at Mrs Williams, but she just made a 'humph' noise and turned away.

'Here, you can take the sugar round if you're that keen.'

'Oh thank you,' replied Grace, picking up the sugar and some spoons and prancing round the room, approaching anyone who had a cup of tea, who happened to be near the new young man. At last she noticed that William was talking to him. Great. Good time to go and talk to William on some excuse.

'Hey William, do you need sugar?' she asked sweetly.

'What for, I haven't got a cup of tea yet.'

'Oh no, silly me. I hadn't noticed. What about your friend?'

'He hasn't got one either.'

'Oh. Well, shall I get you one Mr er er?'

'Greenwood. Robert Greenwood. And yes, I'd love a cup of tea. And you are?'

Grace gazed into his eyes whilst he was talking, deep blue pools she noticed, and didn't realise that he'd asked her a question.

'Grace, what's the matter with you,' shouted William, 'Robert's asked you your name. Come on, he'll think you are simple.'

'Oh, er sorry, I was miles away,' replied Grace, dragging her eyes away from those eyes. 'Well, you know my name now. It's Grace, Grace Butler, sister to William.'

'Pleased to meet you Grace. I was just telling your brother, I've got a new job in the village and thought I'd come to chapel today.'

'Where's your job, then?' asked Grace.

'I'm to be a tackler at the mill in the village.'

'I'm training to be a tackler,' replied William proudly.

'I'm a weaver too, at the same mill. That's good. We'll all be working together,' she replied, her heart beating twenty to the dozen.

'Where are you staying? In the village or down in Burnley?' asked William.

'I'm staying in the village. I don't come from Burnley. I come from Colne, but my parents have both died and I thought I'd have a new start. I'm going to live at Mrs Shapcott's.'

'Where is she today? I haven't seen her yet?' asked Grace.

'No,' Robert replied, 'she's full of cold, so decided to stay at home this morning. I'd better get home to her now, in case she needs anything. It's been good to meet you both. Perhaps I'll see you at work tomorrow?'

'Are you not coming to chapel tonight?' asked Grace hopefully.

'I'm not sure; I'll have to see how Mrs Shapcott is. Bye for now.'

Grace watched him walk away. What a lovely man she thought. He's only just come to live with Mrs Shapcott and yet he was concerned for her. She was wakened from her reverie by a sharp dig in her back and turned indignantly to bellow at William, but it was Katie.

'Put your tongue back in and your eyes back in their sockets, Grace,' Katie said.

'What do you mean?' asked Grace innocently.

'What do I mean? You were nearly slavering over him. I thought you were going to kiss him, you leaned in so close to him,' laughed Katie.

'I did not,' replied an indignant Grace, but blushing at the same time.

'Yes, you did. He is rather nice, though, isn't he?' said Katie. 'I might make a play for him myself. It's a while since we've had any new men at the chapel. He could stir things up a bit.' Grace turned to glare at Katie, so she said she was only joking, she'd leave the new man to Grace.

'He's not my man,' blustered Grace.

'No, but you'd like him to be,' laughed Katie as she hurried away towards her parents.

Yes I would, thought Grace as she went to help Mrs Williams with the washing up. A task she carried out with her thoughts far away from the kitchen sink.

Chapter 6

Grace had never been as keen to go to work on a Monday morning. She chivvied William to hurry up and was almost first past the gates.

'Morning Grace,' shouted Katie as they arrived. 'Are you in a better mood today? You were crammed as a wasp last night at chapel. What was the matter with you?'

'Nothing, I wasn't crammed,' said an indignant Grace. 'Think I was just tired.'

'Huh yes, probably tired with keep turning your head to see who was coming in, or not coming in as the case may be,' Katie chuckled.

'I wasn't,' said Grace.

'Oh you were. You were all excited when we arrived at chapel, but got steadily grumpier as the evening wore on. Could it be to do with the fact that a certain person didn't come to evening chapel? A certain new arrival in town?' teased Katie.

'Who do you mean? I'm certain I don't know.'

'Oh come on, Grace. This is me you're talking to. It was obvious you really liked the new man. What was he called?'

'Robert Greenwood, do you mean him? He was new yesterday morning. But I knew he wasn't coming to chapel, 'cos he said Mrs Shapcott was poorly and he might not be able to come.'

'But you were hoping he would, weren't you anyway?'

'Oh shut up Katie. Look he's here now. Talk about something else.'

'Aren't you going to introduce me then?'

'No, be quiet.'

'Hello Grace,' said Robert approaching them. 'Nice to see you again. Who's your friend?'

'Oh hello Robert. This is my best friend Katie Halstead. We work together. How's Mrs Shapcott?'

'Much better today, thank you for asking. Well, I'd better be going. Better not be late on my first day. I'll see you later.'

'Yes, see you later,' replied Grace.

'Yes, see you later,' repeated Katie in a falsetto voice, copying what Grace had said, but when Grace nudged her sharply she ran off and went to her looms, which were on the other side of Grace's looms.

Grace had to concentrate on her work, but her thoughts were very wayward that morning. Indeed, they had been very erratic ever since she had met Robert Greenwood. She found it hard to believe because men had never affected her before. She spent a lot of time at work with men, and met many men at chapel, but there had never been a man that had interested her before. Usually, she could just take them or leave them; their presence never particularly changed her thoughts.

So why did she keep thinking about Robert? Yes, he was good looking and appeared kindly to others, and he attended chapel, so they were all good things in his favour, but that could be said about many of the other men she met. She'd have loved to talk about it to someone but was scared of their reaction. Grace wouldn't talk to Katie about it, even though they shared all their private hopes and dreams with each other. Katie had already teased her about Robert so she wasn't going to confide in her yet.

Katie was always falling in love with one or other of the men she met, and it was a constant source of amusement to Grace, hearing about Katie's suitors. Mind you, often it was just in Katie's mind, rather than hard fact. But a girl could dream, Katie used to argue.

The day passed without Grace making any catastrophes in her work, despite her mind not being fully on the looms. She had only known Robert for just over a day and as yet didn't really know him, but she felt like he'd been in her thoughts for a long time.

'Grace, wake up,' yelled William as they came out of the mill.

'Oh hello, William. What's the matter?'

'Nothing, I was just telling you to tell mam that I was going to Jessie's for tea tonight.'

'Oh, all right. But you should tell her before you go out to work. She might have made your tea already,' replied Grace, using her elder sister tone of voice.

'Didn't know Jessie was going to ask me this morning, did I?' replied a cheeky William. 'Besides, I'll eat my tea for my supper,' he laughed as he set off at run, having just seen Jessie coming out of the weaving shed.

Grace shook her head, but then set off to go home on her own. As she was starting up the hill, Robert caught her up.

'Grace, I've been meaning to ask you, are there any midweek services at the chapel? I forgot to ask yesterday.'

'Oh yes, we have a Bible Study and Prayer meeting on a Tuesday night for all the church and then a young men's meeting on Friday nights.'

'Do you go to the Tuesday meeting?'

Grace hesitated before replying. Lately, she had often missed going to the mid-week meeting, but she didn't want to give a bad impression to Robert.

'Some weeks, but not all,' she eventually replied, trying to be as honest as she could, without giving the wrong impression. 'Were you thinking of going?' she asked casually.

'Yes, I think I will. Wouldn't mind joining the choir as well. I was in the choir at my last church. Do you have to have an audition?'

Grace laughed. 'Audition? I don't think so. I'd never have got in if we'd had an audition. It's more a question of how enthusiastic you are,' she added, all the time her heart beating wildly inside her chest. Midweek-meeting? Choir practice? That would be two nights a week she could see him. Things were getting better by the minute.

'Choir practice is on Thursday night. Shall I tell Mr Jelley that you want to join?'

'If it is no trouble, yes please,' replied Robert. Believe me, thought Grace, nothing will ever be too much trouble for you Robert, but she simply smiled instead and agreed to leave a note at Mr Jelley's house. 'What voice do you sing?' Grace suddenly remembered to ask.

'Tenor.'

'Great. He'll be delighted. That's what we're short of. It's pretty certain you'll get in,' she laughed.

'Well, I'd better be on my way home. Mrs Shapcott will be wondering what's happened to me.'

'Yes, and I've to tell mum that William won't be coming home. He's going to Jessie's for tea.'

'Are they sweethearts?' asked Robert.

'No,' replied Grace laughing, 'just friends. They're only fifteen years old.'

'Well, I've heard of young ones getting together at that age before. Never mind, time will tell. I'd best be off. '

'I suppose so, see you later then' replied Grace and set off up the hill, pondering just what William and Jessie were to each other. Surely they were just friends? But perhaps not? Did William feel about Jessie like she did about Robert? Is that why they spent all their free time together?

As she walked up the drive at Hillview House, Grace puzzled about the relationships between men and women. Had her mother and father been like this? Her mother said that she had known straight away when she met her father. Knew that this would be the one person for her. Is that how love happened? A sudden knowledge of love? Or was it just a slow burning realisation that grew? Whatever it was, she determined as she went into the house, it was a tiring job. It was taking up all her thoughts and she couldn't keep her mind on anything else. If it was love, but then what else could it be? It was very perplexing.

As she went into the kitchen, Grace remembered to tell her mother that William was away for tea.

'William's gone to Jessie's for tea, mam.'

'That boy'll be the death of me. Why didn't he tell me this morning? Before I made the tea?'

'That's just what I said to him, mam, but d'y'know what he said? He said that Jessie hadn't asked him this morning. He's got an answer for everything, that lad.'

'Well, it's chops for tea, and I've made him one now.'

'I told him that you might have made his tea, and he just said he would eat it for supper,' laughed Grace.

'Huh! Typical! Mind you, he'll probably need it. Jessie Marsden's mother isn't famed for her generosity of table.'

'Ooh mam, that's a bit harsh for you, isn't it?'

'Well, I'll never forget when we were all having a hard time, 'cos the mill was on part time, and it was a Jacob's Join for the chapel anniversary tea and Agnes Marsden brought three buns. Three! I ask you. And her brood always eat loads.'

'Perhaps she made more and they all ate it before she could bring it to chapel,' suggested Grace laughing.

'That might be true. Never thought of that. But you'd have made more, wouldn't you?'

'Perhaps there wasn't time,' offered Grace.

'Maybe. Anyroad, this isn't getting the tea on the table. Can you warm the teapot?'

'Yes, mam. What time is Mr Haynes getting home tonight?'

'He's not coming home for tea. He's got a business meeting tonight. So he's eating in town. So it's just you and me tonight.'

Grace and Mary finished the preparations for the meal in silence and then sat down to eat it.

'You're quiet tonight,' commented Mary. 'Can't usually get a word in edgeways with you and William.'

'I'm a bit tired. Just thinking thoughts really.'

'Oh? What sort of thoughts?'

'Nothing special,' Grace lied. She couldn't bring herself to mention her true thoughts to her mother at the moment, if ever! 'I'll have an early night tonight I think. Catch up on my sleep. I want to read a book anyway.'

'Well, I want you to wash up first. You still need to do your share to help me.'

'Don't worry mam, I'll do my chores,' laughed Grace. But she did them as quickly as she could and escaped to her bedroom, where she could think her private thoughts without interruption. She did try reading a book, but for once, her own thoughts were much more exciting than the novelist's words.

Chapter 7

'Come along. Everybody settle down. We've a lot to get through tonight,' boomed Mr Jelley at the start of the choir practice. 'And also, can I introduce a new member of the choir? This is Robert Greenwood. He sings tenor, thank God.' At which the entire choir laughed, knowing how much Mr Jelley despaired at the small number of tenors in the choir. 'He was a member of Trinity Baptist chapel, in Colne before he came here and they have a fine choir, so we'd better show him what we can do.'

Robert, suitably embarrassed by this introduction, sat down quickly in the tenor part of the choir, but not before smiling across quickly at Grace, who squirmed with pleasure inside, but managed not to show a trace of it on her face; merely nodding her greeting.

'Right,' said Mr Jelley. 'Let's get to work. Now we'll start with the 'For Unto Us a Child Is Born' on page sixty-three. Everybody got it? Here's a copy for you, Robert. We're doing the full Messiah in the chapel the week before Christmas. Right we are then. From the introduction, Valerie please,' he said to the organist.

The organist started the introduction and the choir sang the timeless beautiful words that Handel had created many years before. Apart from shouting at the altos a couple of times for talking, which was normal procedure at most practices, the choir practice went smoothly and Mr Jelley was pleased. After reminding them to learn their parts, the choir was dismissed.

Robert made his way over to Grace and Katie and asked Grace if William was not in the choir. Both girls laughed in reply.

'You've not heard William sing, then?' asked Katie. 'Don't know how a brother and sister can be so unalike in their voices. No, Grace is one on her own in her family. She sings like a lark and yet her mum and dad and William can't sing a note in tune.'

'But both my Grandmothers were good singers, I must have got it from them,' replied Grace.

'Definitely not from William,' Katie laughed.

'I'm going a walk on Saturday afternoon, after work,' said Robert, 'Would you two girls like to come with me?'

Katie and Grace spoke instantly together.

'Yes,' said Grace.

'No,' said Katie, 'we're going down Burnley Market,' then realised what Grace had said. 'Grace, we always go down Burnley Market on Saturday afternoon. I thought you wanted to get a new piece of material to make a dress? You've talked about nothing else for the last week.' Grace glared at Katie but Katie only laughed. 'Well, of course, if you'd rather go a walk with Robert, I'll not stop you. I'll let you two go a walk and I'll go down Burnley Market on my own.'

'Don't be silly, Katie. You know I can't go for a walk with Robert on my own. It'd be the talk of the village before bedtime. Y'know what this village is like for gossip.'

'No, but you'd like to go for a walk with him, wouldn't you?' persisted Katie, whilst Grace tried to get nearer her to kick her on the ankle. 'Why don't you ask your William?'

'Good idea,' said Robert, 'I don't want you to get talked about in the village on my behalf, Grace.'

'That's right, and don't worry about me either Grace. I'm only your best friend. I can go to Burnley Market on my own,' said Katie with a false voice that sounded as if she was offended.

'I know,' said Robert, 'why don't we all go after Sunday School on Sunday afternoon? That way you can still go shopping together on Saturday.'

'I suppose so,' said Katie reluctantly.

'That's a brilliant idea, Robert. Why didn't I think of that?' said Grace. 'That's settled then. Perhaps William would like to go for a walk with you on Saturday as well if you're so keen?'

'No,' replied Robert, 'I'll wait 'til Sunday. Goodbye for now,' he said as he walked away.

The week sped quickly by, but not quick enough for Grace. She was longing to spend time talking to Robert and finding out more about him. On Saturday, Grace had driven Katie mad when they had been on Burnley Market, trying to bring the conversation round to Robert every few minutes.

'Eh, Grace Butler, you've got it bad,' she teased her on the way home in the horse and cart.

'What d'y' mean?' asked Grace innocently.

'You know what I mean. Every time I try to change the subject, you seem to get it back on to Robert rotten Greenwood. I think I'm fed up of him already.'

'I don't.'

'Do.'

'Don't.'

'Do. Do. Do.'

'Well, I suppose I do talk about him a little.'

'Hallelujah! That's the biggest understatement of the year,' laughed Katie.

'But I do like him, Katie.'

'Yes, I have noticed,' replied Katie drily. 'Do you want me to have a convenient upset tummy tomorrow, so that you can have him all to yourself?' Katie saw the longing in her friend's eyes, but Grace quietly said no. Both girls knew that it was more than their life was worth to be seen out alone with a young man. But the look in Grace's eyes told Katie that her friend was indeed smitten with this man, even though they had only just met.

Katie had a momentary twinge of resentment that this man might separate the special closeness of the girls. But then, it would probably happen in the future anyway. Women had to get married and have babies, and friendships had to be put aside. Sighing, Katie reassured her friend that she would be there after Sunday School: ready and waiting to go for a walk. Grace smiled her thanks, and the pair said a cheery goodnight, their former disagreement already forgotten.

On Sunday it poured down all day and Grace was bitterly upset that they wouldn't be able to go out for a walk. In the end, Mary told her to invite Robert for tea after Sunday School, so Grace cheered up.

Robert was a bit overwhelmed when he saw the size of the house until Grace reassured him that they only lived there at the courtesy of the owner and explained her mother's job there.

'Thought perhaps you were a bit higher up in the world than me,' he said shyly.
'Would I be working in the mill if my family owned this place?' Grace laughed.
'Probably not,' replied Robert sheepishly. 'I never thought about that. It just took my breath away to think that you lived here and were far above me.'
'This house takes my breath away every time I come through the gates, but no, I'm no higher than you. Just a poor weaving family, who got lucky.'
'I wouldn't say losing your father was lucky, but I know what you mean. Mrs Shapcott told me how you were asked to leave your tied cottage as soon as your father died and you'd nowhere to go, until your mother got this job.'
'Yes, it was a great relief. My mother has a weak chest and they wouldn't have her back in the mill, so we were going to stay at Mrs Shapcott's before Mr Haynes offered that we could live here. Now come on in and let's get dry.' William had already run ahead of them on the drive because he wanted to tend to Mr Haynes' horses.
Robert and Grace sat chatting in the kitchen with Mary adding her own contribution from time to time. Robert told her that his own father had died when he was thirteen, and his mother had never been the same afterwards. Every one had said that she had died of a broken heart, he told them.
'Can that happen?' asked Grace.
'Oh yes,' replied Mary, 'very easily. When you've loved someone so much, you don't want to go on living. I didn't, but I had you two children to make me get up in a morning and find a living. You just have to keep on going,' reflected Mary sadly.
'That was my mum's problem. She only had me and I was already working in the mill. She just sat at home on her own all the time, brooding. Everyone tried to get her going again, but she wouldn't take anything on board. That's why I wanted to get away after she died. I couldn't stay in the same house. There were too many sad memories.'
'Were you an only one then Robert?' asked Mary.

'Yes, unfortunately, my parents got married later in life and mum lost quite a few babies before she had me. I don't think she ever recovered properly, because she was always tired, all through my childhood.'

'Well, let's have tea,' said Mary suddenly, as if trying to change the atmosphere. 'Go and shout William in, Grace.' Grace went out to the back door but no William appeared.

'I'll have to go and get him,' Grace grumbled, 'when he gets himself in that stable, he's in another world.'

'I'll come with you, or even go for you, if you tell me where to go,' offered Robert.

'That's kind of you, but I can't expect you to find it yourself. No, come with me and I'll show you William's second home,' quipped Grace.

Robert followed her out of the kitchen door and they went across the back forecourt towards the stables. As they were near the entrance, Robert laid his hand on Grace's arm. She stopped instantly: she couldn't have moved because she was shivering just at his touch. She stood stock still, not daring to even look at him.

'Grace, thank you for asking me here today. I really wanted to spend time getting to know you.' Grace just nodded, unable to speak. 'I know we've only just met each other but I feel . . ,' but whatever he felt, he didn't get chance to say, as William chose that moment to come through the door.

'Hello? What are you two doing here? Had enough of mam already?' he quipped.

Robert recovered first. 'We've been sent to get you. We've already shouted for you to come in for tea, but you didn't reply.'

'No, I sing when I'm with the horses so that's why I probably didn't hear you. It's the only time I'm allowed to. When no one can hear me!'

'Too true,' jibed Grace recovering her composure. 'It's the poor horses I feel sorry for. He should be reported for cruelty to animals. Come on, tea's ready. Don't keep mam waiting any longer,' chivvied Grace, and the three of them returned to the kitchen. After an enormous tea, Robert offered to wash up, which shocked both Mary and William.

'No lad, you don't have to wash up,' said Mary, 'but thanks for asking.'

'Eh Robert, don't go giving these two ideas that lads can do housework. That's women's work is washing up. Always was and always will be,' said William.

'I had to do the chores when there was only me and mum, so I'm used to it.' But then he laughed. 'Mrs Shapcott thinks it's a right to-do when I offer to do jobs round the house. Her Bert never lifted a finger!'

'Are you going to chapel tonight, Robert?' asked William.

'Yes, are you?'

'Yes, have you seen the time? We'd best be getting going soon.'

'We've time to wash up lad,' joked Mary. 'It's not that late. What'll Mr Haynes think if he comes home from his nephew's and wants a bite to eat, and comes in the kitchen and sees the pots not washed,' Mary continued, as she bashed the pots around in the sink.

For the rest of the evening, there was no chance for Grace and Robert to speak alone, but when she got home and went to bed, Grace went over and over again in her mind how she had felt when Robert had touched her arm, and pondered what he might have been going to say to her before they were interrupted by William.

She didn't have long to find out. Robert sought her out at the meal break next morning.

'Grace, I hope you don't think I'm being too rude or a bit previous, but I wonder if you would do me the honour of courting?'

'Courting?' squeaked Grace.

'Yes, courting. You know what that means, I suppose? They don't have a different word for it in this area do they? Some words change here even though Colne is only six miles away. I want you to be my girl.'

'Yes.'

'Is that 'yes' I know what courting means, or 'yes' I'll be your girl?' asked Robert.

'Yes to both,' said Grace quietly, feeling her heart would burst.

'I've never felt like this before with anyone, have you?'

'No,' replied Grace, still unable to speak with her usual loquacity.

'Good. That's settled then. Shall I talk to your mum?'

'No. Too soon. Wait a while,' replied Grace.

'I suppose it is. I can't believe what I'm feeling myself. We'll keep it to ourselves.'

'Yes, as much as we can in this village,' laughed Grace, recovering her sense of humour.

'Good. We'll talk some more at the next break perhaps.'

'Look forward to it,' replied Grace softly as he walked away. Grace walked back to her part of the weaving shed to find Katie bouncing up and down in glee.

'What was all that about then? Has he proposed?' said Katie.

'Don't be silly. I've only known him a short time.'

'Well, you were both looking proper soppy, whatever he was saying. Come on, tell your best friend.'

'Nothing to tell,' said Grace primly.

'And I'm a Chinaman. Come on, you can't fool me.'

'All right, but promise not to tell anyone?'

'Promise.'

'He's asked me to go courting with him.'

'He never! Already?'

'Yes, I know it's too soon, but I really feel a lot for him already. I think I'm in love,' Grace gushed.

'Hey, hold hard, Grace. That's a bit soon. Take things easy. You know what they say, "Marry in haste, repent at leisure." '

'I'm not marrying him,' gasped Grace, 'only going out with him, but I'm not telling mam yet, so keep quiet. Or William for that matter.'

'Not a word will pass my lips,' said Katie in mock seriousness.

'Good. I'll keep you informed of any developments.'

'Hmm, I'll look forward to that,' laughed Katie. 'And remember me when you want a bridesmaid. I asked first.'

‘You’re supposed to wait to be asked by the bride Katie, but shut up, that’s a long way off yet.’

‘All right. I’ll give you a year. Bet you’re married by this time next year.’

‘Never,’ roared Grace as she ran back to her looms.

Chapter 8

The weeks sped by towards Christmas. The rehearsals for the Messiah were getting more fraught by the minute. As well as the concert, they had to rehearse for the special services at the chapel and for going carol singing round the village on Christmas Eve.

As each week passed, Grace and Robert spent as much time as possible together, getting to know all the important little details about each other. Their feelings deepened and Grace knew in her heart that she had found the man whom she wanted to marry.

It was impossible to discuss it with anyone as she was too shy to speak about such things with her mother, and she knew that if she mentioned it to Katie, she would tease her mercilessly – she already did.

It was Mary that raised the subject in the end, about a week before Christmas. They were making the mincemeat together to go in the mince pies and talking about various recipes.

'You're getting really interested in baking and cooking now, Grace, aren't you? You were never keen when you were younger. Why the change?'

'Perhaps that's the answer, mam. I was younger then, now I'm older. Time for me to start learning how to cook,' replied Grace.

'Any special reason?'

'Reason? Should there be?' asked a bemused Grace.

'Well, it seems to me like you're learning to make your own nest, y'know, getting ready for marriage.'

Grace blushed. 'I don't know about that, mam.'

'Don't you? You seem to spend all your spare time with Robert nowadays.'

Grace was silent.

'Well? What do you have to say? Is Robert the one for you?'

'I suppose he is. Well, I'm sure he is, but he hasn't said anything yet. How do you know, mam? How can you be sure?'

'Ask yourself how you would feel if you never saw him again.' By watching Grace's face blanch, Mary knew what the answer to that question was without her speaking, so she continued. 'And the other question you have to ask is, do you want him to be the father of your babies?'

'Give over mam, you're making me embarrassed,' giggled Grace, to cover her embarrassment. But secretly, she was thinking that yes, she couldn't live without him now, and she did want to have babies with Robert. She couldn't believe where her thoughts had gone. She'd never really been interested in having babies before, but now it seemed the only thing on earth that she wanted to do. Marry Robert and have his babies. She wasn't sure how she would actually get to be having a baby, but she certainly wasn't going to ask her mum.

Working in a mill shed, she wasn't totally ignorant of the facts of life, but what she heard from the married women in the weaving shed, didn't make married life seem too exciting at times, but she was sure it would all work out. People still kept on getting married and having babies, so something must be all right.

But she knew that when Robert held her tight when no one was looking or gave her a long lingering kiss, her body started doing things that felt very nice, but she didn't really understand them. All she knew was that she wanted him to go on kissing her without stopping. It was all very mysterious, this love lark, she mused.

'I'd give a pound to know what your thoughts were just then, young woman,' Mary said suddenly, startling Grace out of her wayward thoughts, and desperately hoping that her mother didn't know what she was thinking.

'I was just thinking about work,' Grace said lamely.

'Ha! Is that so? I wasn't born yesterday, y'know. I can see the way it is with you and Robert. Enjoy it while you can. Me and your dad were very happy.'

All this talk of love and motherhood was making Grace feel slightly hot under the collar, so she made an excuse to go up to her bedroom for a while.

On her return, Grace made conversation about the forthcoming Messiah, to take her mam's mind off the subject of Robert.

'We're doing all the choruses ourselves, but we're having some soloists in to help us,' Grace prattled on. 'We've got Doris Atkins from Mount Pleasant Baptist in Burnley. She's a soprano. And then there's a bass from Woodland Road Baptist in Nelson, but I can't remember his name. And Robert is doing the tenor part himself. Apparently he's done it before. And Mrs Jelley is doing the contralto part. But it's going to be a real community event, because other local churches are helping us out and taking part in the chorus. There's the Methodist church and the Anglican, St James, too.'

'Yes, I'm really looking forward to it,' said Mary. 'The Messiah always makes you feel like it's Christmas. Are they starting at the same time as if it was the Sunday evening service?'

'That's right, six o'clock. It's instead of the evening service. Now I'd better get off to choir practice or I won't be ready on Sunday.'

As the choir waited to start the Messiah on Sunday, they were all very nervous, but once they got started, it went very smoothly. Everyone praised the singers and enjoyed the cup of tea and a mince pie afterwards. Grace especially praised Robert for his tenor solos. Afterwards, the choir made arrangements for meeting on Christmas Eve to go round the village singing carols.

Christmas Eve was freezing cold, but there had been no snow, so they wrapped up well and went first to the houses of people who were too old and infirm to go to church and then sang outside the Reading Room and the public houses, before going to several of the church member's houses.

When they had finished, they all went to Mr Ormerod's house. He had a large house just past the church, on the road going towards Nelson. Everyone managed to squeeze into his lounge and then mince pies and cups of tea were served.

When they were ready for home, Robert said that he wanted to walk home with Grace, but she said it wasn't necessary, as

William would look after her. But he insisted. William conveniently walked ahead of them so he couldn't hear their conversation.

'Grace, I want to ask you some thing. I know we haven't known each other very long, but I already have very strong feelings for you. I wonder if you would do the honour of becoming my wife?' Robert said nervously.

Grace didn't hesitate or become coy but straightway gave her answer, whilst carrying on walking, without looking at him.

'Yes, I will marry you. Thank you so much.' Robert stopped her walking and just hugged her instead.

'Come on you two, what are you doing canoodling in the street? You'll be thrown out of chapel if you carry on like this,' chortled William.

'Oh be quiet, William. This is important,' bawled Grace.

'It'd better be, or else you'll both be in trouble,' he bawled back.

'Robert and I are going to . . . oh! I'd better not say, should I Robert? Shouldn't we be asking mam first or something?' said Grace.

'I've already spoken to your mam, Grace.'

'When?' said Grace.

'Last week. I couldn't have asked you first, could I?'

'Ah, that explains all the funny remarks she made when we were making the mincemeat,' replied Grace. 'I take it she said yes?'

Robert nodded. 'I thought we could announce it at chapel tomorrow, if you don't mind?'

'Yes, why not. I want to tell the whole world,' said an excited Grace.

'Well, we'll start with the chapel tomorrow and go on from there,' Robert laughed. He left her at the door and a happy Grace went in to tell her mother the news. The news of the couple's engagement was well received at chapel, on the whole, although there were one or two of the older ladies who said that they hadn't known each other for two minutes, but Grace and

Robert ignored them! They were probably just jealous that she was marrying such a handsome man, Grace suggested.

'Talking of marrying, when do you want to get married, Grace?' asked Robert.

'The sooner the better!' quipped Grace.

'Well, not too soon, or else they'll think it's a rush job,' Robert replied.

'There's no chance of that,' said Grace, 'what about beginning of July? The mill will be shut for the Burnley Fair holidays for the first two weeks in July, so perhaps we could have a few days away.'

'Sounds good to me,' said Robert.

'Oh dear, that's only six months away,' said Grace. 'I'd better be starting on my bottom drawer right now.'

Before Robert could reply, Katie came hurtling up to them both.

'Told you, told you. You'll be married within the year. I've won my bet,' shouted an excited Katie.

'Bet? What bet?' asked Robert, 'what sort of chapel girls are you, having a bet?'

'Oh it wasn't about money. I just bet Grace that you and she would marry within the year, and I was right,' Katie laughed. They were interrupted by Mary, who chivvied them along home, so that she could finish off the Christmas lunch. Robert was coming to Hillview House this year for his Christmas lunch, giving Mrs Shapcott more room for all her family that were coming to stay.

Before they started eating, Mr Haynes gave the Christmas presents out. Mary received a new coat from Mr Haynes, which Grace had picked, hat and scarf from William, and a knitted jumper from Grace. James and Jenny Brown had bought Mary some beautiful expensive soaps, as they knew that she loved good soap. It was a far cry from the carbolic soap she had been used to before coming to live in Hillview House.

William received a saddle for the horse from Mr Haynes and was well pleased with that. He also received cleaning tools for the horse from James and Jenny. Grace and Mary had bought him a smart jacket to wear for weekends. Mr Haynes had said that no one should buy presents for him, but Grace had knitted him a jumper for evenings, Mary had bought him some new leather gloves and William had bought him an inkstand with matching pen nib set, for on his desk in the study.

Grace was the last to receive her presents. There was a dress length from her mother and William, a lace collar from James and Jenny, and a crystal vase from Mr Haynes. This last present overawed her, but Mary teased her that it was the start of her bottom drawer.

'It's beautiful,' said Grace, 'I'll be frightened of using it. But it will look well on my dresser, if ever I have one.'

Robert cleared his throat. 'And now my presents,' he said nervously. For Mary and William he had bought a pair of gloves each, for Mr Haynes and James and Jenny he had bought boxes of chocolates, but then he got a tiny package out of his pocket for Grace.

'This is for you,' he said. Grace tore the wrappers off and opened the box to reveal a tiny solitaire diamond ring. She slipped it on her ring finger, with trembling fingers, and had to be helped by Robert. For once Grace was speechless. Well, for a few minutes, then she recovered her usual voice.

'How did you know what I'd want? And how did you know what size I took?'

'For the design, I'm afraid I took your best friend out shopping. She said you often looked in jeweller's shops and she knew exactly what sort of ring you would like. The size was a bit harder, but Katie remembered one ring that you had tried on, so the jeweller measured it. We can have it altered if it's not right.'

'It's perfect. So Katie knew about this and never said? When did you go shopping? How come I didn't know about it?'

'Do you remember when you had a cold and couldn't go to the market with Katie? That's when we went. It worked out quite well.'

'So Katie has known for the last three weeks and never said anything?' Robert nodded, grinning mischievously.

'Wait 'til I see her at work tomorrow. I'll give her what for,' said Grace, but she was laughing as she said it.

'And now we'd better start eating or else the meal will all be cold,' said Mary as she got up and went into the kitchen. After an enormous Christmas meal in the dining room, they all sat round in the lounge, whilst James played some carols on the piano for them to sing to.

'I wish I could play the piano,' said Grace afterwards.

'I could teach you,' offered James.

'No thanks, not now anyway, but perhaps some day, when I've time, I'd like that.'

'Any time you're ready,' replied James. The party broke up soon afterwards as William, Grace and Robert were all working the following day. Mr Haynes and James had shut their shops at eleven o'clock on Christmas Eve and were closed for both Christmas Day and Boxing Day, so Mr Haynes was going to the Brown's house on Boxing Day, as usual.

Grace didn't wear her ring on her finger for work next day, but concealed it under her clothes on a chain, so that the looms didn't damage it. But there was a lot of merriment in the bait room when they had their break, as she sported her ring whilst she was eating. She and Robert got a lot of ribbing from their workmates, but there were a lot of envious glances from the other girls, who had all fancied their chances with Robert.

It was a wonderful close to the year and Grace couldn't believe that by next Christmas she would be a married woman. She couldn't wait!

The winter was a bad one and the deep snow stayed for weeks. Sometimes, Mr Haynes had not even got home from Burnley because the horse couldn't get up the hill, and he'd had to stay at the Red Lion Inn, or one of his friend's houses.

People fell in the ice and broke limbs and after a few weeks, everyone was getting fed up of the snow. Eventually, the thaw started, and caused even more problems as the roads became even more treacherous.

Before they knew it, Easter arrived, quite early that year. The choir had another successful concert at the chapel and repeated it the night after at Aenon Baptist chapel, down in Burnley.

The next big event was the choir picnic and everyone was excited. It was to take place on a Saturday in May and they were to hire the horses and the charabancs from both their own mill and another mill, which was also in Briercliffe.

The trip was to go to Haworth, which was over in the West Riding of Yorkshire, and was the home of the Bronte family. After they arrived, they were to have a meal in the Baptist chapel there, after which they were to give them a short concert in return for the meal. Then they would be free to go round the shops, or go walking on the moors round about. For the older ones, a games afternoon was being set up in the chapel. Tea would be provided at four o'clock and then they would set off back home to Briercliffe.

Everyone was very excited as they climbed aboard the charabancs, which had been given a good clean and the addition of rows of seats for people to sit on. It was not very comfortable, but most of the choir members had taken a cushion to soften the discomfort.

After the lunch and concert, Grace told Robert that she would like to go for a walk. The shops held no interest for her as every penny was being saved for her wedding in a few weeks time. Jessie and William said they would go too, and they set off towards the hills around Haworth. They'd not been walking very long, when William saw the sign for the railway station and said that he fancied going to watch the trains.

Grace pulled a face and said she preferred to be out in the fresh air and not inhaling fumes from a smelly old train. They agreed to part. Jessie and William went to the station and Robert and Grace set off alone up into the hills; so grateful for having some time when they were completely alone.

Second week of July 2012

'Hiya GreatGramps,' shouted Carrie as she hurried through the door, but stopped dead in her tracks when she saw who was in the room.

'Marc, what you doing here so soon? Shouldn't you be at work?'

'Taken a day off today, had things to do,' Marc replied.

'What things?' asked an inquisitive Carrie.

'Oh, this and that, y'know, man's things,' replied Marc, winking at GreatGramps.

'No, I don't know. What have you been up to?'

'Well, I came to ask GreatGramps something.'

'Ask him what? I hope you weren't going on about the rent again. You know how much it upset him last time.'

'No, nothing so important as the rent. Just came to ask him if I could marry you, that's all,' laughed Marc nervously. For once Carrie was silent: differing emotions travelling across her face.

'Well,' said Jake, 'what's it to be?'

'Yes,' gulped Carrie, 'oh yes,' and she strangled Marc in a bear hug, followed by her GreatGramps.

Marc pulled a small box out of his jeans pocket. 'How about this then?' he said, showing Carrie a small solitaire diamond ring. 'If it's the wrong size, I can get it altered. Do you like it? It was my great-grandmother's. As you are so in to family history, I thought you'd like that idea, but I can get you a new one if you prefer.'

'No, no, I love it. It's exactly what I'd have chosen myself. Thank you. But what made you ask GreatGramps first?'

'Just call me old-fashioned. I couldn't ask your father or even your grandfather could I?'

'No, you couldn't,' Carrie replied softly. 'The men in my family don't seem to be long livers.'

'Except your GreatGramps,' laughed Marc, trying to keep Carrie from getting too morose.

'Oh him!' replied Carrie smiling, 'He's a right old creaking gate. We'll probably have to shoot him. Marc, have you thought

about when we would get married? Let's get married soon. I'd love it if GreatGramps could give me away.'

'Hey, love to, . . . but how . . . going to get you. . . . down aisle?' gasped Jake.

'We'll have a wheelchair, complete with oxygen bottle and I'll lean on the wheelchair as I push you down the aisle. After all, the church is only across the car park. I'd want to get married at Sion Baptist, like the whole family has done.'

'You've thought about this, . . . haven't you?' asked Jake.

Carrie nodded. 'Oh yes, I was just waiting for Marc to ask me. We'll get married at half term in October. Can you last 'til then GreatGramps?' she added mischievously.

'Try and stop me,' replied Jake. 'Got something to aim for.'

'Well, I'd better go and ring mum and the grannies and aunties. Boy, they'll be in their element with a wedding to plan. We won't get much say in it, Marc. I hope you're prepared for all this?'

'Just tell me what to wear and where to turn up and I'll be there. But I bet my mum will be as bad as yours. She loves weddings too.' Marc groaned. 'I can see we'll be watching a lot of sport on telly on our own, GreatGramps, whilst the women are out shopping 'til they drop!' Jake nodded, but had a look of quiet satisfaction on his face.

'Right, I'm off to tell my mum, and I'd better check which week half term is,' said Carrie, rooting in her handbag for her mobile. 'Wow, what a year 2012 is turning out to be. First a graduate, then getting a job as a teacher, getting engaged and then a bride. Makes the Olympics and the Queen's Diamond Jubilee pale into insignificance.' Jake nodded, determined to survive until October.

Chapter 9

Grace sat in front of her dressing table staring at the mirror. She looked and looked at her features to see if there was anything different in her face since yesterday. No, nothing seemed different to look at, but what a difference there was in reality.

Trembling, she looked at her engagement ring, glad that it was there, but wishing that she could also see a wedding ring there as well. She couldn't believe what she and Robert had done yesterday afternoon, in broad daylight, and during the choir trip. She blushed with embarrassment, but then remembered it all so tenderly. They'd only meant to kiss and cuddle, but one thing led to another and oh! She couldn't believe what they'd done.

'Grace are you ready yet? What are you doing?' Mary's voice penetrated Grace's thoughts. 'Come on girl, we're going to be late for chapel. William's already gone ages ago.'

Grace grabbed her hat and gloves and ran down to meet her mother, avoiding looking at her: hoping that her mother couldn't see any difference in her either.

They hurried up the hill to Haggate Chapel and took their places inside. It was an overcast day, but the sun kept breaking through. Grace looked up at the great pictures on either side of the minister's platform, which depicted the Ten Commandments. She couldn't look at them today: she didn't want reminding of them. Just then, the light broke through and lit up one of the Ten Commandments. It was the seventh commandment. 'Thou shalt not commit adultery.'

Grace shuddered inside herself. Was this what they had done, then? But no, she reassured herself, adultery is between married people. We're not married. But then another awful word came in to her head from the Bible. Fornication. Ugh. That word sounded even worse than adultery. And yet, that's what they had done yesterday. And it hadn't felt bad at all, quite the reverse. She was glad that Robert was sat behind her with the Tenors. If they caught each other's eyes just at that moment, everyone might guess. Grace kept her head down, studying her Bible or hymnbook for the rest of the service.

At the end of the service, she kept herself busy, collecting hymnbooks and Bibles, trying to avoid Robert. Grace was worried that he would think less of her after yesterday. But eventually he came and found her, and led her outside the chapel.

'Are you all right, Grace?' he said with great tenderness. 'I'm sorry about yesterday. It was all my fault. Can you ever forgive me? I should never have forced you.'

Grace looked up into Robert's eyes, and saw the sheer love shining out for her. 'Forced me?' she asked, 'I don't remember needing much forcing. I was as bad as you,' she giggled. 'Perhaps it's as well we're getting married soon. I must say that I'm quite looking forward to it now,' she said with a cheeky grin.

'I've been awake half the night, thinking you might not want to marry me now.'

'Try and stop me. I want to marry you even more now. Think no more about it,' said Grace. 'Come on, we'd better go back inside.' The two of them went back into the chapel and got immersed in the usual round of conversation with the other chapel members, but giving each other knowing glances every time they met.

The wedding preparations were going well. Mr Haynes had kindly offered to give Grace away at the service, for which she was very grateful. He had offered them the rent of a three-bedroomed house in Briercliffe at a reduced rent of two shillings a week. The two of them had started to decorate the house and buy some second hand furniture. Robert proudly said that with his tackler's wages, and only having to pay such a low rent for a whole house, Grace could stay at home after the wedding.

'But I don't want to stay at home,' replied Grace. 'I want to work. Soon enough time to stay at home when the babies come.'

'Babies?' Robert asked in a quiet voice, 'you don't think we've started a baby already, do you?'

'No, of course not, everyone knows it can't happen first time,' reassured Grace. But she wasn't so reassured the following month when she was sick three mornings in a row. She'd managed to explain the first two days away by saying that it was a tummy bug, but on the third day, she was caught near the toilets by Arthur Jones.

'You seem to be going to the toilets a lot in the mornings, Grace. Have you anything to tell us all? Has little Miss Prim been a naughty girl, then?' he sneered.

'Just a tummy bug,' she replied tersely, trying to keep the vomit from re-surfacing.

'Who do you think you're kidding? Never thought you'd be one to get caught out of wedlock, with your fancy chapel ways. What a story I'll have to tell to the others at bait time.'

'You'd better not say anything. There's nothing to tell. What business is it of yours?'

'Oh, I could make it my business. Although I could be bribed not to tell anyone. Come here and give us a kiss.' Arthur reached out and grabbed Grace by the hair and forced his mouth over Grace's. Grace tried desperately to get away, but he was far stronger than her.

'I'll want more than a kiss to keep me quiet if you don't keep still,' he said, but was suddenly lifted away from Grace with force. It was William.

'Get your filthy hands off my sister, Jones,' he roared, pushing Jones over on to the floor.

'Why should I?' persisted Jones, jumping back up again, 'She was enjoying it! Asking for it.'

'Didn't look like it to me, so clear off.'

'Or else, pipsqueak?'

'Just don't try it. I have friends in this mill. We could make life hard for you.'

'Huh, do you think I'm frightened? You'd better watch it, young Butler. I'll get my own back on you, and that snotty sister of yours. Just watch me. I can bide my time, but I have a long memory. Think on that,' then he slouched off back towards the weaving shed.

'What was all that about, Grace?'
'Oh nothing William, you know what a rotten chap he is. Let's forget it.'
'Are you all right?'
'Yes, I'm fine. We'd both better get back into work now or we'll be in real trouble. How come you were here anyway?'
'I'm just going down to Mr Haynes' ironmongers in Burnley for a part for one of the looms. Otherwise it could have been a different ending.'
'Thanks. I'm glad you were there in time for me. I'll see you later.'
Grace hurried back into the weaving shed and resumed work but not before Katie asked what was the matter. She simply told her that Arthur Jones had been nasty to her and left it at that. She didn't want Katie asking any awkward questions; she was inquisitive enough as it was.
But although she recovered from her shock fairly quickly, the nagging doubt remained in her mind. Had she conceived a baby that day on the picnic? Only time would tell.
The days passed by but her monthly curses didn't come. Although she had previously had little knowledge about the act which caused babies, she knew from talk in the weaving shed, that an absence of the monthly curse, plus sickness was a sure sign that you were having a baby, or up the duff, as some of the coarser women said.
Grace knew that babies took nine months to grow, so she worked out that her baby would be due in the middle of January. At least the baby's birthday would be in a different year than her marriage; then it wouldn't look like she had been already expecting when she got married. What a relief. She would be able to say 'Oh yes, I got married last year.'
The problem now was whether to tell her mother and Robert, or anyone for that matter. Grace agonised for a few days and then decided to tell Robert. She was worried about his reaction but he was delighted.
'I would have liked to wait a little longer and enjoy being married to you first, but it doesn't matter. At long last I'll have a

real family. We'll be all right, me and you and our baby. And the other babies.'

'Hey, let's get over this one first,' she laughed. 'We'll think about other babies after I've had the first one.'

'I wouldn't like to have only one baby. It was miserable growing up as an only child.'

'Oh for goodness sake, Robert. We will have more than one baby; it's just not the right time to talk about it. Better to talk about our wedding day first.'

'Yes, you're right, Grace. Have you got everything ready?'

'More or less. Our dresses are ready and the chapel ladies are organised for the meal afterwards.'

'Have you decided who is standing for you as best man?'

'I've asked your William to do it. I did ask a friend at Colne, but he's written to say that his wife will be near her time then, and he doesn't want to leave her.'

'No, I suppose not. I'm sure William will do instead.'

'He'll do very well. Now I'd better get back to the weaving shed, Ethel Whittaker has been giving me evil looks all through the meal time, so I'd better go and sort her loom out first thing!' said Robert as he went laughing into the shed.

A week later, just a week before the wedding, Katie came back with Grace for a final fitting for her dress. Katie's fitted perfectly and after having some tea, Katie went home.

'And now for your dress, Grace,' said Mary. 'I don't know why you were reluctant to try it on in front of Katie.'

'Oh, you know, brides have their foibles,' said Grace lamely. 'I wanted it to be special between me and you, mam. I'm really going to miss you when I leave home.'

'Don't be soft, girl. You're only going a few hundred yards down the road. You can see me every day.'

'I know, but it's been special since dad died. We've looked out for each other.'

'We'll still look out for each other. And Robert will look out for you too. That's what the Good Book says – you leave your mother and cleave to your husband or wife.'

By this time, Grace had taken off her work dress and was sliding her wedding dress over her head. She smoothed it down over her hips, and then noticed that her mother was staring at her waist. Grace didn't think there was any difference yet, but she knew that one of her skirts was a lot tighter than it had been.

'This dress seems too tight around the waist. I'll have to let it out. That's strange, it fitted perfectly last time I tried it on you.' Grace said nothing, but pretended to fiddle with the trim on her sleeve cuffs.

'Grace, have you something to tell me?'

'What sort of something?' Grace replied, playing for time.

'You've definitely thickened round your waist, and I've heard you being sick one or two mornings. Don't tell me you're expecting,' Mary said with disbelief in her voice. 'I thought you had more sense than that.'

Grace hung her head with shame. 'I think I might be, mam. It was only the once. We didn't mean to. We just got carried away.'

'I am surprised at you, but then you'll not be the first and you certainly won't be the last. At least you're engaged and getting married next week. Thank goodness I didn't insist on a long engagement.'

'At least it'll be born next year, not in the same year as I got married in.'

'Oh, you've worked that out already have you?' said Mary. 'Does Robert know?' Grace nodded. 'And what does he think? Does he think you've been cheap? Some men would.'

'No, he's glad. He feels sad because he has no family so he wanted to start a family straightaway. It's just a little earlier than we intended.'

'And does anyone else know? You seem to have told Robert before me,' said Mary with a hint of pique. 'Who else knows?'

'No one, mam. I would have told you, but I was frightened what you would say.' But then a memory of Arthur Jones attacking her came into her mind.

'What is it, Grace? Is there someone else you've told?'

'Not really, but you know when I said that Arthur Jones had been nasty to me? Well he noticed that I was going to be sick every morning and said some horrible things to me, so I suppose he might have guessed.'

'Oh dear, well never mind. It's over now. Hopefully you'll go overdue, you usually do with your first, then no one will be any the wiser. And it's nothing to do with anyone else anyway.'

'Thanks, mam,' said Grace.

'Now let me see how much I need to let this seam out. Good job I did plenty of seams all round the dress. Eh, I'm going to be a grandma next year. Well I never. What would your dad have said? His little girl going to have a baby. But no more talk of it now. We don't want anyone else knowing.'

'I won't, mam,' replied Grace, and then burst out laughing.

'What's so funny?'

'I was just thinking, when we chose this material, we chose it so that I could wear it all summer as my best dress. I'll probably only fit in it a few more weeks.'

'We could always make you another one in a bigger size, then no one will know?' suggested Mary.

'No, don't bother. Everyone will know soon enough. It'll come in for next year. I do like the pattern, though.' Grace had picked a pale blue material sprigged with little bunches of dark blue flowers, and Mary had trimmed the neckline, wrists and hem of the dress in navy braid. Katie's dress was in plain navy material, with similar braid in pale blue. Grace was to wear a navy bonnet and gloves and Katie pale blue.

Unbeknownst to them, Mary had made William and Robert a waistcoat each in the same colours as the girl's dresses. The two men were just wearing their one and only Sunday suits, but Mary had wanted to make them look a little special for the day. Mary had even made herself a new outfit too, a lilac two-piece trimmed with grey, and she'd trimmed her grey bonnet with the same lilac material.

The wedding was held on a late Saturday afternoon after the mills broke up for the Burnley Fair holiday. On the day, they all looked a treat. Mr Haynes proudly gave Grace away, and then sat with Mary. The choir sang a lovely anthem before the minister declared them man and wife. Robert shyly kissed the bride, in front of so many people, and then a great party was held in the Sunday School.

Mary collected all the presents and cards from the well-wishers, and promised to look after them until they arrived back from honeymoon. The mill's charabanc was all trimmed up for them, and Robert and Grace went down to Bank Top railway station in Burnley to catch the train to Blackpool, along with half the population of Briercliffe and Burnley. They could only afford to stay three days, but were happy with that. It was the first holiday either of them had had anyway, both of them had only had day trips before, so it was bound to be special. They couldn't wait.

Third week of July 2012

Carrie and Marc went in to see GreatGramps holding hands together. Jake nodded his hello.

'Er, we've something to tell you, GreatGramps,' said Carrie cautiously.

'What?' asked Jake, worried by the look on their faces.

'I'm pregnant,' said Carrie.

'Oh, thought . . .bad news. . .look on faces.'

'No, but we just thought you'd be disappointed.'

Jake laughed. 'Thought you could . . . prevent them now?' he said.

Carrie blushed. 'Well, yes, you can, but it must have been that tummy upset I had a few weeks ago. But it's definite. I'm due in January. We're going for a scan on Tuesday.

'Same as rest of us, now then?' asked Jake.

'Fraid so, mum was determined I'd be the first to break the mould. She was so thrilled when I told her I was getting married and I wasn't pregnant. But if I'd only known. I already was! What a family.'

'Children born in love,' said Jake.

'True,' said Carrie. 'And this one will be loved too. We haven't finally booked the wedding reception yet, so we're going to see if we can fast-forward it a bit, so I won't be as far on.'

'Good, no need to last as long,' quipped Jake.

'Oh GreatGramps, you're terrible,' said Carrie, but secretly, she was glad the wedding was going to be earlier. Jake's colour wasn't too good today and she wondered if she should get the doctor in to see him. But then she knew that Jake would only argue with her, so she'd wait and see.

The day after, Carrie told Jake that they had managed to get a cancellation at Rosehill House Hotel for their wedding on August 18th. 'Aunty Gill's really pleased 'cos that's her birthday and she said we can sing Happy Birthday to her as well. Then I can manage a short honeymoon before I start my new job.'

'What about job?'

'Oh it's OK. I've already been to see the head teacher. She understands. Says these things happen.'

Jake chuckled. 'Specially in our family!'

'Yes, you must have passed it down in our genes or something,' laughed Carrie.

'What? Being sexy?' asked Jake.

'Something like that,' agreed Carrie.

'When's scan?'

'Tuesday. I'll let you know what we find out.'

On Tuesday evening, Carrie and Marc came into Jake's sitting room holding an envelope.

'We've got the scan,' said Marc opening the envelope. 'Here it is,' as he offered Jake the picture. Jake looked at the strange swirls and squiggles on the picture.

'Can't see much,' said Jake.

'Oh yes, look GreatGramps, there's the back and there's the little legs and arms,' said Carrie excitedly

'Right, I suppose so,' said Jake.

'Do you want to know what it is?'

'I know what it is. . . a baby,' Jake smirked.

'No, I mean what sex.'

'They told you? Can you tell from that?'

'No, I can't, but they can. It's a little boy, GreatGramps. He'll be your great great grandson. How about that?' Jake smiled and gazed in wonder at the squiggles that were now his great great grandson.

'And we want to call him Jake,' said Marc softly, 'if you don't mind?'

'Mind? Honour,' gasped Jake.

'Good,' said Carrie, 'that's settled then. Little Jake it'll be. Jake Greenwood Spencer.' And she wrote 'Little Jake' on top of the picture. 'This copy is for you to keep. We had an extra one made for you.' Jake smiled his thanks.

'Are you moving out . . . . now baby coming?' asked Jake.

'No, we'd prefer to stay here for the time being, if you don't mind,' replied Carrie.

Jake shook his head. 'Stay as long as you want. Old cot in attic. Marc get it.'

'I will,' said Marc, 'can't have her lifting heavy things now, can we? Was the cot made for you, GreatGramps?'

'No, made for my grandmother's children.'

'For Grace's children?'

'Yes, . . .my father. . . was one of them.'

'Right, I'll go and get it.'

'If it had been a girl, we were going to call her Grace, after your grandmother,' said Carrie whilst they were waiting.

'Nice,' replied Jake. 'Perhaps next one.'

'Let me have this one first,' laughed Carrie, 'never mind the next one.'

Marc was soon back down from the attic with a large cot that was big enough for a child to sleep in until they were about two years old. It was made from oak and had large rockers on either end. After Carrie had wiped the dust off, they stood back and admired it.

'It's lasted a long time,' said Marc.

'Made to last then,' said Jake.

'It'll feel weird that my baby is going to be lying in a cot made for his great-great-great-great-great grandmother, or something like that! Might have got lost in counting the greats,' laughed Carrie. 'Look, it's got Greenwood carved on the side. That's amazing.'

'Perhaps I can carve Spencer on the other side,' quipped Marc.

'Terrific. The two families coming together,' said Carrie.' And now I'll have to get started on making bedding for the cot. Or better still, I'll ask Great Grandma Sandra. And I'll get Grandma Carol knitting. They'll love doing that. Come on Marc, we'll go and give them a ring and let GreatGramps have a bit of peace. ' Jake grinned as they both left the room. He usually needed a sleep after Carrie had been to see him.

Chapter 10

Robert opened the door of their newly rented house and with a flourish, carried Grace over the threshold.

'Put me down, you great lummock,' Grace said, but she was laughing as she said it. 'Oh look, mam's brought all the presents down, and set all the cards out on the dresser. Don't they look nice?'

'Shall we open the presents now or shall we go upstairs and test our new bed?' asked Robert with a glint in his eye.

'What do you think?' replied Grace.

'Oh all right, I'll open the first present,' said Robert. He watched Grace's face fall. 'Oh, isn't that what you meant, Mrs Greenwood?' he teased. 'I was sure you'd want to open your presents first.'

Grace hit Robert round the head with a cushion and then chased him upstairs, with Robert shouting 'you hussy, you. What sort of woman have I married?' But he didn't argue when Grace dragged him into the bedroom.

Quite some time later, Grace made a cup of tea and piled all the presents on to the small table.

'Come on, let's open them. Which first? Biggest or smallest?'

'Biggest,' said Robert gleefully, grabbing the largest parcel he could find. He tore off the wrappers to discover a large Family Bible, bound in leather, with gold writing on. He carefully opened the front page, and there in beautiful copperplate writing was an inscription.

To Robert Greenwood and Grace Butler on the occasion of your marriage
2nd July 1880
From the choir members at
Haggate Baptist Chapel
'As for me and my house, we will serve the Lord'
Book of Joshua chapter 24, verse 15

'Oh Robert,' said Grace, 'that is beautiful. It must have cost them a fortune. We'll treasure it forever, won't we?'
'We certainly will. We'll be able to write all our babies names in here.'
'Hope we don't need too many lines for the babies names,' Grace said fearfully.
'We'll have to accept what we get, my love, there is no way we can control that ourselves. It depends on what the Lord wants to give us.'
'Well, I just hope that the Lord's not too generous in this case. Three or four would be just right for me. Anyway, it's our honeymoon, no more talk of babies, let's open the other presents.'
The two of them tore open the other presents. Katie had bought them some beautiful white towels; William a tea set, the Men's meeting had bought them a bedspread and there were lots of other small presents. Pots and pans and dishes and tea towels; enough to keep them going for years, Grace said laughingly. Robert kept a careful note of each gift and who had sent it so that they could write 'Thank You' letters as soon as possible.
Mary had bought them most of their furniture. Grace had objected to such a large present but she explained that since she had lived at Mr Haynes', she had been able to save money as she lived freely at Mr Haynes' expense, and yet still got a wage.
'You might as well have the benefit now, there are no pockets in shrouds you know, lass,' said Mary. But even so, Grace was overwhelmed at her generosity. She was even more amazed by Mr Haynes' present. He'd bought her a large pine dresser that had been especially made by a local joiner. When Grace objected to the enormity of the present, he laughed and said that she had told him that she wanted one.
'I never asked for a dresser,' said Grace aghast.
'Of course you did, when I gave you a vase. You said you needed a dresser to put it on. So I only did what you told me to do.'
'I didn't mean . . .,' started an embarrassed Grace.
'I know you didn't, but it gave me the idea.'

'But it's too expensive a present.'

'Nonsense. I was the father of the bride for that day, so a dresser is a fine present for a father to give. Now say no more about it. Besides, the man who made it for you, is just setting up in business on his own. He's served his time now and he needs commissions, so I've helped him as well.'

'That's so kind of you and I'll never part with it. Thank you, and my vase and all my crockery does look well on it.'

Robert and Grace reflected how well they had done with their presents.

'I'll have to hold a thanksgiving tea to show off all my fine crockery and furniture. Let's do it next weekend before we go back to work,' suggested Grace.

'Good idea. Whom shall we invite?'

'Let's see, mam and William, and Jessie, and Mr Haynes, and Katie. Who else?'

'Mrs Shapcott?' suggested Robert.

'Oh yes, I'd better not forget her. I'll make sure we use the milk jug and sugar bowl that she bought us.'

'Will that be too many people for one tea? Do you think we need two separate meals? We haven't enough chairs to sit everyone down at the table,' asked Robert.

'No, one tea is enough. We'll sit them all down and we'll serve them, like servants. That will be fun and it'll get round us not having enough chairs.'

'I could always borrow some from Mrs Shapcott,' said Robert.

'No, I like the idea of serving our friends and family. That's what we'll do. We could start a new fashion.' And so they did! All the family and friends approved of the new fashion tea and felt like members of the gentry when their hosts served them.

But on Monday morning, it was back to work with a bump. They could no longer play at being newly weds and the grim reality of the working week took over. During the Burnley Fair holidays, the mill had been cleaned and the engines overhauled and everybody had a lot to talk about when they returned to work.

The routine carried on; work, chapel, choir, meetings and enjoying being married. Fortunately, Grace carried the baby like Mary had carried hers; their wide hips meant that the baby didn't show straight away, and Grace got away without anyone realising that the baby was already on the way when she got married. She waited until a few months after the wedding to announce that she was expecting. The pinny that she wore over her work dress also covered up her bump at first.

The Christmas period was almost on them again. The choir were again doing a choral work and carol singing was being planned. There was great debate as to where the Christmas meal would take place that year. Grace would have liked to hold it at her house, but Mr Haynes' overruled that, and said that everyone should still come to his house, especially as Grace was getting near her time. Nearer than you think, Grace thought, but acquiesced eventually.

The Christmas morning service had been truly beautiful this year, with the children from the day school performing a nativity on Christmas morning, to the delight of everyone present.

The meal was plentiful; a rich goose with all the trimmings and a flaming Christmas pudding to follow. Grace had eaten little, as she had quite a lot of backache. Mary had reassured her that it often happened in the last few weeks, and encouraged her to put her feet up and rest, banning her from helping with the washing up. Grace didn't need telling twice. The backache was becoming quite uncomfortable.

James Brown was playing the piano to entertain them. He had his fiancée with him this year; a lovely girl called Louise. She was accompanying his playing by singing in her warm soprano voice.

'Grace, why don't you come and join us? You and Louise will sound lovely together,' James suggested.

Not wishing to appear ungrateful to her host's nephew, Grace agreed. She heaved herself out of the chair and as she did, something happened which took her by surprise. As she stood up, a gush of water ran down her legs.

'Oh,' she cried out, 'what's happening?'
Mary soon realised just what was happening.
'I think it's the baby coming early. Can we use one of the bedrooms, please Mr Haynes.'
'Certainly. Jenny, you help Mrs Butler organise everything. This is women's work. William, go and get Doctor Astle. Take my horse and buggy. Robert? You come and have a cigar with me. It's going to be a long night.'
'But I haven't booked a doctor, only a midwife that lives in the village,' said Grace.
'Well get her as well, William,' directed Mr Haynes. 'Two heads are better than one at these times, I suppose.'
Suddenly everyone got busy and Jenny and Grace went upstairs whilst Mary got the kettles on the stove and collected some old linen.
'I'll put you in the spare guest room at the front,' said Jenny Brown.
'Don't you think we'd better try and get home instead? It all seems a lot of trouble for Mr Haynes.'
'Nonsense,' replied Jenny, 'it'll do him good, and this house. There hasn't been a baby born here since it was built. The parents bought it just after William, Hilda and I were born.' But she pursued this thought no further as Grace was doubled up in pain.
'My, that's a strong pain. How long have you been in pain, my dear?' asked Jenny when the pain had passed.
'All day really, but it was only backache at first, but then it changed into feeling like a strong dose of monthly troubles. Nothing bad really, but it's getting stronger now. The pain has moved into the front, rather than just the back. Oh, here it comes again.'
'I reckon that's only about three minutes since the last one. I think you are quite well on. You've a few weeks to go yet, haven't you?'
'Yes,' said Grace, 'perhaps this is just a practise run?' she said hopefully.
'I don't think so,' said Jenny. 'Oh, here's your mother.'

Mary rushed in with bundles of bedding, and then ran out again to get the dishes of hot water.

'Here, put this old nighty of yours on, Grace. It was still here from before.' Grace managed to get the old nighty on before the next pain engulfed her. The pain was becoming unbearable now, and that last pain had made her cry.

'Keep walking about as long as you can,' said Jenny. 'It helps the baby go down the birth canal.'

'It is easier when I'm upright,' said Grace, and then stopped again as another wave of pain swept over her. Mary and Jenny sat or walked with Grace, encouraging her and praising her as she coped with each contraction. They were coming faster and closer together now. Grace was worn out and eventually had lain on the bed.

'How much longer, I can't stand this anymore?' screamed Grace, but before they got chance to answer, the door opened and both Doctor Astle and Midwife Wilcox arrived together.

'Now then young lady, what's going on here? You're not due until the middle of January. Is all this Christmas excitement getting too much for you?' said Doctor Astle but before Grace could think of an answer, she cried out in pain again. 'Let me have a look at you,' he said, as he pulled back the covers. He felt her tummy and then put a little funnel to her tummy and listened in.

'Yes, heartbeat loud and clear. This is a strong baby,' he grinned. 'Strong contractions too,' he said, as another pain came on. There was a knock at the door. It was Robert, wanting to know if there was any news, but he was browbeaten out of the room, and told to go away as it was women's work. 'Ask again in a couple of hours,' shouted Midwife Wilcox, at which Grace groaned. Could she stand another couple of hours of this agony? But as it happened, after another hour of strong pains, Grace felt the pains change in nature.

'I think I want to push,' she shouted to the room in general and there was a rush to the bed by midwife and doctor, prospective grandmother and family friend.

'Out of our way,' said Midwife Wilcox, 'you two stand at the side and talk to her.' They were quietly obedient.

'All right Grace, time to push,' said Doctor Astle and Grace pushed with all her might, until she thought she would burst in two. It seemed as if she could never get this baby out, and she would be pushing for the rest of her life, when Midwife Wilcox told her to stop pushing.

'The baby's head is being born, just pant and don't push.' Grace did as she was told. 'Now you can push,' instructed Midwife Wilcox, and she did. Out slithered the baby in a rush to get born, crying loudly as soon as it did.

Midwife Wilcox picked the baby up and looked to check her breathing was satisfactory, but the loud wailing was a pretty good testament to the health of the baby.

'It's a little girl,' Doctor Astle said, 'and everything seems to be there. About just over five pounds wouldn't you say Mrs Wilcox?' Not bad for an early baby. Probably would've been a whopper if you'd gone to term. Better for you that you had it early.'

'A girl, let me see,' said Grace, sitting up in the bed.

The sticky bundle was placed in her arms. Grace fell in love with her instantly. She was so beautiful and was waving her arms about energetically.

'I shall call her Helen Mary,' she said quietly.

'They're lovely names. Why have you picked them?' asked Midwife Wilcox.

'I had a friend called Helen when I was a child. We were very special friends, but she died in the cholera epidemic in 1866. I said that I would name my first girl after her. And Mary is of course for my mam.'

'Well my dear, you are the first to have a baby today in Briercliffe that I know of. If it had been a boy, you could have called it Noel, on account of it being Christmas Day,' said the midwife. 'Now somebody had better tell the father, but don't let him come up yet. I've to sort the afterbirth out.'

Grace soon delivered the afterbirth and after inspection, Doctor Astle declared that he was happy to leave Grace in the care of Midwife Wilcox.

The proud grandmother came and held out her arms for a cuddle of baby Helen, and kissed her daughter.

'You were very brave, Grace. You behaved far better than I did when I had you,' she admitted.

'Made for childbirth, is Mrs Greenwood,' said Doctor Astle cheerily as he left. An exhausted Grace gave him a murderous look. Never again would she have another baby. Never. Ever.

Next the baby had to be suckled, and after a little help, Helen took to it as if she had been feeding for years. Eventually, Robert was allowed to come in and see his wife and daughter. The other women discreetly left the two of them together to share in the most intimate of moments as they gazed at their new creation.

'Are you happy that it's a girl?' asked Robert.

'Yes, are you?'

'Yes. I'm just glad you are both safe. The pain sounded terrible from downstairs.'

'Doctor Astle says that I'm made for childbirth,' Grace said with a cynical voice.

'Oh good,' said Robert, but Grace gave him the same murderous look, so he changed the subject.

'It will be lovely that we always celebrate the birth of our first child at the same time as we celebrate our Lord's birthday.'

'Yes,' replied Grace, 'we can have birthday candles on the Christmas cake for both of them, but oh Robert, why today? Of all days?'

'Why not today? It's a lovely day to have been born.'

'Well, it's still 1880. I wanted our baby to be born in 1881. It won't look good in the Family Bible in years to come.'

'Oh Grace, you do think of the weirdest things. Just enjoy the baby today and forget the future. What does it matter when she was born? You are both safe. That is all that matters.'

'All right and now if you don't mind, I'd like a sleep. No wonder it is called labour. I'm exhausted.' And before Robert could reply, she was fast asleep.

Chapter 11

Next morning, Grace woke from a deep sleep, with the cries of her newborn baby ringing in her ears. She stirred in the bed, but winced as she moved around. She'd had no idea that giving birth would be so painful afterwards, although the pain of labour was almost forgotten, in the joy of holding her baby girl.

Grandma Mary was soon in the room on hearing the cry.

'I'll get her out for you,' she said. 'Oh, she's a beautiful baby, even though I'm biased. Here you are, Helen Mary, go to your mummy,' Mary said, in the soppy voice of a new grandmother. 'She sounds hungry Grace, so I'll change her afterwards. She'll be needing a bath later anyway.' Mary passed the precious bundle over, still wrapped in a towel, in the absence of any baby clothes, and Grace started feeding. After the feed, Mary put little Helen back in the drawer, whilst she went down to the kitchen.

Shortly afterwards, Robert arrived in the bedroom.

'How are my two special girls this morning?'

'Robert, where did you sleep last night? I don't seem to remember much from last night after the baby was born.'

'No, you just flopped straight asleep. Didn't leave much room for me in the bed,' teased Robert.

'And where did Helen sleep?' We've nothing ready for her here.'

'I slept in James' old bed and Helen slept in a padded drawer, but Mr Haynes wants to come in and see you, if that's all right with you?'

Grace gathered her nighty together and pulled a shawl round her shoulders.

'What will he be thinking? Giving birth in his house. It's so embarrassing.'

'Don't worry. He was quite excited, like the rest of us. I'll go and get him.'

Grace wriggled in the bed to get in a more comfortable position, wincing as she did at the pain in her nether regions, but her face changed as Mr Haynes walked in with Robert.

'Good morning Grace. How are you feeling today?'

'Sore, but happy,' replied Grace. 'I'm sorry that I inconvenienced you yesterday. It took me by surprise. The baby wasn't due for a while yet.'

'Think nothing of it, but unfortunately we are not geared up for receiving babies here. I've arranged to have a cot made by my joiner friend, but I'm not sure whether it's finished or not yet, with you being early.'

'That's very kind of you. You shouldn't have gone to so much trouble,' said Robert.

'It's nothing. I think of you as my family now. You've lived her for so many years. And now I must get along. I'm going to Jenny and James' house today, it being Boxing Day. I'll get the cot delivered to your house as soon as it's finished.'

'Thank you. We hadn't got round to getting a cot yet. Most babies in Briercliffe spend the first few months in a drawer anyway!' laughed Grace.

'Well, stay here as long as you like. Don't feel you have to rush off home.'

'Thank you,' said Robert and Grace simultaneously

It was a week before Doctor Astle would let Grace go home to her house in Ernest Street. During that time she was able to get used to having a baby and managing the care for herself, ably helped by her mother. Robert had gone back to work, but had received well wishes from many of their workmates.

Katie arrived in a flurry after work one day, cuddling a tiny cardigan that she had knitted.

'You caught me on the hop there, Grace! I had to sew it up last night, so that I could bring it round. My, you were quite early, weren't you? You are lucky she's so big.'

Grace looked at Katie sharply, but there was no hint of criticism or suggestion in Katie's face. If she had her own private thoughts about the very early arrival, she kept them to herself. No doubt there was a lot of discussion and speculation in the weaving shed, but at least Grace wouldn't hear it.

The new family were soon settled back in Ernest Street. The cot had already been delivered. It was beautifully made in oak and would probably last Helen until she was about two years old. It had rockers on both ends and a wooden hood at the head of the cot, and the name 'Greenwood' was carved along one side of the cot. Jenny and James had sent some exquisitely embroidered cot bedding and warm blankets to go with the cot. Mary had knitted enough garments to last Helen until she was at school, Grace laughingly said, but she had also added to Grace's own efforts at making little vests and sewing napkin squares. Now, they would be able to sew pretty dresses and frilly undergarments to their heart's content.

Grace ably tried to get Helen into a good routine of regular feeding during the day but Helen was having none of it. Born during the night, Miss Helen Mary Greenwood liked the night. She would sleep most of the day, hardly waking for any feeds, but as soon as it was bedtime, Helen would cry and wail and want regular feeding. Grace was exhausted and Robert wasn't getting much sleep either, and had resorted to sleeping in one of the other bedrooms, on a single bed. Their tempers were frayed and for the first time in their marriage, they were continually falling out.

Fortunately, daytime sleeping had worked well when it came time to take Helen to chapel for her dedication service, as she slept throughout and was impeccably behaved. Being of the Baptist persuasion, a service of dedication was given, rather than christening. Grace had tried to explain the difference to Jane Leaver, one of her friends at the mill. She was a member of St James church in the village.

'Why don't you baptise babies then?' she'd asked.

'Well, the parents just give thanks for the baby's birth and promise to bring the child up in the Christian faith.'

'That's similar to baptism, so why not baptise them?' Jane persisted.

Grace thought for a moment. 'The Baptists believe that in the Bible, the way to become a Christian, is that a person must repent of their sins, accept Jesus as their Saviour and then become baptised. And what baby could repent of their sins?'

'But the parents can repent of the baby's sins for them, can't they?'

'Well, not really, it should be the person themselves,' replied Grace. 'We get baptised when we are adults, but it is when we want it to happen: when we've made the decision. You can be nine or ninety, but it's your choice.'

'And don't the church members take part in this dedication as well?' asked Jane.

'Yes, they promise to help bring the child up in the Christian faith.'

'Yes, we do that,' replied Jane.

'And we have a full immersion, not just a sprinkling, like you do. Usually in the river down Lane Bottoms.'

'Oh, I don't like the sound of that,' shivered Jane.

'It's amazing fun actually. You don't think about the cold, just about what you are doing.'

'I think I'll stick to my way and you stick to yours,' laughed Jane.

'That's fine,' replied Grace, 'that's what it's all about, we work it out for ourselves and do what we think right.'

'Besides, I like the fact that I'm a Godparent. You don't have them, do you?'

'Not usually, but you can if you want to, but it saves having family arguments about who is going to be the Godparents,' said Grace. 'I know, why don't you come to Helen's dedication service, then you can see for yourself.'

'I might just do that,' replied Jane, and Grace was pleased to see Jane and her husband at Helen's dedication service, and invited them to stay at the chapel for something to eat afterwards.

Helen might have been well-behaved at her dedication service, but it didn't occur at night and Helen continued to wear her parents out. Inevitably, Robert slept in the spare bed more than he slept in the marital bed. They tried everything. Each new piece of advice that they heard from relatives and friends, they put into practice, but to no avail. Helen had a mind of her own, and a routine of her own. They tried ignoring her, giving her extra feeds and even solids, trying her with water, gripe water, and many other tips, but nothing worked.

Eventually one night, when she was about eight months old, Robert grabbed the cot and pulled it in to the other bedroom and slammed the door.

'We are going to have a night without Helen in the room. I want to sleep with you Grace; it's been ever so long since I cuddled you. Come here,' said Robert and pulled Grace towards him. At first Grace couldn't bear it that Helen was crying but eventually her body took over and she forgot everything, as Robert loved her. Long afterwards, they both suddenly realised that Helen was quiet. Grace's instinct was to jump up and go and see to her, but Robert wouldn't let her go. Grace didn't argue very much, because she was falling asleep: the result of too many sleepless nights.

Next morning, Grace couldn't believe it when the 'knocker up' banged on the window to get Robert up for work.

'Helen! She hasn't woken us all night,' cried Grace, and ran in to the other bedroom, fearing the worst. But no, Helen was sleeping peacefully, her little fist curled round under her chin. That one night seemed to be the turning point, and Helen settled into a routine that had been long in coming, and they left her to sleep in her own bedroom from then on. It was perhaps as well, because a few weeks later, Grace realised that she was probably expecting again.

Chapter 12

Whenever possible, but not often, Grace would escape down to Burnley Market on a Saturday afternoon with Katie. Such a change had come over Katie whilst Grace was expecting. She started by being a bit vague about where she was going on a Saturday afternoon, instead of spending it with Grace and little Helen. Sometimes she said she was going to Burnley with her sister, but was quite evasive.

Eventually, Grace got to the bottom of it, and it was a man, as Grace had expected. Katie had met him at the bandstand concert in Thompson's Park, in Burnley. They had been meeting secretly for several weeks, but now it was on an official basis; they were engaged and were getting married in December.

His name was Edwin Procter and he was a rope maker in a local factory. Katie was besotted and Grace was pleased to see that her friend had found the man she wanted.

'I wanted you to be my bridesmaid, or dame of honour, but now you've told me you're expecting again, I can't. I'll just have to have my sisters instead,' moaned Katie.

The wedding was on a bright crisp day and Katie and her sisters looked beautiful. Grace managed to find a dress that was very loose fitting so that she didn't look too big, as her next baby was due in April.

Before her second baby was born, Katie told Grace that she was expecting a baby too, and they both looked forward to their forthcoming motherhood, although Grace's views on it were far more realistic than Katie's.

After her marriage, Katie got work in a weaving shed in Burnley, as Edwin's work was there. They set up home in a terraced house, not far from the centre of Burnley, and also near to Edwin's parents. But as often as she could, until she got too big herself, Katie would come and take little Helen out for a walk, to give Grace some time on her own.

* * * * *

The next ten years were a trial to Grace. All she seemed to do was look after babies, who inevitably came along at regular intervals, as well as trying to cook and clean. Sometimes, she would have preferred to go out to work in the weaving shed, than be at home with the children, even though her mother was a great help. She missed adult company during the day, but Robert would not hear of her going out to work, so Grace had to suffer it.

It wasn't that she didn't like being a mother and she passionately loved her children, but she felt frustrated staying at home, and got out of the house as often as possible, even if it was only to walk to Hillview House, or go to a shop so that she could talk to an adult.

The next child born was William Albert, named after his uncle and Mr Haynes, and also Robert's father. William Albert was born on Easter Sunday 1882, again at a family luncheon at Hillview House. Grace came in for a lot of ribbing that it had happened again. Robert even suggested booking in for the next birth now, but the murderous look from Grace was enough to cure him. At least William Albert was on time, though, not that it mattered as much this time.

After William, who they called Will, so as not to get confused with his Uncle William, came Samuel Jack in 1884, followed by a little girl called Eliza May in 1885. Sadly, Eliza was born too early and only lived for three days. Robert and Grace comforted each other as much as they could during this sad time, but Grace's arms ached to hold her, even though she'd only known her for three days. But Grace had to put sadness behind her and think happy thoughts when she discovered that she was expecting again in 1887. This time it was another boy called James Peter. Another boy was born called Isaac Joshua in 1889.

'It seems as soon as I get one of them out of the cot, then I'm expecting again,' said Grace in exasperation to Robert. 'Perhaps I should lend the cot out to someone else, and then I can't have another baby.' They'd rearranged the bedrooms, so that the largest bedroom was for the boys, whilst Helen had the littlest bedroom as her own. As each boy was born, Helen complained that it was another boy, and desperately wanted a sister. Grace didn't mind really, as long as they were healthy; the memories of Eliza's short life were never far from the surface. Despite having five children, she still yearned for Eliza.

Katie had had another two children quite quickly, a boy called Stephen in 1883 and another boy in 1884 called David. Grace was amazed that Katie had had three babies in three years, but then she seemed to stop. Katie didn't have any more children, whilst Grace seemed to carry on regardless.

By 1889, William had married Jessie and had just found out that they were expecting their second child. Their first-born was a little girl, whom they had called Maud. Grace offered them the cot with the first child, but Mr Haynes had already promised to have one made for them. After an uneventful first confinement, things weren't going too well for Jessie this time. She was vomiting constantly and was going thinner by the minute.

'I've usually stopped vomiting by three months,' said Grace trying to cheer Jessie up, 'it shouldn't be much longer now.'

'I hardly vomited at all with Maud,' replied Jessie

They lived in the terraced house next door to Robert and Grace, again owned by Mr Haynes, and spent time in each other's houses. But in the following weeks and months the vomiting didn't stop and Jessie was getting weaker. Mr Haynes brought in a specialist doctor to see Jessie, but his advice made no difference. Still the vomiting continued.

Jessie had had to give up doing any housework, and was made to rest as much as possible and so Grace went round to look after her as often as her brood would allow her. Mary sent food down to tempt Jessie, or sat with her to keep her company, or took Maud out to give her peace. It was a trying time for all of them.

Eventually, Jessie got to the eighth month, and then went into labour. The labour was long and painful, and with Jessie being in a weakened state to start with, the midwife was very worried and insisted that Doctor Astle came to see her.

A small boy was eventually delivered, who was barely breathing. Doctor Astle worked hard on saving the little boy, and told Grace to give him some diluted cow's milk, as Jessie was too weak to suckle him. The midwife was having trouble delivering the afterbirth, too. Once she managed to deliver it, she thought that things would improve, but then Jessie started to bleed. Doctor Astle massaged her stomach to try and stop it, and raised the foot of the bed, but nothing worked. Jessie continued to bleed; nothing seemed to stop it.

Within two hours of giving birth, Jessie was dead. She had only barely held the baby, but knew that it was a boy; her joy showing on her face, even though she was in pain and frightened. William had to be told, and Grace held him to her and cuddled him, just like he was one of her children.

'What am I going to do without Jessie?' he wailed to Grace. 'I don't think I'll be able to live anymore. I need her so much. I always have, ever since we were children. And she needed me too. We were just two halves of one, if you understand what I mean.'

'I do, William. Robert and I are a bit like that. But I'll help you to go on. And so will mam. Now come and see your little boy.'

'Where is he?'

'Just having some milk off mam,' replied Grace.

'Milk? He's alive then? I thought he'd died too. I never heard him cry.'

'He's only tiny, but with good nursing, he'll pull through, Doctor Astle reckons.'

'Did Jessie see him?'

'Yes, and she held him for a short while.'

'What did Jessie call the little boy?'

'She didn't: you'll have to chose.'

'We'll call him Richard, after her dad.'

'Yes, that will be good. Shall I go and tell them?'

'No, I must go myself. I'll meet them outside the mill at the end of the shift. Now I'd like to stay with Jessie for a while. Leave us alone, Grace, but thank you for what you've done,' said William. Grace hugged him again, and then left him alone as requested: her own heart heavy as she went downstairs.

Jessie's sister, Martha, was at home with her children, so it was decided that she would care for little Richard and Maud during the day. As she had recently given birth herself, and had plenty of milk, she was able to be a wet nurse for the baby. William insisted on paying for a young girl to come in and help Martha each day. Martha refused at first, but was glad as time went by, as looking after three healthy children and one sickly premature baby was taxing, to say the least.

Richard had to be fed almost two hourly during the day, yet Martha managed to express extra breast milk and put it into a bottle for William to give him at night.

The family did their best to help William during his grief, but often he just wanted to be left alone with his children, or if he were on his own, he would sit in the graveyard, near to the grave.

For the first year, Grace and Mary worried about him; he seemed to have lost so much weight, but during the second year, William seemed to come round a little. He would never get over losing Jessie so young, but life had to go on.

Despite the initial worries, little Richard did thrive and although he always had a weak chest, he became an engaging toddler, with a wicked sense of humour. He looked on Martha as his mother, but little Maud bossed him around too, so it was like having two mothers for him. But it was having Jessie's children to remind him of her that gave William the strength to go on with his life.

And by the time little Richard was two, Grace realised that she was expecting again. This time, Helen got her wish. A little girl was born in 1891 called Florence Katie, followed far too quickly by another girl in 1892 called Pearl Alice.

Robert and Grace had hard words after Pearl's birth.

'We just can't keep on having more babies, Robert. The house is getting too small, and I'm exhausted all the time.'

'What can we do about it? We've tried everything we've heard about that prevents babies. You always breast feed for as long as you can, and we've tried not making love, but we never last very long do we?' Robert laughed.

'It's not a laughing matter,' she cried back at him, 'it's not you who has to carry them, or give birth to them, or bring them up. You just go to work, away from it all.'

'Oh yes, I just sit at work all day, twiddling my thumbs,' he said angrily. 'I do my best, Grace, I work hard, I bring all my wage home and don't stop off at the pub and waste my wages, like a lot of the men do. I try and help you in the house, and try and take the children out of your way so that you can have some peace. What more can I do? Do you want me to stay at home with the babies and you go to work?'

'Yes, I'd love that some days,' Grace screamed, but then collapsed in laughter at the thought of Robert looking after all the children all day. Then Robert started laughing, and then they had a hug, and before they knew what was happening, they were making love.

Grace was furious a few weeks later to find that she was expecting again.

'This is definitely the last,' she said, 'even if I have to go and live in another house on my own.' But whilst she was expecting, she went to visit Katie and whilst they were talking, Katie told her about the use of vinegar sponges to prevent babies being born. That's why Katie had only had three babies.

'Why didn't you tell me before?' Grace railed at Katie.

'It's not the sort of thing you talk about, is it? It's a very private thing, what goes on between a man and his wife in the bedroom.'

'Well, I shall be definitely trying it after this one is born,' said Grace. 'Anyway, who told you?'

'My midwife. Doing herself out of a job, really, isn't she? But she believes that women should only have the number of children that they want or can afford.'

'I like the sound of her. She sounds like my kind of woman. How are your three, anyway? We never get chance to have a long chat nowadays,' moaned Grace.

'Perhaps we will if you stop having babies,' teased Katie.

'If only,' said Grace with feeling. And the two of them chattered an hour away before Grace had to leave. But when she got home, Grace was determined to talk to Robert about this new fangled thing that Katie had told her about. The thought of no more babies was just too tempting.

Chapter 13

Her next baby, whom Grace announced to all and sundry was her last, was another boy. Grace had a very difficult and hard labour this time, and Doctor Astle had to be called. He was muttering with the midwife about using instruments to help with the birth, and despite Grace trying her best to push the baby out, the instruments had to be used.

Grace felt like she was going to split in half: more so than with her usual births. She also had the worry that the instruments might damage the baby, although both doctor and midwife assured her otherwise.

Eventually, Thomas Andrew was born, and Grace could hear the doctor and midwife muttering quietly together again.

'What's the matter? Is there something wrong with my baby?' asked Grace, fighting through the exhaustion.

Doctor Astle brought the baby round to show Grace, and he looked and sounded good, as he was screaming lustily.

'Not really,' said the doctor, 'but there's something not just right with one of his feet.'

'Let me look,' demanded Grace, and stared at the little foot hanging limply and twisted. What's the matter with it?' asked Grace, 'will it get better?'

'I'm not sure,' said the doctor, 'it might just be because the baby has been in a funny position in the womb, or it might be a condition called Talipes. Only time will tell.'

'Can anything be done for it?' asked Grace.

'Well, we could try; exercise and stretching might help. We'll know as time goes on what it really is, if the foot doesn't revert to a normal position.'

'I bet it's those instruments you used,' said Grace crossly.

'No, they didn't affect it at all. This happened in the womb.'

'Is this what they mean by club foot?' asked Grace more quietly.

'Yes,' said Doctor Astle, 'it is known by that name by laypeople.'

After everyone was gone, Grace looked down at her little son and grieved for the fact that he wasn't perfect. She tenderly stroked his foot and tentatively stretched it as the doctor had shown her. It felt cruel, but Thomas didn't seem to object. When Robert got home from the mill, she told him what the doctor had said and they discussed the implications this would have on his life as a child and when he was older.

'Whatever happens, we will protect this little one, Grace,' promised Robert, as he cradled them in his arms.

'At least he seems healthy otherwise,' Grace commented.

'Good, for that we must thank God,' he replied.

Life dragged on for Grace. A long round of housework, and caring and cooking for Robert and all her children; not to mention all the washing and ironing. Grace usually had a great big pile of washing in the scullery, waiting for Monday morning washday. And alongside all this, Grace had to do exercises on Thomas. Sometimes Helen, Robert or Mary would do them for her, but it was usually Grace that did them.

There wasn't much improvement, and as time went on, Doctor Astle said that it was Talipes. All he could offer Thomas was a caliper; a sort of ugly splint that tried to straighten his leg, and make his leg longer, so that his limp wasn't as pronounced. Throughout all the treatment, Thomas was very brave and didn't cause any fuss when his treatments were carried out, or his calliper was put on.

But besides all the hard days, there were good days too. Days of going out walks in the local countryside, days of picnics or teas at the chapel. Sometimes, there were even day trips to beauty spots with either the chapel or the mill. Days of going up to Hillview House with the children, and letting them play in the gardens and fields around about.

Holidays had gone by the board, because there were too many children to be accommodated, and it was too expensive, so the smaller treats meant much more to them all.

Grace was pleased that the children all enjoyed school. None of them were reluctant to go and at least she had some peace when they were there.

It felt strange when Helen went to work in the mill; her firstborn old enough to work. Grace had suggested that she try for some other job, but Helen was insistent that she wanted to be a weaver, along with her friends from school. Her closest friends were Doris, Elsie and Alice. All of them managed to get a job at the same mill and were forever giggling together, and talking about votes for women, and how they were never going to get married.

Unfortunately, Arthur Jones realised who Helen was, and immediately set about taunting her. Helen took it all in her stride, and often gave as good as she got. But this only riled Jones even more. He still had a downer on the entire Greenwood family, in which he included William Butler as well.

After Helen gave him a verbal onslaught in front of other workers, Jones walked off with venom in his heart. Helen just laughed with her friends, and thought nothing more of it. That night she was late going home, as she had been chatting to her friends.

As she went down by the side of the mill, through the alleyway, a hand reached out and grabbed her. She started to scream but a rough hand was pushed over her mouth.

'Shut up, or you'll be sorry,' the man said. Helen realised with a sinking heart that she recognised the voice. It was Jones. Absolutely panic stricken, Helen fought as best she could, especially when he started grabbing her clothes and pulling them upwards. Working in the mill and listening to the older women, Helen knew what he intended doing and was terrified.

Fortunately, he had to let go of her mouth so that he could force her to the floor. Helen took the opportunity to scream as loudly as she could, even though she knew that all the workers would have gone home by now. Jones slapped her hard across her face, which temporarily stunned her and stopped her screaming.

'I told you to shut up, you bitch. You're going to get what you need. I'll show your family that you don't mess about with me.' He carried on trying to get under her clothes and had just managed to get hold of her drawers, when she bit him on his shoulder. For that she received another slap, but she carried on screaming anyway.

Just as he managed to get her drawers down, he was suddenly lifted up bodily, away from her. Helen jumped up quickly and moved away, only to turn round and see that her father was fighting with Jones. Jones seemed to be getting the upper hand, as he was wirier than her father.

When Jones was on top, bashing Robert's face, Helen kicked him with her clogs in the small of his back and again in his head. This gave Robert the chance to get hold of him properly. Just at that point, Uncle William came down the alleyway and Helen screamed for him to come and help.

Between the two of them, they dragged Jones back into the mill, and told the mill manager what he had done. He was instantly sacked on the spot. Jones tried to argue with the mill manager, calling Helen names and suggesting that she was agreeable, but the mill manager said that he had had enough of Jones, as there had been other complaints about him, that had never been proved. His dismissal was final. Jones walked away from the mill and screamed over his shoulder that he would get the family back. He could wait, he said, but just watch out. No one got him the sack and got away with it.

Robert hurried home with Helen and quickly told Grace what had happened. Helen had calmed down considerably by the time they got home, but just kept saying how grateful she was that her dad and uncle had stayed behind to attend a tacklers' meeting in the mill.

Grace took her upstairs and asked her questions to ascertain if any real damage had been done and was relieved that Helen hadn't been violated, apart from the blows to her face. Grace was happy for Helen to stay off work next day, but Helen insisted on going, now she knew that Jones wouldn't be there. But she never went home on her own again, and was nervous for quite some time after that: constantly checking if anyone was following her. She took the threats seriously.

Life carried on; the children all growing up happy and healthy, even if the family didn't have any money to spare. The children were all very different in looks and temperament. Will was soldier mad. Mr Haynes had bought him some toy soldiers for Christmas when he was three, and he'd never looked back. All his games were about soldiers and war. It drove Grace mad at times, but it kept Will quiet at least. Will insisted that he wasn't going in to the mill when he was older, but joining the army.

Grace had her own thoughts about that, but kept them to herself. But despite her thoughts, Will joined the army when he was eighteen in 1890, before the last three children had been born. Prior to that he'd had a spell working in the mill until he was old enough to enlist. Grace knew that she couldn't have dissuaded him, but was glad that the country wasn't at war. But it was very hard that Christmas when they all gathered at Hillview House and Will was missing.

Samuel loved sums and was showing himself to be a good teacher to the younger children in the school. Robert wondered if this was where his future would lie and Grace was secretly proud that they might have a schoolteacher for a son. But it wasn't to be. As soon as he was fourteen, he begged to go in to the mill with his father. It was with a heavy heart that Grace kitted him out in working gear ready for his entry into work.

James was a scamp. There was no other word for it! He was always at the centre of any trouble that happened. And when he was remonstrated with, he always had an answer.

'But I was just . . .' he would start each sentence with, to justify why he was misbehaving. He frequently received the cane at school, and further chastisement when he got home from Robert, for misbehaving at school. But it didn't change him. Nothing seemed to get him down or make him sad. He was a happy-go-lucky scamp all the time. But people loved him, whatever he did. Grace came to dread the opening sentence of any conversation with her friends or relatives that began 'You'll never guess what your James has done?' Grace would hold her breath until she knew how serious the next misdemeanour was.

Isaac was the exact opposite. A serious, shy child who never had his head out of a book and could get completely lost in his reading and be oblivious to the outside world.

Florence was a proper little girl, who loved nothing better than playing at being a mother to her dolls; continually dressing and undressing them, and taking them out for walks up the front street. Pearl was a gentle soul who loved everyone. She was quite shy but always giggling, and was never happier than when Isaac sat her on his knee and read to her. She also worshipped Florence.

The children often fell out at home, but when they were outside or at school, they stuck together through thick and thin, and would stick up for each other in the playground. It became known that if you kicked one of the Greenwood's, they would all come to each other's rescue, so woe betide you.

They were particularly careful of little Thomas and made sure that no one took advantage of him, because of his limp. Not that Thomas let his limp stand in his way of anything that he wanted to do. At long last, the babies seemed to have stopped coming and Grace frequently thanked Katie for giving her the information to limit her family.

Eventually, Grace got all the children to school, but just as Thomas went to school, Samuel left and got a job at the mill with his dad. Suddenly, Grace had a little more time on her hands during the day and she relished it. Sometimes she would meet up with Katie or with Jane Leaver whose three girls were all at school as well. Other times, she would spend time with her mam.

Grace tried to persuade Robert to let her go back to work as a part-timer, but he was having none of it. He insisted that she stay at home, so that the children always had someone there when they got home from school. As it happened, it was as well she was not working in the summer of 1896. Diphtheria broke out in Briercliffe.

At first, the disease was sporadic and hardly any children were infected. But soon it spread rapidly throughout the village. The school was getting empty as another child went down with the dreaded disease.

It was Florence who came down with it first. She came home from school complaining of being tired, hot and a sore throat.

Grace asked Florence questions quite casually, but inside her heart was racing at the thought that she might have got the dreaded disease. The doctor soon confirmed it. Grace went in to a panic and packed off all the other children to stay at Hillview House.

But it was too late for Pearl. Two days later, Pearl had the same symptoms and was brought back to Ernest Street with Florence. Grace followed all the doctor's instructions to the letter, but the children were getting worse; Grace could easily see that. As the membrane grew over their throat, their colour got poorer and their little chests were gasping to get enough breath in to their lungs. And they didn't have any energy at all, but lay there listlessly on their beds.

It was very hard work trying to get any drinks into them, as they couldn't swallow at all. As soon as they were settled, a bout of coughing would start up. Grace would get one of them settled, and then the other would be ill and needing help, and would wake the other one up. Grace was exhausted.

Later that day, William came running round to see Grace in a panic. Young Richard was showing signs of the disease, and seemed to be far worse than her own girls. Grace offered to look after him with the girls, and suggested that Maud should go up to Hillview House for safety, with the rest of Grace's children. William agreed, but not before telling Grace that Jessie's sister, Martha, had already lost one of her children to the disease yesterday. And she was still caring for Williams's children when he was at work.

The brother and sister looked at each other with horror. What if it happened to them? Surely not, they both thought. Not us. Surely the Lord would protect them? But on this occasion, he did not. Richard died the following morning with William and Grace both sitting with him. It was hard having to go straight on to nurse the other two children, but mercifully they were too ill to realise that something had happened to Richard.

Florence and Pearl were being nursed in the same bed, as that seemed to give them both comfort, to touch their sister and know she was there. But next morning, when Grace went in to the bedroom, she saw that Florence was struggling to get her breath and her lips were going blue. Grace held her upright in her arms, rocking her and trying to give her relief. But with a big shudder, Florence stopped breathing and lay still in Grace's arms. Grace wanted to scream out loud, but she knew that she would upset Pearl. She quietly moved Florence, releasing her hand from Pearl's, and placed her in the boys' bedroom, where Richard had died so recently.

Pearl seemed agitated when Grace got back in and seemed to be reaching out for Florence's hand, so Grace gently held Pearl's hand until she quietened down and went back to sleep. She dreaded her waking up and asking where Florence was, but she would meet that when it happened. For now, all her efforts must be concentrated on Pearl.

But it was to no avail. Later the next day, Pearl too died in her mother's arms. Three children in the family dead. Now Grace let herself go, in wild howls that would have scared the wolves themselves. It was how William found her. Wailing and rocking on her bed, with Pearl still in her arms. He gently took Pearl off Grace and laid her on the bed, before he took Grace in his arms and cuddled her. The mill owner had given him the day off work to sort out a funeral for Richard. Now they would have a joint funeral for all three children.

A message was sent up to Hillview House to let them know, but with the instructions that the other children hadn't to come home yet. Just in case. But fortunately, no other children in their family came down with the disease. It was sad enough for Mary to be burying three of her grandchildren at the same time.

Mr Haynes bought the family a Vault up at Haggate chapel to bury all the children in, rather than have them all in their own graves. He said that he would arrange for Eliza to be put in there as well. Grace and William just accepted the kind gift, not realising how much it must have cost Mr Haynes, but grateful that the three cousins were together, or four once Eliza was moved.

Robert was as silent as the grave. He couldn't talk about his feelings with Grace, which was difficult because she wanted to talk about the children and how they had died. The two grew apart for a time, as they grieved separately. Grace also had to cope with the children's grief, because Robert couldn't articulate his feelings with them and didn't want to talk about the children who had died with anyone.

But eventually they both broke down one night when Grace accused Robert of not caring about the children. The healing tears helped more than each other's grief, but rekindled their deep love for each other. But it was a hard year for both of them. And William too, who had no wife to support his grief. But at least he had a mother, who was grieving in her own way at the loss of her grandchildren, but could still help her son.

The whole village had been under a cloud as twenty-two children died within the village that year. Grace was glad when the New Year came and they could look forward to new things happening. Let good things happen in Briercliffe in 1897, she prayed fervently at the New Year's Eve Watch night service.

Chapter 14

It was a rare quiet moment. The children were all at school or work. All was silent. Grace had a lot of baking to do for the New Year's Eve Watchnight service at the chapel tonight. There would be a service about eleven thirty, followed by a party when the New Year arrived. It was such a special New Year this time, 1899. A new century. The twentieth century was about to start. She and Robert had been wondering what the New Year would bring them. No more babies I hope, Grace had quipped. She'd managed to go six years without a baby now. But their thoughts had pondered on what might happen to them both, and their family in this new century.

Grace had made herself a cup of tea once she'd put the baking in the oven, and was sat savouring three things; the drink, the thoughts about the New Year, and her momentary free time. Her peace was shattered by a hammering on her door.

'Mrs Greenwood, Mrs Greenwood, come quick,' a little voice was shouting through the letterbox. Grace went to open the door; her heart in her mouth, wondering what might have occurred to one of her loved ones. Her first thought was Will, out with the army in the Boer War, but it couldn't be him. It would be a letter, or one of those telegram things if anything had happened to her precious son. She cautiously opened the door. It was young Annie Wareing, whose mum was the new cleaner at Hillview since Mrs Croft had retired.

'What's the matter, Annie?' Grace asked.

'My mum said to tell you to come, quick.'

'But what for? What's the matter?'

'Mr Haynes. He's just been took bad.'

'But the children will be coming home from school. I can't leave them. Can you stay here and wait for them and I'll get our Helen to come home from the mill. I expect your mum told you to come straight back, didn't she?'

Annie nodded, still a little out of breath.

'Right, let me get my shawl on, and then I'll be off to the mill. If the children get home before Helen gets here, could you sort them out and then help her bring them up to the house for me? No better still, leave them here. I could do without them being under my feet if there is nursing to do. Oh, and tell Helen there is baking in the oven,' she shouted as she went through the door.

Grace set off up the street to the weaving shed and called Helen from her work. After explaining the situation, Grace ran, puffing a bit, up to Hillview House. She wasn't as fit as she was as a young girl. Arriving in the kitchen, there was no one around, so Grace ran into the lounge. Eventually after searching all the downstairs rooms, she went upstairs. Mr Haynes was lying on the floor outside his bedroom door; Mrs Wareing and Mary bent over him.

'Oh Grace, thank goodness you're here. Quick, go and ring Mr James and Mrs Jenny on that dratted telephone thing. You know I don't like using it. Annie went for the doctor before she came for you, so he shouldn't be very long now.'

'Don't you think we should get him on to the bed?' asked Grace.

'Can't move him, he's too heavy,' Mary replied.

'Where's our Annie?' asked Mrs Wareing.

'I've had to leave her waiting for my young ones coming home from school. I've been and told Helen to come home from the mill to look after them. Annie's going to come up as soon as she can.' Mrs Wareing nodded her thanks.

'Mam, what happened to Mr Haynes?'

'I rang the gong to tell him his breakfast was ready and he didn't appear, so I went upstairs to see why he hadn't come down, and I found him here. He doesn't seem to be with it, although he is breathing. I covered him up with this blanket to try and keep him warm. I didn't know what else to do.'

'That was probably the best thing to do. Now I'll go and ring the family.' Grace went downstairs to the hall where the implement was situated. Should she ring Mr James or Mrs Jenny first? Deciding on Mr James, she picked up the speaker handle and wound the other small handle to get through to the exchange.

'Could I have the premises of Mr James Brown, the department store in St James' Street, Burnley please,' said Grace, trying not to show her nervousness. She'd only used the implement a few times before, and only to make telephone calls for her mother.

After a short wait, Grace was put through to a man who answered the telephone confidently.

'Brown's Store. Mr Saunders speaking.'

'Oh, er, hello, I'm Mrs Greenwood, and I'd like to speak to Mr Brown, please.'

'Is it urgent?' he asked, 'only Mr Brown has a customer with him.'

'Yes, it is urgent, it's about his uncle Mr Haynes.'

'Oh, right then. I'll get him for you immediately,' replied Mr Saunders, a totally different tone to his voice.

Grace didn't have to wait very long before Mr James came to the phone.

'Grace, what's the matter? Saunders says it's about my uncle?'

'Hello Mr James. Yes, I'm afraid your uncle has collapsed at home. My mam and Mrs Wareing are with him, and we've sent for the doctor.'

'I'll be with you as soon as I can. Thank you. Oh Grace, have you told my mother?'

'No, I thought I'd better tell you first.'

'Good, that's right. I'll ring her myself now. Thank you Grace. See you shortly.'

Grace put the handle down on the holder and hurried back upstairs. She'd just got to the top when the front door bell rang. Running back downstairs, Grace was relieved to see that it was the doctor, and he had young Annie Wareing on his pony and cart.

Doctor Astle ran upstairs with Grace running behind, telling him what little she knew.

'We need to get him in to bed. Do you think we can manage it between us?' asked Doctor Astle.

'We'll try,' they all replied. They all gently took hold of him, with the doctor giving the most strength, and lifted him on to the large bed.

'We'll need to get his clothes off. Has he a nightgown, Mrs Butler?'

'Yes, I'll get him one,' said Mary as she dashed into the dressing room next door. As she returned, she asked what the doctor thought had happened.

'Could be several things. Could be a seizure, or a brain haemorrhage or his heart. I'll have to examine him first.'

Mary and Mrs Wareing put the nightgown over Mr Haynes and then undid his other clothes and slipped them off, covering him up with a sheet, to save his modesty.

Doctor Astle examined Mr Haynes and put a small trumpet to his heart, listening carefully, and then he checked his pulse. After that he tested all his limbs.

'Heart sounds fairly strong. But he's not responding to my touch. He doesn't appear to be feeling anything, so that's a good thing, he won't be feeling any pain,' said Doctor Astle eventually. Just at that moment, Mr James rushed into the room.

'What's happened? How is he, Doctor?' asked Mr James.

'Not sure yet. Seems to be unconscious, but his heart is fairly strong, so that suggests to me that he's had a seizure or a brain haemorrhage, rather than his heart.'

'And how long will he be ill for?' asked Mr James.

'Hard to say. The next two days will be able to tell us more. It's a waiting game really.'

'But he will get better, won't he Doctor?' asked Mr James.

'As I say, the next two days will tell us more. I can't promise anything. It depends if and when he comes out of being unconscious. Would you like me to arrange a nurse?'

'No,' said Mary suddenly. 'No nurse, he wouldn't like it. He's used to me and Mrs Wareing being around and doing things. He wouldn't like strangers. Begging your pardon, Mr James.'

'No you're right, Mrs Butler. If both of you don't mind, I'd be very grateful?'

'It's the least we can do, after all he's done for us,' replied Mary quietly.

'Well, give me a list of anything that you are going to need and I'll get it sent up from town. I'll just borrow my uncle's pony and cart and go and get my mother. I think she'd like to be here too. I only came on my horse.'

Doctor Astle gave his list of instructions to care for Mr Haynes, whilst Mr James left them to get his mother. After the doctor had gone, Mary checked with Mrs Wareing that it was all right for her to stay.

'I'm sorry, Mrs Wareing, I should have checked that you were able to stay. That was wrong of me to assume.'

'Don't worry. I agree with you. Mr Haynes has done a lot for us both. I'm in the same boat as you, Mrs Butler, a widow, so I've no man whingeing because I haven't come home. The only problem will be my Annie. I can't leave her on her own at home. She's a sensible lass, but I don't want to put her under that sort of stress.'

'She can stay here. There's plenty of bedrooms. I'm sure you'll be able to do errands for us, Annie, won't you?' to which Annie nodded, a little overwhelmed at staying in this large house.

'And by the way, my name is Mary,' she added.

'And mine's Thelma,' replied Mrs Wareing.

'I'll come and help as much as I can, mam, you know I will. I'm grateful for what Mr Haynes has done for me too. I'll go down to Doctor Astle's house now and see if the prescription is ready, shall I? And I can check up on Helen to see that everything is all right at home with the little ones. I'll see you both later.'

Grace made her way home to find that the little ones were fine. Helen had got them helping her to bake, or rather hindering her.

'Thought I'd better finish your baking for tonight, mum,' said Helen. 'I know you'd still want to send some even if you can't go yourself. How's Mr Haynes?'

'He's not good, Helen. He's unconscious and is just lying there. The doctor says that the next two days will tell one way or the other.'

'That doesn't sound good.'

'No, and I'd like to help with the nursing if I could. Would you be prepared to stay at home and look after the little ones so that I can help up there? Your Gran and Mrs Wareing will get tired if they do all the work themselves. But Gran refused to let a nurse come and care for him.'

'Ah, that's typical of Gran. But she's not so young herself now, she needs to be careful.'

'Less of your cheek, she's only in her sixties.'

'I know, but that's ancient.'

'Enough, cheeky girl. Now, do you think that you could sort tea out for the others? Did you get chance to tell your dad what happened?'

'Yes to both things. What did you promise for the Jacob's Join tonight?'

'Buns and egg sandwiches. We'll need some more eggs, could you send James to the farm for some when he comes in from school?'

'Yes, I will. You go back to Hillview House now, mum. I'll be fine.'

'You're a good girl Helen. I don't know what I'd do without you. You'll make a lovely wife one day soon.'

'Huh! Not me. I don't want to be tied to a man and have babies every year like you did. I'd rather be a Suffragist instead. Women have rights as well as men.'

'Oh no! If you're going to get on your soapbox, I think I'll go straight away.' Grace hurried out of the door, not wishing to get in to another battle about Votes for Women. Helen had been instrumental in inviting one of the Suffragists from Clitheroe to come to the mill to talk to the girls, but it hadn't gone down very well with the management, or the men for that matter, who had booed the girl and tried to drown out what she was saying, during the lunch break. What with Helen with her Suffragists and her brother William trying get a Trade Union accepted, their name was becoming one of troublemakers.

But she had others things to occupy her mind right now. How to help her mam and Mrs Wareing? On arriving back at the house, Grace found that both Mrs Jenny and Mr James had arrived. Both were visibly upset, and Grace went back downstairs to make everyone a cup of tea. The universal panacea for all ills, thought Grace as she waited for the kettle to come to the boil.

Apparently, Mr Haynes had just wet the bed, and that had upset everyone, as if that was a sign of how ill he was. Mary knew that he would have been mortified if he'd known what he'd done.

That night, Grace stayed up and made her mam and Mrs Wareing go to bed, as they would need their strength for tomorrow.

'But what about Robert and the children?' protested Mary.

'Helen is going to stay off work, and Robert will be fine about it. Stop worrying and get off to bed. Has Annie already gone?'

'Yes,' said Thelma, 'she was a little upset by the strangeness of the room.'

'Do you think she would like to go to my house and sleep with my lot? One more won't make much difference,' laughed Grace.

'That's kind of you, but I think she'll settle. It all depends how long this goes on for.'

'Mm, and that's something we won't know. We'll just have to take a day at a time from now on.'

'And pray,' added Mary.

'Oh yes, and pray, that's all we can do,' agreed Grace. The two older women went upstairs to bed and Grace resumed her stay by Mr Haynes bedside, watching carefully for any signs of change. Occasionally she dozed, but mainly she watched and waited throughout the night. Once she changed his bed again; twice she gave him medicine. She was glad when dawn appeared.

Quite early, Doctor Astle arrived to check up on Mr Haynes.

'Well, he's no better, but then he's no worse. I think you need to keep doing what you are and I'll call again tonight after my surgery.'

'Thank you Doctor. I'll see you out,' said a tired Grace.

When the other two ladies got up, Grace gave them a report, and then went home to bed. The children weren't getting ready for school, just playing about.

'Hello mum, you missed the Watch Night service. I ate loads of food and we didn't go to bed until two in the morning,' crowed James.

'And I ate a lot too,' piped up Isaac.

'Hush boys, get off to school,' said Helen.

'There is no school today, it's a holiday,' shouted Isaac.

'Oh no. Well, I'm going to bed, so you'd better play out a long way from here, because if you wake me up, you'll be sorry,' replied Grace.

'How was Mr Haynes, mum?' asked Helen.

'Just the same. I think it's going to be a long job. Do you mind missing work Helen?'

'No mum. As long as you don't mind missing my board money on Friday,' Helen quipped. 'It just confirms my feelings. I don't want to sit at home with babies all day, but I'll enjoy it for a while. Just give me the mill any day!'

Chapter 15

As it happened, it wasn't a long job. For seven days and nights, the ladies took it in turns to watch over Mr Haynes, doing all the nursing care for him. All without any sign of improvement. Mr James and Mrs Jenny attended for long periods during each day, and William Butler visited during the evenings, and just held his hand, telling him how his horses were. Grace teased him about that, but William argued that he didn't know what else to say, and anyway, Mr Haynes would want to know about the horses.

On the eighth day, Mr Haynes seemed agitated. When Doctor Astle came to visit, he was quite optimistic.

'This could be a sign that he is waking up. We'll have to wait and see. Report anything unusual at once, or if you are concerned about anything, but I must admit, you are all doing a sterling job. Couldn't have better nurses if I'd sent them myself,' which pleased all three of them.

Throughout that day, Mr Haynes was restless. Whilst Mary was caring for him, he suddenly made a noise. Mary jumped up out of her chair and moved towards the bed, holding Mr Haynes' hand.

A funny gurgle came out of the side of his mouth that sounded like the name Beth. But then he let out a large sigh and stopped breathing. Mary shouted out for Thelma, who came running.

'I think he's gone. What do you think?' Mary said quietly.

Thelma nodded. 'What happened, Mary?'

'He just made a noise and then a gurgling sound, then stopped breathing.'

'Shall I ring the doctor? And Mr James and Mrs Jenny too?'

'Yes please, you are more confident with the telephone.'

Thelma set off downstairs to the telephone, but was interrupted by having to answer the door. It was Mr James.

'Oh Sir, I was just coming to ring you. I'm afraid Mr Haynes has just passed away. Quite suddenly. I'm sorry, Sir.'

Mr James paused with his hand on the banister, his head bowed, his breathing ragged.

'Are you all right, Sir? Can I get you anything?'

'I'll be fine. Just give me a minute. It's just such a shock. He's been more like a father to me than an uncle. My own father died whilst I was still a toddler. I'll go up and see him, if you don't mind.'

'You do that; Mrs Butler is up there with him. And I'll bring you a cup of tea.'

'Thank you Mrs Wareing. You are so kind. No, on second thoughts, I'll ring my mother first.' Mr James moved towards the telephone, then shouted, 'Have you rung the doctor?'

'No Sir, I haven't had time yet.'

'Righto. I'll ring him as well.' He picked the receiver up and Thelma went towards the kitchen, leaving him to his sad task.

After making the telephone calls, James went upstairs to Mr Haynes' bedroom. Mary jumped up when he entered.

'I'm so sorry, Mr James. He went peaceful, though.'

'What happened, Mary?'

'He was a bit agitated this morning and when Doctor Astle came, he said that could be a good sign, so we were all quite hopeful. But then he made a funny noise, then a gurgling noise and then just stopped breathing,' said Mary. 'I might have been imagining it, but the gurgle sounded like the name Beth, but that might just be my fancy,' she added quietly.

'Beth?' Are you sure?'

'Yes,' replied Mary, worried that she had upset Mr James.

'Yes, it probably was Beth. That was his wife's name.'

'His wife? I didn't know he'd had a wife.'

'Yes, she died in childbirth: the child with her. They'd only been married a year.'

'But he never said anything about it.'

'No, he wouldn't talk about it at all. Said it was his way of coping.'

'Oh no, and our Grace has had two of her babies born here. What a trouble that must have been to him. Oh, why didn't he say?' said Mary getting upset.

'Don't worry about it Mary. Those births did him good. He said he felt like he and the house were living again. He looks peaceful, doesn't he?'

'He does that, Mr James. I haven't done anything yet. Not until the Doctor arrives.'

'No, that's for the best. Oh, there's the door; it might be him now. I'll go down and let him in,' said Mr James, but before he could get downstairs, Thelma was showing Doctor Astle upstairs.

'Sad day, James,' Doctor Astle said. 'When I saw him this morning, I didn't know which way it would go, but you always hope for the best.'

'At least he was still working. I don't think he could have stood it if he'd had to retire.'

'No, he was an active man, despite his age. Seventy eight, wasn't he?'

'Yes, I hope I'm not still working when I'm that age.'

'Me neither, James, me neither' replied the Doctor. On arriving in the bedroom, Doctor Astle confirmed what they already knew and signed a death certificate. On showing the doctor out, James' mother arrived. She too, wished to be escorted to her brother's bedroom. Mary discreetly retired from the bedroom and left mother and son to grieve alone.

'That's our jobs gone, now,' said Thelma morosely.

'Yes, I suppose so,' replied Mary. 'It's my home gone as well,' added Mary. But the thought of what would happen to her was horrifying, so she rallied Thelma and said 'Come on, we've a lot of work to do. We won't be going anywhere yet, and we won't get a good reference if the house isn't up to standards, when it's sold.' The two women decided to start cleaning the main drawing room: just to give themselves something to do. It was there that Mrs Jenny found them.

'I just wanted to say how grateful I am – we both are – for all the care and attention you have given to my brother. You will be rewarded. And now we have a funeral to plan. Mary, do you know anyone who can do the last offices for him?'

'I'll do it,' said Mary quickly, 'it'll be an honour. The last service I can do for him.'

'Are you sure? Well, that's very kind of you, and I must say, I quite like the idea that it's you. He would have approved of that. And now I must ask an awful imposition of you both. Could you manage to prepare a funeral meal for us here?'

'Of course,' replied Mary and Thelma together.

'We've already started cleaning the house ready,' added Thelma.

'Thank you, I'll leave it to you both. I'll let you know about menus and numbers nearer the time. I'm going out with James now to see the undertakers.' Mrs Jenny left the room and soon afterwards, Mr James and Mrs Jenny left the house.

Thelma and Mary cleaned most of the downstairs and then it was time for Thelma to go home. Left alone, Mary started getting upset about the morning's events. She would really miss Mr Haynes. He'd been a fine companion. They'd had many a comfortable evening, talking about old times together. She would miss that, and she would certainly miss living in this house. Then her fears reappeared. Where would she live now? Certainly not with Grace – it was too crowded! Perhaps with William? But then he had his own problems. Oh well, I'll just have to trust God again, Mary thought. He didn't let me down last time. And now she'd go and get her black clothes out of her wardrobe and put them on. It was the least she could do for her employer.

Three hours later, the undertaker arrived from Burnley and took Mr Haynes body away to the Chapel of Rest. After preparation, he would be returned to Hillview House until the funeral, which had been arranged for the following week.

By the following week, the house had been cleaned until it was spotless. Thelma, Mary, Grace and Helen had spent all morning preparing a sumptuous cold meal for the mourners. Everything was laid out in the dining room, with small tables being arranged in the drawing room and lounge as well, so that people could sit down to eat.

Mary had said to Mrs Jenny that she wouldn't go to the funeral so that she could be at Hillview House, in readiness for the funeral guests, but Mrs Jenny wouldn't hear of it.

'I want you at the funeral; it's what my brother would have wanted. I know women don't go to funerals very much but you're different. You played a very important role in his life for the last few years. Leave Helen and Grace here to get ready, but you must come Mrs Butler, and William, I insist.' Mary eventually gave in, and was transported down to St Peter's Church of England church in Burnley, with Mrs Jenny and Mr James, as if she was the chief mourner. And she and William were made to sit in the front pew with the Browns, despite them heading for the back of the church. Mary was very uncomfortable and felt that she was stepping out of her rank, but couldn't argue with Mr James.

The church was packed. Mary couldn't believe how many people were there, but then her practical head stepped in. Would there be enough food if all these people came back to the house afterwards?

Many worthy dignitaries paid moving tributes to Mr Haynes; one of them was Mr Ormerod from her own chapel. Mary struggled to stop the tears from rolling down her face, surreptitiously wiping them with her best black gloves.

Eventually, the service in the church was over, and they moved to the churchyard, where the family vault had been prepared. Mary watched as the coffin was lowered into the vault. This was the end of an era, she reflected. Life would change, that was for sure. But she had no idea what that change would be. Help me to trust you, Lord, she murmured to herself as they moved back to the horse and cart.

As soon as they got back to Hillview House, Mary joined Thelma, Annie, Grace and Helen, in setting out all the food and serving cups of tea for the mourners. Fortunately, not all the mourners had come back to the house, Mary was glad to see, and there was an abundant supply of food for everyone.

After the last mourner had gone, the women hurried off to start the mammoth task of clearing up after the meal. They cleared the tables first and piled all the pots in the kitchen, with a view to Helen and Annie starting on the washing up; large sinks of hot water were ready.

Mr James came into the kitchen and Mary spoke to him straightaway.

'We'll sort all this washing up out as soon as possible, Mr James. And then can you tell me how soon you want me to leave the house? Or will you want me to stay until it is sold and the next owner comes in?' But Mr James just laughed.

'You don't think we're going to throw you out tonight, do you Mary? We're not that cruel. Now I want you all to come in to the drawing room, please.'

'The drawing room? Whatever for? We've too much to do,' replied Mary.

'Just do as you are told for once, without questioning it,' Mr James said, but he was laughing as he said it. 'And bring Thelma and Grace with you, for that matter.'

As they got in the drawing room, they saw that Mr Ormerod was still here. Grace thought that was strange but didn't say anything. Mary was just surprised to see him because she thought everyone had gone.

'Come and sit down all of you,' ordered Mr Ormerod as they came in. Even stranger, thought Grace, when it's not his house. They all sat down and then Mr James told Mr Ormerod that he could start.

'Right, thank you,' said Mr Ormerod, 'this is the last will and testament of William Archibald George Haynes.' He proceeded to say some very flowery legal language, which none of the women really understood. Then he was saying about leaving Hillview House and the business to Mr James, along with certain properties that he owned, on condition that he always provided a home and catered for the financial needs of his mother. But the next beneficiary was a shock.

'To Mary Butler, my constant friend and companion, I leave number five Ernest Street, Briercliffe, with an annuity of £100 per annum, until her death.' Mary gasped. That was the house next-door to William and next door but one to Grace and

Robert. He'd left her a house, and £100 by the sound of it. She would never want again.

'To Grace Greenwood, I leave number one Ernest Street and the sum of £1000.' Here, it was Grace's turn. She too, gasped out loud.

'I can't, I can't have that. That's not fair,' she stuttered.

'Shush Grace,' chided Mr James gently, 'it's what my uncle wanted. Now just listen to the rest. Go on Mr Ormerod.'

'To Mr William Butler, I leave number three Ernest Street and the sum of £1000, plus my horses and carts.' William wasn't present, as he'd had to go back to work, but Grace and Mary gasped on his behalf.

'To Miss Helen Mary Greenwood, I leave my sister's gold locket and the sum of £100. To Mr William Greenwood, I leave the sum of £100.' Mr Ormerod proceeded to name all of Grace's children, saying that they had got £100 each. Then he mentioned Maud Jessie Butler, and she had got a hundred pounds as well. Next it was Thelma's turn. Mr Haynes had left her £100, even though she had only worked for him for a few months.

'But I've only been with him for a few months,' Thelma gasped.

'That doesn't matter. A labourer is worthy of his hire, or her hire, as your case may be,' said Mr Ormerod gently. 'He was forever changing and making additions to his will. I was used to it!' he laughed. There was also a small legacy for Mrs Croft and for the gardener, Scott, and larger ones for St Peter's Church and several charities that he supported.

There was a stunned silence at the end of the reading. Mr Ormerod thanked everyone and then left.

Mr James was the first to speak. 'Did you all understand what your inheritance meant?'

'Yes,' said Grace, 'but he's given us so much. Surely it all should have come to you?'

'No, I've got plenty left, don't you worry. Why, just getting this house would have been enough, but I got a lot more. I'm also overwhelmed by his generosity. Mary, did you understand the word annuity?'

'Yes, I've got a hundred pounds and the house.'

'No, you've got £100 every year, to live on. You won't want again. You gave up your life to come and live here with my uncle, and he was very grateful.'

'But he saved my life by giving me a home when I was turned out of the tied cottage. It's me who should have been thanking him.'

'Never mind, you're financially safe now. And Grace, he wanted you and William to make a go of a business or something. That's why he gave you so much, so that you could get out of the mills.'

'But we love the mill, even though I'm not working there at the moment,' replied Grace.

'Leave it for now. I'll let the truth sink in first, but in a couple of weeks, I'll meet with you and William to discuss what you are going to do with it and give you any help that I can. And now I want to get my mother home. Will you be all right staying here on your own, Mary?'

Mary nodded, too overcome by her sudden wealth.

'Helen could stay here with you, mam,' suggested Grace.

'No, I'll be fine. I'd rather be here on my own, with my memories tonight.' Mary shook herself. 'So, when will you be moving in, then Mr James?'

James laughed. 'Oh not for a while yet. Wills take time to sort out. I'll give you fair warning. And any way, I'd love it if you stayed here and worked for me, at the same wage, of course.'

'That's very kind of you Mr James, but if I'm as rich as you say I am, I'd like to retire to my new house, near to my grandchildren and spend time with them.'

'Perhaps you would stay on, Mrs Wareing.'

'Yes please, Mr James. I'll still need to work, however generous Mr Haynes has been. But could my Annie stay?'

'That's fine. We'll sort out the details later. And now we're going. Thank you all for the wonderful meal you made for us today. Goodbye.'

'Goodbye,' echoed all the women, still reeling with the news of their inheritance.

'Well, that's a turn up for the books and no mistake,' said Grace eventually and they all nodded. 'Come on Helen, we'd better get home. Your dad will have forgotten what we look like; I've been here for the last two weeks more than I've been at home. Besides, I can't wait to tell him he's married to an heiress,' she chuckled. The two of them set off for home, marvelling at the change in fortunes that all the family had received that day.

Soon after they arrived home, Robert got home from the mill with Samuel, and the children returned from the neighbours where they had gone after school. Grace had warned Helen not to say anything to them until they had had tea and then she would announce it. When tea was finished, Grace cleared her throat and told them that she wanted to have words with them all. The younger lads looked guilty, desperately searching their minds for any misdemeanours they may have done, for which they were going to get into trouble.

'As you know, it was Mr Haynes' funeral today.' The children all looked suitably grave when she said this. 'Well, he left us all something in his will.' She looked at each person in turn, prolonging the suspense. 'What do you think it might be?' she asked them.

The children made various suggestions from a horse through to a sovereign. Robert suggested a small sum of money.

'He left us this house, for all of us. No more rent to pay, so we shall be much richer,' she said, teasing them. 'And he left Will £100.' All eyes stared at Grace, with incredulity. They couldn't imagine £100. It was too vast a sum for their reasoning.

'£100?' said Robert in disbelief, 'for Will? Only him?'

'No,' said Grace, really enjoying this, 'he left £100 to each and every child in this family, and to your cousin Maud next door as well. Oh and he left Helen his sister's locket.'

'Oh poor Helen, only getting a locket,' said Samuel.

'No, I got £100 as well as the locket,' explained Helen.

'But why did you get a locket?' persisted Samuel.

'Oh when she was a little girl, Mr Haynes found her in his sister's bedroom, playing with the locket, and saying it was hers, because it had a letter 'H' on it. I was mortified,' explained Grace. 'He must have remembered that all these years. It is a lovely locket. I hope you will treasure it, Helen?'

'I will, but come on mum, stop teasing. Tell them the rest,' said Helen.

'The rest?' said Grace with a mystified air, 'oh you mean your gran's got a house next door to Uncle William, and a £100 per year for life?'

'And the rest, mum,' demanded Helen.

'Oh yes, Uncle William has got his house, like us.'

'Muuuum,' screamed Helen.

'Oh yes, and me and Uncle William have got £1000 each as well.'

'£1000?' screamed Robert, but then all the children went crazy, running up and down the room.

'I couldn't believe it either,' Grace softly said to Robert, as she drew him to the corner of the room away from the children. 'Apparently, he wants me and William to go into business and improve our lives.'

'I can't take this in,' replied Robert eventually.

'Mr James is going to come and talk to us and advise us later. It'll take a while for the money to come through anyway. But I think we can afford a week's holiday this year, don't you?'

Robert grinned. 'If not a fortnight,' he laughed. It was a happy family that went to bed that night, full of plans for their amazing amount of money.

Chapter 16

Although Mary was sad that her employer had died, she quite enjoyed living in the big house alone. The grandchildren vied to be allowed to stay with her, ostensibly to 'look after her', but usually it was more that she was looking after them – making large amounts of food and clearing up after them. During this interim period, before Mr James moved in to the house with his wife Louise and their family, Mary spent time getting her own house ready, once the previous tenants had left. She was so excited, she had never owned a house before, and was enjoying making curtains and looking for second hand bargain furniture.

It would be so good to live next door to both her children and all her grandchildren. It was also good to know that she could please herself whatever she did. It was a very happy situation to be in, with no financial worries ever again. God had been good to her again, she reflected.

About four months after the funeral, Mr James called round in the evening to talk to Grace and Robert and brother William.

'The will has been proved now, and the money is ready to pay out. The deeds to the houses will take a little longer, of course, but I have your cheques with me now. I suggest you all go to Burnley Building Society and open an account, whilst you think about what you are going to do with it. At least your money will be making money whilst you deliberate.'

'That's a good idea,' said William. 'We've had lots of talks about the money during the last few months. We still can't really believe it's happened to us.'

Mr James pulled the cheques out of his inside coat pocket. 'Well, you'd better believe it now,' he said with a big grin on his face. The three of them looked at the cheques in awe. Even though they'd known about it, it still looked much bigger when written down.

'So what ideas have you had about the money? Are you going to go with my uncle's suggestion and buy a business?'

'Probably,' said Grace, 'but we're not sure what sort of business. Or whether to do something for the good of others, like a children's home. We sort of feel guilty that we were picked to receive so much money when others have nothing.'

'Don't feel guilty,' replied Mr James, 'you can help others by being good employers and giving work to people who haven't got jobs. That's what's so good about having money. You can make things happen for other people; you can improve their lifestyle.'

'I've never thought about it like that,' said William. 'I've got a lot of ideas about what makes a good employer.'

'I bet you have,' laughed Mr James. 'I've heard you going on about Trades Unions often enough. Well, you could start a business where Trades Unions were welcomed.'

'But what sort of business would you recommend?' asked Grace.

'It really depends on what you want. And what is available to buy at the time. Or if there is a demand for a new product that isn't available locally. Go for what you know, is my recommendation.'

'Go for what we know? You mean weaving?' asked William.

'Why not? You could be much better employers than a lot of other mill managers because you have been through it yourselves. What do you think, Robert? You're very quiet, not saying much.'

'It's not my place to say anything, is it? I didn't inherit the money.'

'Oh Robert, don't be so daft,' declared Grace. 'What I inherit, you inherit. Of course it's up to you as well.'

'I'm just happy as a tackler. I've no design to be anything better.'

'But wouldn't you like to help in managing a mill, if we bought one?'

'No. I've just said, I'm happy as a tackler.'

Grace stared at her husband. She loved him dearly but sometimes she didn't really understand him. This was such a golden opportunity to make their life secure, not just for them, but for the children as well. But she knew better than to press him in company. They would talk about it later, if and when they decided to buy anything.

Sensing the tension, William cut in to the conversation. 'Is there anything out there for sale that you think might be worth looking at then, Mr James?'

'I thought you'd never ask!' laughed Mr James, 'and less of this Mister. Just call me James now. If we're going to be fellow businessmen and women, we shouldn't stand on ceremony. As it happens, there is a very good opportunity that has been brought to my attention. Do you know Wilfred Bainbridge's place in Burnley? It's across from St Peter's church.'

Grace shook her head but William knew of it.

'Well, it's for sale at a very reduced price,' continued James.

'Could we afford it?' asked William.

'It would stretch you, but I think it's feasible. Would you like to go and have a look at it?'

'Yes please,' said Grace and William together.

'How about Saturday afternoon, after you've finished work?'

All nodded agreement.

'Good. I'll fix up a viewing for Saturday then. Shall we say about three of the clock?'

'Yes, that'll be fine. I'll ask my mother to mind the children. I think Helen is going out,' said Grace.

'I'll come and pick you up in my horse and cart about half past two, then.' With that, James left the house, leaving the others shocked at the way the evening had gone.

'Just think, William, us being mill owners,' said Grace.

'You aren't yet,' replied Robert, bringing them back to reality. 'It might not come off.'

'Well, let us dream for a day or two. Reality can come in on Saturday when we've seen it. You are miserable, Robert. I thought you'd be thrilled.'

'I don't hold with being above your station. We're just poor weavers, not mill owners.'

'But don't you get it, Robert? We're not poor weavers anymore. We're rich, compared to most of our neighbours and friends. We can make a difference.'

'We'll see,' replied Robert, refusing to be drawn.

Grace couldn't wait for Saturday to come round. When James arrived, they all set off, including Robert; Grace had managed to persuade him.

The horse and cart drew up outside Bainbridge's mill. It was a long low building as befits a weaving mill, with a north-angled roof, to maximise the light. To the left was a four-storey office block attached to the weaving shed. Just after that was the engine house, which powered the machinery in the mill. Next to that was a yard where the horses and carts were stabled. On the right was a detached house, and then a long row of back-to-back houses, across the road from the mill.

'There is more than just the mill for sale here,' said James, 'that's why I thought it would be ideal for you. Besides the mill, there is this row of houses included, plus the detached house, and then a large house in Reedley.'

'A large house in Reedley?' asked Grace, a little surprised.

'Yes, that's where Walter lived. With Walter being a childless widower, and not leaving a will, there has been trouble finding the next of kin. Now they've found some obscure second cousin who will inherit. But he's an academic in Cambridge University, and is not interested in keeping the business. That's why he wants a quick sale and has vastly reduced the price.'

'Can we look round the houses?' asked Grace.

'Never mind the houses, what about the mill?' asked William.

'Mill first, then the houses,' decided James.

The weaving shed looked like any other mill. Every available space packed with row upon row of looms.

'They all look in good order,' said Robert, speaking for the first time. 'How long have they been idle?'

'Over two years,' replied James. 'Do you think you could get them working again?'

'Probably. I'd need to get the power up first, but I'd soon know then. At least the looms are from Howard and Bullough in Accrington. That's what we have at Briercliffe. When I worked in Colne the looms were made by Pickles of Colne, so it took me a while to get used to them when I moved to Briercliffe.'

'It will certainly save a lot of money if we already had a working mill, then trying to set up from scratch,' said Grace.
'What happened to all the workers?' asked William.
'They just got laid off.'
'But did they move out of the houses as well?'
'I don't know,' replied James, 'but they're not here now. The houses are all empty. Perhaps they got jobs with other houses.'
'Where did Mr Bainbridge live? In Reedley?' Grace wanted to know.
'Yes, he spent a lot of money on that house. It was all done up in the best of taste, and then his wife died in childbirth. I think that broke him. He was never the same after that,' replied James. 'Why, are you and Robert thinking of setting up in Reedley if you buy the mill? It is a lovely house, and it includes the furniture.'
Grace laughed. 'Certainly not. And anyway, it would be up to William. He might want to live there in fine style.'
'Not me,' replied William, 'I'd rather live nearby, so that I could see what was going on, even when the mill was shut.'
'More likely so that you wouldn't have to get out of bed too early to get to work,' teased Grace.
'There is that fact as well,' laughed William, 'but I wouldn't want to live in a big house anyway. I think that's where a lot of mill owners go wrong. They start thinking they're the gentry!'
'Me neither, just think of all the cleaning!' quipped Grace. 'I quite like this house, standing on its own, next to the mill. Whose was this house, James?'
'That belonged to Mr Bainbridge's grandparents, then his parents. They lived here when the mill was first built at the beginning of the last century, but Walter moved out, as he got richer. I think the foreman was living here before it closed.'
'I'd like to live here,' said Grace, 'would you, William?'
'No, too big for Maud and me. It'd be fine for you and Robert and all your brood. What do you say, Robert?'
'It is a fine house, but we already have a house, Grace.'
'Yes, we have. But it's a long way from this mill if we decide to buy it.'

'That's true. But we're making plans before we've seen everything. Let's look round the rest of the mill,' urged Robert.

The trio then went into the four-storey section of the mill. The ground floor housed a large storage room that was empty; the next floor had a similar room, where tables and chairs were set out, as if people ate there. The whole room was drab, with tiny windows and dark brown paint on the walls.

On the next floor were offices: several small and one large and ornately furnished office.

'I guess this was Mr Bainbridge's office?' laughed Grace.

'That's right,' replied James, 'he liked his comforts.'

'Oh look, he's got a telephone,' said Robert, who liked contraptions and would have loved a telephone in their own home. That was one idea he had come up with when they inherited the money; he wanted a telephone.

'Bainbridge was a man who liked all the latest inventions. Everything in the mill is of the latest design or best quality. This was only the second mill in Burnley to get electricity installed. He was quite annoyed that he was beaten by another mill. Pity he didn't give the same care to his workers.'

'Well, the foreman that lived here must have got a good deal,' said Grace.

'But that probably made him unpopular with the other workers who had to live in sub-standard conditions,' said James.

'What's on the top floor?' asked William.

'Come and see,' said James grimly. He led them upstairs and there was a large open room, crammed with narrow metal beds covering most of the room, with large hooks on the wall.

'What's this? An orphanage?' gasped Grace.

'Almost,' replied James. 'This is from the days of orphan apprentices. The children would be 'bought' from the workhouses and given a home. They would live and work here and rarely leave.'

'But that's awful. What sort of life did they have?'

'Not much. Their life was grim, but grim as it was, it was better than the workhouse. At least here, they got slightly better food than the workhouse, and could eventually become an adult worker for proper wages.'

'Didn't they get wages as children, then?' said Grace, appalled.

'No, they were expected to be grateful for board and lodging. But the hours were long and hard, the food only fair, and many of them didn't survive childhood.'

'And we thought we were hard done by when we went into the mill in Briercliffe,' moaned William.

'That's why I said you could make such a difference, by running the mill on humane grounds,' said James. 'Come on, let's go and look at the houses.' They went out of the mill and down to the row of houses. The houses were very basic but the overwhelming stench of damp was the first thing that hit them all.

'What's that smell?' asked Grace.

'Damp,' replied James. 'These houses were built on boggy land, but the builders just wanted quick money and didn't care that the foundations were on a bog. I suspect that the foundations were very shallow.'

'Is there anything that can be done?' asked William.

'Yes, but it'll be costly. But once you had it sorted, the houses would be fine for years. Each house has a large room downstairs and another upstairs. Very basic and yet sometimes, more than one family lived in them. All the houses are the same. Do you want to see them all?'

'No,' said Grace quietly, her mind already working overtime as to how she could improve these houses and make them habitable.

'Let's see the large house, then,' said James.

This house was much larger and had several rooms downstairs and four bedrooms, with four attics above the bedrooms. There was even a kitchen with a large black-leaded stove, which could heat up water, cook and keep the house warm. Each bedroom had a fireplace, even the attic bedrooms.

'It's far grander than the others, isn't it?' said Grace. 'You can tell it was built for the owner originally. I could live here quite happily.'

‘Before you decide, Grace, I’ll take you up to Reedley. Who knows, you might fall in love with that house, and want to move up there. After all, you did live in Hillview House for many years. You might have become accustomed to it!’ James teased.

‘I doubt it, I’ve lived in Ernest Street for many years since then,’ Grace quipped back.

Chapter 17

They got back in to the horse and cart and drove the mile long journey to Reedley. Here the houses were much grander, with long gardens and several stories high. It was obvious that these were rich men's houses.

James showed them round the house and although it was very elegant and beautifully furnished, with lots of modern equipment, Grace had no desire to move in. After seeing the house, they all returned to Grace's house, where after cups of tea and cake were sorted out, the four adults had a long conversation.

'I suppose we can't afford it, now you've fired us up about it,' said Grace mournfully.

'It would be tight, and I know that you would want to spend money on improving the houses as well, but now I've shown you all the properties, I do have a plan.'

'Gone on, then,' said William, 'we're all ears.'

'Well, you obviously don't want the Reedley house, either of you, so you could sell that. There are many up and coming businessmen in Burnley who are looking out for larger houses to show off their wealth and rise in prominence. I'm sure you would be able to sell it easily.'

'But would that be enough to sort the houses out?' asked Grace.

'Only just, and you'd need to buy yarn and get your first orders in, so you'd need some capital to tide you over for the first few weeks. But I've another idea. If you are going to buy it and be living down here, do you need your houses on Ernest Street? You could either sell them or rent them out.'

'But what if the mill made a loss and we had to sell, we'd have nowhere to live then,' suggested Robert, who was still very wary about the whole venture.

'But you would be buying the business outright, so if it failed, you'd still have a lot of money to come back when you sold it. More than enough to buy you all a house,' reassured James.

'Don't be so miserable. Why should you fail? You are all hard working and know how a mill should run. You can't go wrong.'

Grace, Robert and William sat for a while in silence, digesting what James had said.

'If we bought the mill, and if we moved down there, who would buy our houses? And would mam want to come? And would she want to sell her house? And what if we couldn't sell them?' asked Robert out loud.

'Oh, you'll sell them all right. I bet the person who owns the rest of the street would be keen to buy them,' James suggested.

'But how can you be so sure?' demanded Robert.

'I can be very sure,' replied James. 'I own the rest of the street. Don't forget I inherited everything else from my uncle, but he wanted you all to have your own house, so that you were secure. If I bought them off you, you would be doing me a favour, because I'd have the whole street again.' The other adults sat in silence, ruminating on what he had just said.

'The money you release from these houses would make you have more funds to start the business. But I've an even more radical idea for you to think about.' Three pairs of eyes were riveted immediately on James. 'You could use your children's inheritance to start with, and pay them back once you had got straight. That would release getting on for eight hundred pounds.'

'No,' said Robert immediately, 'that's for their futures.'

'But don't you see, it would be for their futures. You could either give them shares in the business, or re-invest the money once you were making a good profit,' replied James. 'You could pay them back with interest fairly quickly.'

'Yes, I see it,' replied William, 'and it would be an incentive for them to work in the mill if they owned a little part of it.'

'I'm not sure that all my children will want to work in the mill. Look at Will. He couldn't wait to go in the army,' said Grace.

'But having this money will allow them to do any job that they want to do. For the little ones, they can't spend it until they are adult anyway, so you might as well use it for now,' argued

James. 'And you could always sell your mother's house, too,' said James as the back door opened.

'What's that? Are you planning to bump me off and sell my house?' asked Mary as she entered the room with the younger children, who quickly went into the tiny front parlour to play away from the adults.

'No, of course not mam. It's a long-term plan, if we buy the mill we've seen today,' said Grace laughing. 'We would have to use all our money to buy the mill, and we are working out how we can afford to do the worker's houses up and get the mill working.'

'So you'd sell my house to fund it? The cheek of you! And what were you going to do with me?'

'If we bought the mill, we'd all move down there. There are plenty of houses. So it would be up to you whether you stayed here in your own house, or whether you came down and lived in one of the houses near the mill.'

'I'd have to think about that. I've a lot of friends here in Briercliffe. But then, I'd also want to be near you lot. I'd hate to be too far from my grandchildren, even though they drive me daft at times,' Mary laughed.

'Talking of grandchildren, where is our James? I thought he was with you last night?' asked Grace.

'He's gone to young Peter Watson's house for tea.'

'And what about my daughter?' asked William.

'Oh, she's gone as well. You know that those two are inseparable. I've told them to come back here afterwards, not to outstay their welcome and to be polite at all times.'

All the adults laughed.

'That'll be hard for our James,' said Robert, 'he's a scallywag at the best of times.'

'He's not that bad,' Grace defended her son hotly.

'Oh, you can't see any wrong in him, can you?' replied Robert.

'He's not bad, just lively,' said Grace.

'Lively, is that what he is?' said Robert laughing.

'I'm going to leave you now,' said James. 'You've a lot to think about. Let me know if and when you want to make an offer on the business.'

'We will,' said Grace as she showed him to the door.

When Grace got back into the kitchen, everyone seemed to talk at once. They were full of ideas about what they could do. Slowly, Robert and Mary were brought round to the idea of buying the mill and Mary said that she could see the benefits of her moving down with them as well.

'But what about my friends and the chapel' she asked.

'Your time will be your own, mam,' said Grace, 'and you can come back to see your friends and go to the chapel if you want, but it'll be a hard journey up this hill in time for morning service. We'll just have to find another chapel down here; there's plenty of them. Why, Sion Baptist is only round the corner in Yorkshire Street. We could easily go there. Anyway, we haven't made the final decision yet, it's all idle talk.'

'Haven't you?' asked Robert sternly, 'you sound pretty decided to me.' Grace blushed and tried to bluster but Mary chipped in.

'Yes, she's got that determined look in her eye, hasn't she Robert? Not much we can do about that when she makes her mind up.'

'No,' said Robert, 'she had that determined look in her eye when she first met me. I was a lost cause. Couldn't refuse that look!' he quipped. Grace pushed him lovingly and said she didn't know what he was talking about but Mary and William just laughed at her.

Once the decision was made, things moved very fast. Mr Ormerod organised all the legal side of transferring the mill over to William and Grace: Robert still refusing to have anything to do with the management of the mill. Whilst William, Helen and Robert carried on working in the Briercliffe mill, Grace and Mary spent all their spare time down at the new mill. Grace drove the builders mad with her demands about the new houses, but William had to give credit where it was due; she had made a tremendous difference to the houses.

The main living room of each house had been partitioned to make a little kitchen, which had running water, and a sink. The living room had a black-leaded stove, which could cook and heat the house. Now that the damp problem had been dealt with, the houses smelled much better. Each house now had an outside toilet, whereas there had only been four toilets for the whole double row of houses before.

Upstairs, the large room had been divided into three smaller bedrooms. Robert said that was unnecessary, but Grace insisted that most families had boys and girls and it would be nicer if they could have a room for each sex, as well as one for the parents, not all sleeping in the same room as before. It made the bedrooms much smaller, but perfectly big enough for sleeping in.

In the large house, Grace indulged herself by having a bathing room installed. It was her one desire from the days when she had lived at Hillview House. She told her mother and brother that they would be welcome to use the bathing room at any time, as she was feeling a little guilty because of this unaccustomed luxury for working class people. The rest of the house, she left as it was, deciding that it was adequate for now, and they could decorate it at their leisure.

Whilst the houses were being made ready, Grace also had workmen in the mill itself. The large room on the ground floor was going to be made over for the children of the weavers, as a playroom. And Grace knew exactly who was going to be in charge of the children. Jane Leaver had had to go back to work following the death of her husband, but was finding that the dust was getting on her chest. Only last week, Jane had been telling Robert how much she was struggling to keep up with the work.

When Grace contacted Jane, she was delighted at the thought of her new job.

'But how will I get to work?' she asked Grace.

'That's the other good thing I've got to tell you. There's a house that goes with the job.'

'Where?'

'Right next to the mill. You'll be able to look after all the older children before they go to school, and look after the little ones during the day, so that their parents can work,' replied Grace

'That sounds amazing. I always wanted to work with children, but I had to go in to the mill, like most of us did. Thank you so much, Grace.'

'Don't thank me; just thank Mr Haynes. We couldn't have done all this without him.'

'When will the job start? I'll need to give my notice.'

'Fairly soon. We haven't got a starting date yet. But I'll want you to be here for the open day.'

'What open day?' asked Jane.

'The one we're trying to organise as soon as possible. We haven't got any workers yet, so we're going to have a day where people can come and look round and we can get some workers. I'd like you there that day to tell people about how you'll be looking after their children, so that they can work. I think it's an important part of our mill and should get some good weavers in.'

'You will, when I think what sort of women look after children whilst their parents work. That first woman I used was terrible. She used to dose them up so that they'd sleep all day and not bother her. I'm just glad I caught her out. How many children do you think there will be?'

'I've no idea. It'll depend on how many women come to work here. But I'm sure there'll be enough to keep you busy,' Grace laughed. 'I'll let you know when the open day is.'

During the renovations, Grace had found all the original ledgers, customers and bills that Walter Bainbridge had used. She also found a list of all the workers. William decided that they would write to all the addresses they had of the weavers, although some of them had been living in the mill houses. William suggested that Grace go to the Burnley Express and get some publicity for the open day, so that was what she did. The male reporter who interviewed her was a little scathing of a woman being involved, but Grace argued her corner and cited several women who successfully ran businesses in the town.

Despite his reservations, the reporter did give them a good write up in the paper, albeit not mentioning Grace's managerial role at all. He did, however, mention that they were having an open day. They were all set. The weaving shed had had a good clean and paint; the eating room was transformed into a pleasant clean, light airy room, with lots of comfortable tables and chairs.

The children's room was also light and airy, with lots of smaller tables and chairs and large toys for the children to play with. The top floor which had been the orphans' dormitory was left untouched for now, although Grace had made some workmen empty the room and tidy it up, so there was no evidence of its former use.

On the office floor, the large office had been left almost unchanged, but two of the other smaller offices had been made into another larger office. William and Grace were to have an office each, so that they didn't get under each other's feet, Grace quipped. Robert remained adamant that he wanted to be a tackler, and so there was no special provision made for him, beyond a small office on the weaving shed floor, where he and the other tacklers could see the whole shed from the window.

Word was getting out in Burnley that the mill was re-opening and before the open day, several people came and asked for a job. Grace took their names and addresses and told them all to come back on the open day, where interviews would be held. She also wrote to all the old employees, informing them that the mill was re-opening. Grace was getting excited.

Chapter 18

Before the open day, Robert and the children moved in to the detached house. It was a chaotic day, but Grace had given all the children their own jobs to do. Robert and Grace had the large front bedroom, and Helen claimed the other front bedroom, saying that she was the oldest and should have first choice. That left the other two large bedrooms at the back for the boys to share.

There wasn't quite enough furniture to fill all the downstairs rooms, but Grace wasn't bothered. Time enough to spend on the house when they were making money. The second front room looked well anyway with Mr Haynes' dresser taking up a large part of it.

Mary moved into the first of the terraced houses, nearest to Grace's detached house, but at the rear of the back-to-back terrace, farthest away from the mill. In the front part of the first house, William and Maud moved in, so all the family were near to each other.

William, Helen, Samuel and Robert had given their notice at the Briercliffe mill so that they could finish the last week of August, and have a few days to move house and prepare for the open day.

The open day was held on the second of September. Mary had baked all day on the previous day, as Grace had decided that it would be good to have refreshments available for the visitors. It could also show them the lovely facilities for mealtimes as well, Grace thought with glee.

William was astounded at the numbers of people who came through the doors that day. Grace wasn't. She knew that two mills had closed down the month before. And besides that, many of the Burnley folk were coming to have a nosey round the mill, to see what it was like. It soon got round about the refreshments too and children appeared from nowhere to sample the wares.

The first man through the door was an engineer who had worked at the mill previously and knew the engine. When Bainbridge's had shut, he'd moved to one of the mills that had closed down the previous month. He couldn't believe his luck when William offered him the job. His son was also an engine room assistant, so that was the pair of them back in work.

'We'll work hard, I promise you, Mr Butler,' said Jed Hanson.

'Yes, you will, I'll work you hard, but you'll find we're fair employers.'

'Are there any vacancies for weavers?' asked Jed tentatively, not wanting to push his luck.

'Yes, why?'

'My wife and daughter both got finished at the mill same as me.'

'Where are they?' asked William.

'Still at home, minding the little ones. It was more important for me to get work, but if there are vacancies . . .'

'Yes, go and get them. It's going to be a family business anyway, so having whole families together will be good.'

'Thank you sir, I won't be long,' said Jed, setting off at run.

'Just a minute, will you want to rent a house here as well?'

'Yes please, if we can.'

'Righto, I'll just make a note of that. It's first come first served for the houses, but you're the first man I've hired, so you're all right,' laughed William. Jed set off at a run.

Grace and William had decided that they would take on sixty weavers to begin with, even though there was capacity for far more. James had got them their first order from another mill in the town. Tattersall's mill had got a large order for some cloth that they didn't usually weave, so were quite happy to off-load it onto William and Grace, to help them get started.

Jethro Tattersall had been very helpful to Grace and William and had given them a lot of useful information about management, prices, and other important facts, such as workers' rights and safety matters, especially that they had adequate numbers of fire buckets.

Grace had also written to all the former customers of the mill to tell them that it was back in business, under new management. James had kindly told lots of his friends and fellow businessmen about the venture.

On the Sunday, the family decided to go to Sion Baptist Chapel instead of trailing up to Haggate. They were warmly welcomed and told of all the activities that were going on in the chapel. By the second week, Helen, Robert and Grace were all in the choir, and Samuel had joined the young men's class.

Helen's face had never stopped smiling, since she saw all the young men that were in the chapel. She'd never really liked anyone at Haggate as she'd grown up with them all, and been to school and worked in the mill with most of them, so this was a golden opportunity for her. But first she would have to find out who was courting with whom, so that she knew who was free. She just hoped that Jack Ashton was free, as she quite liked the look of him. Tall, dark and handsome, what more could a girl want? Time would tell, she decided. Time enough when they had got the mill sorted out.

The mill was going to open officially on September fifteenth. After long considerations, the mill itself was named Victoria Mill, in honour of the Queen, but the business was called Greenwood and Butler. They'd debated for quite some time which way round the 'Butler' and the 'Greenwood' should go, but decided it sounded best with the 'Greenwood' first. The townspeople, however, soon came to call the mill 'GreenButs', and ignored the 'Victoria' part of the name altogether.

Robert had worked hard, with his best friend John Coates, to get the looms ready for the opening day. John had been happy to come from Colne to work at the mill and become the other tackler.

Many of the town's dignitaries such as the Mayor, councillors and Aldermen were invited to the opening event, and even a small brass band had been paid to play. Again, refreshments had been made ready and there was a party feel to the whole proceedings.

James Brown officially opened the mill for them and then Jed Hanson, who had fired up the boiler earlier, let the steam through by opening the main valve, to loud cheers from the new workforce. Grace looked across to William. They were in business. The only thing to mar the whole day had been that most of the men who attended had totally ignored Grace and only spoken to William. She had a moan about this to James.

'Am I invisible? Do they think that it's only William's mill? Don't they know how to talk to a woman?' she fumed, whilst James tried to calm her down.

'It's what men are like in business. They think that only men can do business. Think the woman's place is at home, by the sink,' he said sympathetically, 'they'll get used to you. Just give them time.'

Robert wasn't much help either, when they were alone in her office and she was complaining to him.

'Well, I did tell you that would happen, but you were so full of yourself, that you wouldn't listen,' he said to Grace.

'Full of myself? What do you mean?' shouted Grace, 'if you had taken part like I wanted you to, there would have been two men to talk to today.'

'Don't start that again. I've talked to plenty of men today. Weavers, engineers and tacklers.'

'That's not what I mean, and you know it,' fumed Grace, but they were prevented from it becoming a full-scale row as Helen came in the office.

'Mum, Uncle William said to come down. The Mayor and his entourage are going.'

'Huh! Why would he want me? I'm only a woman!' snarled Grace. But she left the room and went downstairs anyway. Helen looked at Robert with raised eyebrows, but Robert just shook his head and followed her downstairs.

Grace joined William and said her goodbyes to the Mayoral party and thanked them for coming. They were impressed with the changes to the mill and specially commended them on the cooking facilities that were available. Grace had made the eating area much cleaner and brighter, with small tables and chairs spread about.

A cook had been employed to make a basic nourishing meal each day, so that the weavers didn't have to go home or eat a cold meal at work. There would also be hot drinks for everyone, even those who still brought their own food. The food was going to be at cost price, so that most weavers could afford the meals. William and Grace had decided that they too would eat in the eating room, so that their workers would get to know them, and any potential trouble could be nipped in the bud.

Robert and Grace didn't speak again until they got home on the first day, and it took quite a long time of talking for them to agree to differ, and be friends again. But they were soon back to their loving selves. They couldn't stay mad at each other for long.

As the first week went past, some of the old customers came to the mill to meet the new owners and discuss their requirements. Grace and William were thrilled that they hadn't all found new weaving sheds and were prepared to give them some orders. Grace however, was not so impressed, when most of the men ignored her and spoke only to William. She tried hard to bite her tongue and not butt in, but that wasn't her style. Sometimes she was rebuffed, other times they politely listened to her, but then made the final deal with William.

'Why are they ignoring me? Why can't they deal with a woman?' Grace fumed when they had gone, but William just kept quiet. He knew it was better to just let Grace rant and rave and have her say. Besides, there was nothing that he could do. Men were men. And most of them wouldn't like Grace being around in the office.

Being more comfortable at accounts, Grace was going to be responsible for the money side of the deals and balancing the books, and William would deal with day to day running arrangements and hiring and firing of staff.

William had deliberately given a job to a man called Joseph Robinson, who was keen on unions. They had met at one of the meetings at the new Mechanics Institute in Manchester Road in Burnley. From talking to him, William knew that he wasn't a hothead and wouldn't bring disruption to the mill, but Joseph had a quiet persuasive way with him, which William valued; a foil for his own hot-headed sister!

Joseph was encouraged to start a union within the mill, and he was given one of the smaller offices to carry out his union responsibilities. William insisted that the two men had a regular meeting, so that they could discuss any worker's worries or problems.

By the end of September, the mill was running smoothly. They had a few orders in that would easily take them up to Christmas. But William was worried about what would happen after that. He invited Jethro Tattersall round to ask his advice. The types of cloth they were weaving were different, so there would be no conflict of interest between the two firms.

'How do you get the bulk of your orders, Jethro?'

'Change,' said Jethro.

'Change?' asked William. Jethro nodded.

'I go to Manchester Cotton Exchange most days; certainly every Tuesday and Friday, which are the main market days. That's where I do the most of my trade. Yes, you can get orders from your regular customers, as they renew each time and they want more cloth, but if you want your name known, and to improve sales, you need a spot at 'Change.'

'How do we go about that?' asked Grace, who had just come into the room.

'There's no 'we' about it, I'm afraid Mrs Greenwood, they would not tolerate a woman on 'Change. I'm afraid it'll have to be William that goes there.' Grace bit her lip and flounced out of the office.

'I'm sorry, William, I hope I haven't offended your sister.'

'Not at all, Grace gets angry when she can't be treated as a full business partner just because she's a woman. So how do I get a spot on 'Change as you called it?'

'You would have to be introduced. Best thing is if you come with me one day and we can sort you out. What about next Monday?'

'How do you get there? By horse?'

Jethro laughed. 'No, that'll take far too long. No, we go on the train.'

'We?' asked William.

'Yes, all the other cotton mill owners. We all go on the seven forty five from Bank Top station. Takes us straight to

Manchester Victoria Station, then it's a short walk to the 'Change. We have quite a lark on the train. Some of them play cards, others read. Others just chat. It's like a gentleman's club really. And then we usually all come home on the same train at night. I'll meet you at the station on Monday, then?'

'Yes, that would be great. Thanks for your help. I'll see you then.' Jethro Tattersall picked up his bowler hat, gloves and cane and went towards the office door.

'Just a thought, William. You need to dress up a bit for 'Change. I hope you don't mind me saying so,' he said looking at William's rough work clothes.

'Of course,' replied William blushing, 'Sunday best suit?'

'Yes, that would be fine, although I don't wear my best suit for 'Change, I keep my next best suits for work.'

'Good idea,' said William as he left. 'Thanks for the advice. I appreciate it.'

'Wouldn't want you looking out of place on the train or on the 'Change, would we?' he laughed, as he went downstairs.

As soon as he had gone, William went to find Grace. She wasn't in her office. William had a good idea where she would be. He was right. She was talking to Helen. Grace knew that she would get no sympathy from Robert about a woman's place, but her almost militant Suffragist daughter would give her all the sympathy she needed.

As he thought, Grace was telling Helen all about the 'Change.

'Only change I'll get is hot flushes and the like,' Grace was saying as he approached.

'Grace, I need to go and get myself kitted out to go on 'Change next Monday. Are you all right if I go now? Apparently they all wear hats and good suits. I'll have to look the part.'

'Oh, yes, do go. Can't have you looking under-dressed, can we?' said Grace with a sarcastic voice. 'Don't worry about me; I'll be here looking after the mill, you just go and play with your new friends. And have a haircut whilst you are out. You're a disgrace.'

William made a quick exit and when he had done his shopping, and had his haircut, he went straight to his house and put his new clothes away in the wardrobe. No need to antagonise Grace any further today, but secretly he was excited. He was looking forward to going on the 'Change, especially if he got more business.

After he had gone, Grace went back to her office, chatting to many of the weavers on her way. It seemed to be a happy bunch of people that were working for them and she was pleased with the way the work was going.

When she got back to her office, she realised ruefully that she had spent quite a bit of money on her work outfit when she had started at the mill, so she shouldn't resent William decking himself out. William had just tended to wear any old shirt and jacket at the mill, but Grace had had to think carefully about her outfits. It was inappropriate to wear her old weaving clothes – not that they would fit her after all those children! Neither could she wear her Sunday best clothes, as they were often light in colour and not made of a very serviceable fabric.

In the end, she had decided on a matching long skirt and jacket, almost like a man's jacket, but with different coloured blouses underneath it. Her favourite blouse was an emerald green one with a high neck. The skirts were fairly straight, with no bustle, but a small vent at the back, to help her walk easily. A lady in Burnley had a dressmakers shop and she had made her two suits, one in navy, and one in a medium grey. And she had bought lightweight boots to go under her outfits, not wearing the clogs that many of the weavers wore.

Grace felt comfortable in her new apparel; not too dressed up, but smart enough to meet businessmen – if they would condescend to talk to her, that is. No, she would not carry on about William's new clothes, she decided, and would make her peace when he came back.

On Monday, William was at Bank Top Station in plenty of time for the train. It wasn't very far from the mill houses so it was an easy walk. There were already several men on the platform; almost all dressed in the same way. Smart suit, top hat or bowler hat, shirt and tie, waistcoat, and a watch and chain hanging across their often ample waists. It was almost like a uniform, thought William, but he was grateful that Jethro had warned him, so that he was similarly dressed himself.

'William,' a voice shouted. William turned round and saw Jethro.

'Jethro, good to see you,' replied William. 'Oh look is this our train?' he asked as a large steam train puffed in to the station.

'Yes, that's the one. I'll introduce you to all the men when we get on.'

Once the train was in motion, Jethro took William round all the other men. As they reached each station, more similarly dressed men got on the train, from mills in Huncoat, Hapton, Accrington, and Blackburn. All greeted William on Jethro's introduction. Some of the other men asked what type of cloth William wove and whether he did carding or spinning as well.

William replied that he only did weaving and was asked what sort of looms he had and where he got his yarn. Jethro interrupted. 'Let the man get to the 'Change before you start bombarding him,' he laughed. 'Mind you William, there's many a deal done on this train, before we get to 'Change.' The other men laughed and agreed.

'Yes, it's like a miniature 'Change on here,' said a man from Blackburn, 'but we all look out for each other, even though some of us are in competition.'

'Listen to him,' said a spinning mill owner from Accrington, 'look out for each other? Cut each other's throats more like.' And the whole carriage roared in laughter.

On arrival at Manchester, William was keen to go to the 'Change, but most of the men went straight to a coffee house, or to their offices.

'I don't have an office in Manchester, it's far too expensive, but many of the bigger firms do. Come on, we'll go for a coffee first.'

Jethro led them to a coffee shop, where the air was thick with cigarette smoke. Jethro lit up a cigarette and offered one to William, but he declined. He'd never seen the fun in smoking, perhaps due to the fact that if you were a weaver, you wanted fresh air in your lungs. But he suspected that none of these men had ever worked in a mill, only inherited or owned them. There seemed to be several of the men from the train in the same coffee shop, and business did seem to be taking place unofficially here, too. He wasn't too keen on coffee either, but manfully drank it, not wanting to cause a fuss.

Eventually, they got to the 'Change and Jethro took William to the office to register as a trader; Jethro being William's introduction and referee to the management. William was assigned a space, number H7, on the floor of the 'Change, which was near to Jethro, and he stood and watched all that was going on.

At lunchtime, the men went out for a meal and then returned to the 'Change, until mid afternoon. After that, they returned to the train station and caught the train home, back to Burnley.

'How did you get on?' asked Jethro on the way home.

'Not many people spoke to me, but someone did come and ask me to quote for weaving a large order that he wanted in a hurry. I said I would give him a quote tomorrow. That's what you usually do, isn't it?'

'Yes, it's too tricky to work it out in your head, in case you make a mistake and undercut yourself. Then tomorrow you can make a deal. If he's in a hurry, it might bode well for you if you can make the deal and get the order out to him quickly. It could lead to other orders.'

'Will I need to go on 'Change every day, then,' asked William.

'Not necessarily but I would for the first week or two, to get your face and name known.'

When they got off at Bank Top Station, Jethro wished him goodnight and went off to his own home, which was up Manchester Road. His servant had met him at the station with the pony and trap and was ready to take him home.

William pondered all that had happened to him as he walked home and was ready for a good sit down, but Grace was round at his house before he had got his coat off. She wanted to know all about his experiences and was pleased when William told him about the rush order. She was less pleased when William told her that Jethro had recommended that he go every day initially, but for once, she kept her mouth shut, knowing that getting business was so important if they were to continue with this venture.

The weeks took on a pattern: William going to Manchester and Grace running the mill in his absence. They managed to get a good price for the rush order and fulfil it in the required time, so the man gave them further work.

It was soon Christmas and Grace realised that they had made a small profit already, and they had paid Helen and Maud their hundred pounds back as well. Things were looking good. The workforce that they had employed had worked hard for them and Grace suggested that they give them all a present for Christmas.

'What sort of present?' asked William.

'I don't know. Money or food?' suggested Grace.

'I think food would be better. Unfortunately, some of our weavers would just drink any money we gave them, but if we gave them food, at least all the family would benefit.'

'That's true,' said Grace. 'What about a plum pudding each, Or a turkey?'

'Mmm, but what about the Hanson's? They would get four puddings or turkeys with all the family working here.' They both laughed at that, visualising the Hanson's having too much of the same food.

'I know,' said Grace, 'we could give them a sort of voucher that they could spend at James Brown's food shop. That would benefit James as well. After all, he's been so good to us.'

'Good idea. What do you think we should give them?' They both thought for a while and then William said 'What about one pound each?'

'One pound each?' said Grace. 'It'd be the equivalent of more than a weeks wages for some of them. That would cost us sixty pounds in all. Can we afford it?'

'You are the one to answer that, Grace. You've just said we've made a profit.'

'Yes, we have. And I don't suppose we'd have made it if we hadn't got good workers. Yes, let's do it. One pound each.'

'And anyway, it's sixty-two pounds, not sixty,' said William
'Why, have you taken some more weavers on?'
'No, but you're the one that's good at maths. Don't we count? Don't we deserve a Christmas bonus too?'
'Oh, of course. Do you think we ought to have one? Is it fair?'
'We've worked hard too. As long as it's the same as the weavers. I don't think it would be fair to have a big bonus,' replied William.
'Neither do I. All right, we'll have a pound bonus as well.' But in the end, they didn't take one. Shortly before the Christmas season, many of their customers brought gifts of chocolates or port or other seasonal things into the office. Fortunately Jethro had warned them that this would happen, so they had got a stock of chocolates in themselves, neatly wrapped by Helen.
They decided that they would keep all the food gifts instead of a bonus, and gave James the alcohol, as neither of them drank. He was very pleased, not just about the alcohol, but also about all the tokens they had purchased for their workforce, from his food shop.
On the last day before Christmas, they gave the tokens out and let the weavers go home early, so that they could spend them in time for Christmas Day. During the lunch break, they also opened some of the boxes of chocolates and handed them round the room. It was a very happy workforce that went home that Christmas. And Grace and William were both relieved that things were working out well.
But it was not to last.

Chapter 19

1901 started off well, with the order books full and production in full swing. William found that he needed to go to the 'Change most days, but managed to share the work between him and Grace, in an amicable way. The horse and carts were kept busy taking newly made up orders to their customers, who were getting farther and farther afield. Robert predicted that the new horseless carriages would change the way that they lived, but Grace was adamant that they wouldn't last. Noisy, dangerous things, she insisted. She much preferred the graciousness of the horses and carts, and the steady pace of driving.

The whole country was plunged into mourning when they heard the sad news of their Queen's death on January 22nd. In honour of the Queen, and partly copying off the display in the window of the Burnley Express, Grace put up a picture of Queen Victoria in the eating room, trimmed with black ribbon, and the dates of her life underneath. As the funeral took place on a Saturday, February 2nd, William and Grace decided to close the mill that day in respect for her. The entire workforce was supplied with black armbands shortly after her death, to wear until after the funeral. Many of the local people were very sad to hear of her passing, as she had been the longest serving queen ever.

The reign of the new King appeared to bring in a breath of fresh air to the country, as King Edward the seventh was visible to everyone through newspapers, unlike his mother, who had stayed away from the public eye for many years. Mechanisation seemed to be growing apace, and William heard of many new innovative experiments and new practices when he was on the 'Change.

It was about the beginning of March when Grace got a message from Jed Hanson, to say that a man was asking for a job. As William was in Manchester, Grace said that she would come and see him. As she walked downstairs, she saw the man waiting, with his back to her. As she approached him, she saw that he was a thin, shabbily dressed man, with straggly hair.

'I believe you are looking for a job?' Grace said. The man turned round, causing Grace to gasp. It was Arthur Jones, looking very down at heel. He stared at her for a long time, whilst Grace was shivering inside because of the feelings that welled up inside her at the sight of this horrible man. He looked like he hadn't had a decent meal in months and his clothes were threadbare.

'You! What are you doing here?' Jones said, in a disrespectful manner.

'I own the place, that's why I'm here,' replied Grace in her haughtiest voice.

'Own it? Huh. What did you have to do to get a place like this? Don't tell me, I can guess,' Jones leered, whilst Grace blushed.

'I own it jointly with my brother William, and it's no business of yours how we came to own it. Now what do you want?'

'I was looking for a job, but I didn't know you'd taken over this place. I've been working in Darwen for four years, since I got sacked at the Briercliffe mill, all through your brother and husband. I think your family owe me something, don't you?'

'No, I do not. You deserve nothing,' Grace spitted venomously. 'Now get out.'

'Or else? Will your fetch your stupid husband and your soppy brother to get me? Eh? Will you?' he sneered back.

'Is this man troubling you, Mrs Greenwood?' asked Jed Hanson, who had stayed in the background just in case, not having liked the looks of the man who had come asking for a job. Grace had never been as glad to see Jed Hanson in her life. It gave her courage again.

'No, no trouble, he's just leaving, Jed. Perhaps you could escort him off the premises,' said Grace with great dignity, and more calmness than she was feeling.

Jed started to take the man by the arm and push him towards the door, but Jones reared up and shook his fist at Jed. Jed stood his ground; not intimidated by this bully. As Jones got to the mill door, he turned back and stared at Grace.

'You'll be sorry for this, just you wait,' growled Jones, with a threatening look, but Grace had already walked away, she didn't want Jones to see that she was shaking.

Hurrying back in to the weaving shed, Grace sought out Robert and told him the whole story. Robert was all for going out and chasing after Jones, but Grace told him not to. She was worried that Jones would retaliate and she didn't want any harm to come to Robert, even though he was well able to look after himself.

It was clear that it had shaken Grace, so after comforting her and holding her close, Robert took her into the eating room and found Peggy, the cook.

'Could you make my wife a cup of tea, please Peggy? She's in need of it.'

'Certainly, just sit there, Mrs Greenwood. I'll be with you in a minute. The kettle's just boiled.' Peggy bustled around in the kitchen, whilst Robert sat with Grace, listening to the full story. Eventually, after the restoring cup of tea, Grace went back to her office and Robert returned to the weaving shed. The whole story had to be told again when William came home, but he wasn't worried that there would be any repercussions, and reassured Grace as such.

The next morning, when Robert and Helen came to open the mill doors, they noticed that a pane of glass was broken in the ground floor, where the children stayed.

Robert was the first in, telling Helen to stay outside until he checked that there was no one inside. Helen offered to go back to the house and get her mother. Robert swept up the shards of glass that were sprinkled on the floor, after quickly looking around and ascertaining that there was no one about.

When Helen got back, closely followed by Grace, Robert showed them the brick that he'd found on the floor.

'Who would have done this?' asked Helen. 'Do you think that it was children larking about?'

'It could have been, but I've got other ideas,' replied Grace.

'Don't jump to conclusions,' said Robert, 'we don't know it was him.'

'I bet it was,' said Grace viciously.

'Bet it was who?' asked Helen, as they hadn't told the children about the incident yesterday.

'Never mind, it probably was children, Helen, can you tell Uncle William to call in before he goes for the train?'

'All right, but why do I think that you aren't telling me everything?' Helen moaned.

'We tell you what you need to know,' replied Grace primly, but Helen just walked off in a mood.

'Well that was well handled Grace, wasn't it? You've set Helen off on her high horse again. We'll get no peace for days,' complained Robert. 'Pity the man who takes her on as wife,' he laughed. 'I'd better have a word with young Jack Ashton. He doesn't know what he's taking on.'

'Jack Ashton? Is she keen on him?' asked Grace.

'Haven't you noticed them? They're always together at chapel do's.'

'Well, yes, I suppose they are, but you know what Helen's like. More interested in the Suffragists than men. And always saying she'll never get married and have a load of children.'

'If you took your head out of the mill's accounts and looked at your children sometimes, you might know what's going on.'

'Robert, that's not fair. I do my best for the children,' but William's arrival prevented any more discussion.

Grace quickly told him what had happened and asked him to call in at the glaziers on Bridge Street on his way to the station.

However, the following week, another pane was broken, this time at the back of the mill, on the second floor. William was all for getting the constable involved, but Grace wanted to hold back. If it was just children playing, she didn't want to get them into trouble. She was also reluctant to name names as to whom her suspicions were about.

But on the third week, another pane was broken, again on the children's floor so Grace reluctantly called the constable. One of his first questions was if they knew anyone who had a grudge against them, as three consecutive broken windows, seemed more than just children playing. Grace and William looked at each other, and then Grace nodded.

'We have had a man threatening us because we wouldn't give him a job,' said William quietly.

'What's his name?' asked the constable.

'Arthur Jones,' replied William.

'Well, we'll look in to that and let you know. Do you know where he lives?'

'No, we knew him when we all lived in Briercliffe, but we don't know where he lives in Burnley,' replied Grace. The constable left, and Grace and William carried on with their work.

'Do you think we've done the right thing?' said Grace quietly. 'You don't think he'll retaliate, do you?'

'Oh no,' reassured William, 'not now the constable is involved. He's not that daft.' But Grace was left with an uneasy feeling for the next few days, especially after Jones was seen outside the mill shouting threats to the family.

The following week, in the early hours of the morning, an urgent banging on the door wakened Grace and Robert. They both jumped up wondering what was happening.

'Can you smell smoke?' Robert asked, as they were getting dressed quickly.

'Yes, you go down and open up, I'll be down shortly,' said Grace as she struggled in to her working clothes.

It was William at the door. The mill was on fire and the fire brigade had been telephoned. Grace and Robert ran after William, telling Samuel to stay with the younger children and watch them.

Looking at the outside of the mill, the fire seemed to be contained in the four-storey section of the mill, but as they stood there, they saw flames leaping across to the weaving shed.

Running in to the mill, Grace, Robert and William got all the new water buckets that were positioned around the mill and started filling them up, throwing them over the flames and even on the dry cotton that the fire hadn't reached. They were soon joined by many of the workforce who lived in the mill houses. They made a chain of people passing buckets of water to put out the fire. They concentrated on the weaving shed as there was likely to be more damage there than in the four-storey section. Eventually, the fire brigade arrived, from their headquarters in Manchester Road, and ordered everyone out of the mill, whilst they used their more powerful hoses. After two hours, the fire was under control, and Grace and William could go in and check what damage there was.

Virtually all of the cotton waiting to be woven and all of the finished cotton pieces were destroyed. Fortunately the looms weren't damaged and at least no lives had been lost, but it could have been a very different story, thought Grace as she viewed the mess that was left, not just from the fire, but also from the water that had been sprayed everywhere.

'Are we insured for all this?' asked a grim Robert.

'Yes, thanks be to God, but all our completed orders have burnt, so we'll have to contact all of our customers to ask for a few days grace, until we can get back into production. And all our stock of cotton thread has gone as well,' said William.

A constable arrived as the fire was being dampened down and asked if he could have a look round the premises with the Chief Fireman. On the ground floor of the four-story section, they found empty bottles on the floor, near a broken window.

'I think this might be arson, these bottles could have had paraffin rags in them, and been thrown through the window alight,' said the constable to William. 'We'll have to make more inquiries.'

Grace was sat on the chair in Robert's office, totally weary from the efforts of saving the mill. Once the fire brigade said that the fire was completely out and the mill was safe, Grace told her workers to go home and get some rest. If they would come in later in the day, they could help with the cleaning up process, and help get the mill ready for work again. She also added that none of them would be out of pocket because the mill wasn't working. They would all receive an extra bonus for coming to help.

William, Robert and Grace stayed up and started sorting out the other sections of the mill. Whilst there was smoke damage throughout, the fire had stayed on the ground floor, so it was just the children's play area that was damaged. The eating area, kitchen and offices were all intact. The play area was temporarily housed up on the top floor, until their own floor could be redecorated and made safe again.

Only one order was lost through the customer not understanding about the fire; most of them were very sympathetic and helpful. Both Tattersalls' and Pickles' mills offered William some yarn to help them over their difficulties. Both men knew just what total devastation could occur with a fire in a weaving shed. Grace was just glad that they had taken advice about having lots of the fire buckets spread around the weaving shed, as it was through them that the shed had been saved. She was so thankful; it could have been a lot worse.

Eventually, Arthur Jones admitted that he had started the fire and was sent to prison. Grace was just glad that he was out of the way for some time and they could forget about him. But the whole episode made her a lot less complacent about safety, not to mention upsetting people.

Chapter 20

With all the fuss of the broken windows and the fire, Grace forgot to watch Helen and Jack together, but things came to a head a few weeks after the fire. Jack came to see Robert at the end of his shift. He seemed ill at ease and was screwing his hat around in his hands.

'Now lad, what's the matter? Come into my little office. You look fair worried. You've not lost your job have you? Are you wanting a job here?'

'Er, no, none of those things. I was wanting to talk to you Mr Greenwood, if I may?'

'Oh yes?' said Robert, not making it easy for young Jack, 'what about?'

'I, er, I want to, er . . . '

'Spit it out lad,' replied Robert.

'I want to ask for your daughter's hand in marriage please,' Jack gasped out all in a rush, his head bowed, his hat nearly pulverised.

'You do? And what does she think about this? Our Helen has always said that she's not getting wed, nor having children. What do you think about that?'

'Well, er, Mr Greenwood, er, I think er, that you'll find she's changed her mind. Well, on the wedding bit of it. I'm not as confident about the children.'

'Let's ask her then, here she comes. Helen, this young man wants to wed you. What do you think about that?' And for the first time in his life, Robert watched Helen blush and go all coy. Wait 'til he told Grace, wouldn't they have a laugh about this.

'Yes, I'd like that, dad,' said Helen demurely.

'Well I never,' said Robert. 'This is very good news. No more having to put up with her temper tantrums and her messy ways. You do know about her temper tantrums, I take it Jack?'

'Dad, stop it. Leave us alone,' shouted Helen.

'I haven't asked the right questions yet. What is your job, Jack? Can you look after my daughter to the standards she is used to?'

'I'm am engineer at Pickles' mill and I earn twenty–five shillings a week. My dad and mum's still working, so there are no worries about losing my wage. And I can have a small house that goes with the job, down on Croft Street.'

'Well, that all seems satisfactory. Perhaps I'll think about it for a few months, then let you know.' Jack's face fell, but he still managed to thank Robert, even though he was bitterly disappointed.

'Dad, stop messing about. Give us a straight answer.'

'Are you sure that it is what you want Helen?' to which Helen nodded excitedly. Robert seemed to think for a minute, and then he said 'All right then. When were you thinking of getting wed?'

'Soon,' said Jack.

'Hey, there's no reason for any hurry, is there?' asked Robert, remembering his own wedding.

'Definitely not. I respect Helen, but we are keen to get wed soon.'

'Right. Well, get engaged now, and then we'll talk to your mother about it all.'

Right on cue, Grace appeared.

'Talk to your mother about what?' she asked Helen.

'Dad's just said that me and Jack can get wed, mum.'

'Oh has he? Don't I get a say in the matter?'

'No,' said Robert, 'you just have to sort the wedding out.'

'But we barely know him,' objected Grace.

'It's Helen's life, and she seems to know him quite well. So let's leave them to it, shall we?' said Robert sharply.

Grace recovered her manners. 'Would you like to bring your parents to our home for supper on Sunday after church, Jack?'

'Yes, I would. I'm sure they'd be pleased to do that. Can I go for a walk with Helen now? Now we're engaged,' he added with a grin.

'Go on, then,' said Grace, 'but tea will be in about an hour, so don't be long.'

'We won't,' Helen laughed as the two of them ran off down the street, hand in hand.

'Well, that's taken the wind out of my sails,' said Grace. 'You were right, Robert, there was something between them. I thought that they were just friends, as they go out in such a big gang together.'

'But they have to do that. We wouldn't have allowed it if they were wanting to go off on their own together, would we?'

'I suppose not,' replied Grace, 'and I suppose that's how we got to know each other, isn't it? Going out in the big gangs from church on outings and walks. And we always paired off when we could. So nothing's new. At least the trouble with Arthur Jones hasn't put her off. I wasn't sure if that was part of why she didn't want to get married.'

'That's true, but no, I think she just fancied herself as a Suffragette. But I agree; I can't believe our daughter is getting wed. After all she's said about it. What a change about,' said Robert.

'We're getting old, Robert. Our first child getting ready to be wed.'

'Nonsense, you'll never be old. You are too busy all the time,' laughed Robert. 'Although I did see some white hairs the other morning when you were brushing your hair.' Grace landed out at Robert because of his cheek and they went over to their house laughing, to start the evening chores.

After saying she would never get married, Helen suddenly had a lot of plans about the wedding, but fortunately they weren't extravagant. The wedding would be at Sion Chapel but the minister from Haggate would help at the service as well. Having no sisters herself, Helen was glad that Jack had three young sisters. Primrose, Daisy and Rose were to be the flower girls, for which they were very excited, and Maud was the chief bridesmaid. They planned the wedding for winter.

The day soon came around and Grace struggled to keep the tears from her eyes when she saw Robert walking down the aisle with Helen, looking radiant in her light grey wool dress, with matching hat. The three little girls and Maud looked pretty in their pink long sleeved dresses with bonnets and knitted stoles.

After the ceremony, a great party was held in the Sunday school, after which the newly-weds went to their own house. They had decided against having a honeymoon, but would wait until the weather was warmer.

Even though she saw Helen at work, Grace missed having her around the house, and often stopped to have a chat with her in the weaving shed. Being a thoroughly modern woman, Helen insisted on working after she got married, until she had children, she told Grace.

'Children?' asked Grace, with a teasing smile. 'What children? I thought you were never going to have any?'

'I don't mind two or three, but I don't want to keep going like you and dad have.'

'You get what you are given sometimes,' said Grace, a little annoyed at the comment that Helen had made.

'Oh, not nowadays, mum, there are things you can do, you know,' said Helen blushing.

'Yes, but they don't always work, do they?' replied Grace. 'I should know.'

'I'll just have to see what comes, then,' said Helen and quickly changed the subject.

During Easter of 1902, Helen shyly told Grace that she was expecting a baby later in the year.

'Are you pleased, Helen,' Grace asked tentatively, fearing the answer.

'Very, we both are,' was the reassuring reply.

Grace wasn't sure how she felt about being a grandmother, but all the other women in the mill said that they were better than your own children, because you could keep them as long as you liked, but then give them back at the end of the day and get a peaceful night's sleep.

One of the women asked Grace if she was going to give up work to look after the new grandchild, but Grace was horrified at the thought. No, she had replied, I work. Helen can look after her own.

The work in the mill carried on, with full order books, and more weavers had been taken on to cope with the increased demand. William and Robert had joined with Jethro Tattersall and some of the other mill owners and businessmen to form the Burnley Chamber of Commerce. James Brown had introduced them to the idea, as he had seen the same thing at Blackburn, which had been going since the seventies. It was around this time, that William got interested in local politics. Managing to get himself on the Town Council, he was soon going off to meetings regularly and Grace frequently had to have Maud for tea and make sure she got to bed safely. But she was happy to do this for him, as it was giving him an interest in life outside the mill.

Young James had come to work in the mill as soon as he was fourteen. He wanted to learn all the jobs there were to do in the mill and his great ambition was to be a tackler, like his dad, he would tell anyone who would listen. Grace had been surprised by that, she thought that James would have preferred to work elsewhere than the mill, but he seemed happy enough.

Samuel had developed Grace's keen ability with sums and could do them in his head. He would often work out the sums for his Uncle William after he had been on the 'Change. After a lot of pestering, Samuel was allowed to go and have a day at Manchester with William. The train journey and all the chatter that went on during the journey amazed him. But when they got on the 'Change, Samuel was starting to do the sums in his head for William.

'That's two hundred and sixteen pounds, twelve shillings and eleven pence,' Samuel whispered.

'What is?' replied William.

'That order that the man just asked for. I've just worked it out.'

'Keep quiet, you might have made a mistake, and then we'll have to honour the quote,' said William.

Samuel did keep quiet as told, but when William got home and worked out the sum, he realised Samuel was correct to the very last penny. He proudly told Grace how clever Samuel had been, and so Grace and William decided that Samuel could be trained up to learn all about the office work, and go on a regular basis to the 'Change, so that if ever William couldn't go, Samuel could stand in.

After the first few correct quotes that Samuel had done in his head, William risked using his figures for smaller quotes. Very soon, Samuel became known as the quickest young man on 'Change. Often Greenwood and Butler would get the business, because they could give a quote straightaway, without having to go back to their offices to work it out.

As William's work for the Council increased, Samuel was allowed to go to the 'Change on his own: a very proud day for both Samuel and his parents.

During the Burnley Fair Holidays in July, several of the mill owners got together and organised a special train that took all the workers for a day trip to Blackpool. It became such a popular event, that they decided to do this on a regular basis, each July. Added to the excitement of the Fair coming to Burnley, followed by the annual Pot Fair, when many a bargain of crockery could be bought, there were some happy Burnley folk.

Having the mills shut for two weeks, meant that essential maintenance and cleaning could be done, and there was always people that were out of work in the town, who were happy to work when the others were all away having fun.

That first year, Helen had to stay at home, being too near her time to travel easily. Grace and Mrs Ashton helped her prepare tiny baby garments to have ready. Grace also offered her the cot that Mr Haynes had given them, joking that she had no further use for it now.

On the 25th September, Grace got a message that Helen had gone in to labour. Fortunately it was a day when William was at the mill, so she abandoned her post and went to be with Helen. It was so hard watching her own daughter bearing the pains with great courage. Her labour had started the day before, but it had been mainly backache and short-lived pains. Now it was moving on strongly.

By the time she started to push, Grace was almost pushing with her, but the midwife warned her against it, saying she might give herself problems 'down below' if she did that.

After waiting patiently, Grace was amazed to watch her first grandchild being born. Although she had given birth to so many, yet she had never seen a baby being born and was fascinated by the whole process. It was a little girl, with lots of thick black hair, just like her dad. With Jack still being at work, after all, labour was a woman's job and men were just in the way; Grace got to hold her first grandchild straight after Helen.

Grace looked down at the small crying baby and felt the same rush of love that she had felt with all of her own children. And yet there was a different feeling with a grandchild. It was as if you became aware of the generations going forward. You had already produced the next generation yourself, but now your own offspring were producing their own children. The future was starting: the bloodline would continue.

'How does it feel to be a grandmother?' asked the midwife gently.

'Great,' laughed Grace, 'you get the baby, but don't have to go through the labour, although I feel so emotional, as if I had been in labour myself.'

Helen groaned. 'Why didn't you warn me it was that bad?'

'There's no point. Once you are expecting, there is no way out. You just have to put up with it. But it's surprising how soon you forget your pain, once you hold your baby. It doesn't stop you having another child, either,' Grace laughed.

'I'll never have another child,' gasped Helen as the afterbirth was being delivered. Grace and the midwife laughed.

'They all say that,' said the midwife, 'but fortunately they don't mean it or I'd be out of work.'

'They should invent a pill that means you don't have to have babies until you want them,' said Helen.

'That'll never be,' said Grace. 'Perhaps if men had babies, then they would try to invent one, but never whilst it's women having babies.'

Several mill engine's hooters were heard outside at six o' clock and soon Jack came dashing in to the bedroom. He picked the little baby up and held her gently in his arms, then tenderly kissed Helen.

'What have you called her?' Jack asked eventually.

'Nothing yet, I was waiting for you. What do you suggest?' asked Helen.

'Can she be called Mary, like we talked about? That's my mother's name, and your Grandma Butler's name, so it's good on both sides.'

'Yes,' replied Helen, 'Mary sounds good. What about Mary Grace?'

'Mary Grace Ashton. Sounds perfect,' said Jack as he cuddled both of them in his arms.

With tears welling up in her eyes, Grace decided that it was time to go.

'Thank you for calling her Mary Grace. I'd better get home now and see to the tea,' said Grace as she left the bedroom.

Back at home; Grace had to tell all the family about their new relative. The little ones wanted to go round straight away, but Grace persuaded them to wait until tomorrow, to give Helen time to rest. Mary was especially pleased about her great grandchild's arrival, not to mention her name.

It felt good that a new life had joined their family and put some of the stresses of the fire behind them all. It was time for celebrations in the family, and besides, there was a dedication service to plan, thought Grace.

Chapter 21

Christmas 1902 was the best she had had for a long time, Grace reflected as they all sat round the table after their meal. All the family was together; all her children, her grandchild, mother, brother and niece. This year was also extra special, as Jane Leaver and her children had joined them for their meal. William had proposed to Jane on her birthday in the middle of December and so it was her first family gathering with the Butlers and Greenwoods. Being both widowed, they didn't intend to wait long before they got married.

Grace was glad that they had got together, as they were both lonely, and caring for their children on their own; all four girls. Samuel teased his Uncle William that he had only proposed to her to get help with Maud, but got a cuff from his father for giving cheek.

They were just about to start on a second round of eating: a light tea of sandwiches and Christmas cake, when there was a hammering on the door. Grace instinctively thought of the last time she had heard hammering, and worried that it was another incident like the fire. She couldn't have been more wrong. James got to the door first.

'What are you doing here?' they heard James ask, then 'Come in, do come in.' The others looked mystified, wondering who could have arrived on such a special day.

It was Will, in his smart red army uniform, but he was not alone. He had a young woman and a baby with him.

'Hiya mum, dad, everyone. May I introduce my wife, Rachel, and our son Henry.' he said proudly. Behind Will stood a tall, elegant, fair young woman, who was smiling broadly, if a little nervously. It was Robert who recovered first.

'Welcome, son, and welcome Rachel, and Henry, for that matter. This is all a surprise. Why didn't you let us know you were coming?' Robert said.

'We wanted it to be a surprise.'

'It's certainly that!' replied Grace. 'You could have let us know you were getting married. What a shock.'

'But I did,' said William, 'didn't you get my letter?'

'Obviously not. Where were you married?' asked Grace.

'At the army barracks chapel in Catterick. I'm in charge of training new recruits now, especially since the Boer War is over. Rachel's dad is my commanding officer, so we wanted to get married at the chapel. I knew you wouldn't be able to come, but I did let you know,' pleaded William.

'Never mind all that,' said Helen, 'let them sit down. And anyway, I want to show them my daughter, you're not the only one to have a baby, Will. This is my daughter Mary Grace. And Jack, my husband.'

'Whoa, Helen, you are married? I never expected that. Good to meet you Jack. I hope she isn't leading you a dog's life. She did us, when we were children.'

'I did not,' said Helen. 'Anyway, how old is your baby?'

'He's two months old,' answered Rachel.

'Oh, he's younger than mine; Mary is four months old now.'

'How long are you staying for?' asked Grace, bringing them some food and hot drinks.

'Just for three days, then I have to get back to barracks.'

'Good, I'll organise some beds for you all,' replied Grace. 'Do you remember Jane Leaver from Briercliffe mill?' Will said that he did, and then he was told about the forthcoming nuptials between Jane and his Uncle William.

'Seems weddings are in the air,' replied Will laughing.

'I'm not getting married, ever,' piped up Samuel, but the family all laughed and said that that was just what Helen had always said.

'I didn't intend getting married either,' said Will, 'soldiers are often better single. But then I met Rachel and I was a lost cause. It could happen to you as well, Samuel, so don't say never. I haven't regretted a minute of being married.'

'And so say all of us,' replied Grace laughing. 'Just think, Robert, two grandchildren now. We're getting quite a brood.'

'How's things at the mill, Uncle William?'

'Doing well, thanks. We've set on more workers and have a full order book. Did your mum tell you about the fire?'

'Yes, I heard about that. Fancy it being Arthur Jones. Mind you, I'm not surprised; he was always an evil man. He got away with far more because everyone was frightened of him. But the mill is back on target now?'

'Never better, and Samuel is coming to the 'Change with me sometimes, to help sell the cloth. In fact, he's better at it than me. He's a right charmer when he gets going. Charms the orders out of the most reluctant businessmen.'

'That's because I can do the sums, that's all,' said Samuel modestly.

'Yes, he's a wonder at sums. Sometimes I let him make the deal before I work the sums out myself at home, and he's always right,' said the proud uncle.

'Never thought I'd be told that Samuel was a charmer,' laughed Will, 'he was always the one that was mucky when we were children, and being told off in school for saying the wrong thing to people. Well, well, what a turn up for the books. And what about the rest of them?'

'I'm working in the mill now. Dad's going to train me as a tackler soon,' said James.

'Well, I will if he stops being such a scamp. He's always teasing the older weavers,' said Robert.

'Don't you want to go into the management side, like Samuel then?' asked Will.

'No chance. I'm going to be like dad. A tackler's life for me. And looking after the horses when I get the chance.'

'And what about Isaac? You're being quiet?' asked Will.

'I'm still at school. I don't really want to go into the mill. I'm going to Burnley Grammar School next year' said Isaac.

'A scholar? That's good. Every family needs a scholar, what do you say, Rachel?' Rachel agreed with him, but Henry was getting restless and she asked if she could feed him. Grace jumped up instantly and took Rachel upstairs to give her some privacy to feed Henry.

'I'm so pleased to meet you all at last,' Rachel said to Grace whilst they were in the bedroom.

'And I'm pleased to meet you. Will's obviously made a good choice of wife in you. I'm proud to welcome you to the family. It's just a pity that you will be living so far away from us, so I'm especially glad that you've come this Christmas, although I'm sorry that we weren't prepared for you. You can have this room tonight. Robert and I will sleep in Helen's old room.'

'Oh no, we couldn't take your room, it's not fair.'

'Nonsense. You'll need a comfortable bed after the long journey that you've had. You're welcome to it while you are here.'

'Thank you. I think Henry's had his fill now; may I go to the privy? Is it outside?'

'No, it's just next-door. When I was a girl, I'd got used to the bathing room at the house where my mother worked and we all lived, so when we moved here, I had one installed. My one little weakness! I'll leave you to go there, and I'll see you back downstairs.' Rachel smiled her thanks and Grace returned to the party. It was a very late party that night, but everyone agreed that it was the best Christmas that they had ever had.

The three days went past too quickly for Grace and Robert, and although glad to get back to their own bedroom, they were very sad to say goodbye to Will and Rachel and especially little Henry. Nobody knew when they would get back again to Lancashire.

The mill was working flat out and the workforce seemed to be happy. Having a union did a lot to engender good working relationships. And the good quality houses were always a bonus, but the happy working environment went a long way towards the harmony that William and Grace had created.

In 1903, Helen gave birth to a little boy called Joseph, and Grace was again delighted to be a grandmother. Shortly after the birth, Helen started working part time at the mill, helping Jane with the children. It was ideal, as she could take her own children to work with her, so Jack was happy about that, but they had to take on another girl to help when Jane found out she was expecting a baby.

The next year passed, and Grace found that she was getting very tired. Mind you, she was working hard at the mill and running the home, although she had now got some help, in the form of a widow called Maggie. Maggie would do the cleaning and make or start the evening meal for them all. And the best part, as far as Grace was concerned, was that Maggie did some ironing for her. There was always a massive pile of washing to get through each week, as well as the subsequent ironing, so Grace was glad of any help on that score.

The tiredness persisted and Robert tried to encourage her to go to the doctor, but Grace was having none of it. I'm just tired, she kept insisting. But one day at work, she actually fainted, so Robert wouldn't take no for an answer. He bundled her off to bed and sent for the doctor.

Grace tried to tell Doctor Phillips that there was nothing wrong with her, and she was probably going through the change, but Doctor Phillips told her that he would make the diagnosis, not her. He prodded and poked her and asked her some questions, and then said that he knew what was wrong with her. His face was grave.

'Tell me, doctor, what is it? Will I live?' Grace asked in fear and trembling.

'Oh I think you'll live, Grace. You're going to have a baby that's all.' Grace sat bolt upright on the bed.

'A baby? I can't be.'

'Why not?'

'Well, I'm too old, I've got grandchildren. And anyway, I'm going through the change; have been for months.'

'Sorry to disappoint you, but you're having a baby, probably next Spring. Some women do get caught on the change.' Grace was stunned, so Doctor Phillips called Robert into the room. After he'd told him the news, Robert was just as stunned too, so Doctor Phillips beat a hasty retreat, to allow them to come to terms with it on their own.

'What will people think at our age,' moaned Grace, 'this is so embarrassing. We're grandparents.'

'Why do you always worry about what people think? They'll just think that we're a normal loving couple. We are married after all; it is legal. And anyway, we won't be the first couple who've had another baby after they've had grandchildren.'

'How will I tell our Helen?'

'Don't tell her yet. Just keep it to yourself for a while. Everyone will guess eventually, anyway.'

'I suppose so. I still can't believe it. I'm too old.'

'No you're not. You're only forty six.'

'But it's eight years since I had one.'

'Well, it's too late now. You're expecting and we'll just have to get on with it. Now come downstairs and I'll make you a cup of tea.'

'That won't cure it,' said Grace grudgingly.

'No, but you'll feel better for it. Come on,' coaxed Robert.

Grace went downstairs felling despondent, but let Robert cosset her. Already she was worrying about how she would manage the mill and a new baby. But Robert told her that she would take it all in her stride, like she always did.

As she got bigger, Grace got the dressmaker to make some cleverly designed jackets that covered her swelling girth, but the workforce soon made comments. And Helen was one of the first. She couldn't believe her eyes at first. Grace just kept a dignified silence about the whole matter, and discouraged any talk about it. She just didn't think about this baby like she had with her others. It wasn't welcome and Grace wasn't going to love it.

After three hard days of labour, Grace was sure that she would never love this baby. In fact, she thought that the baby wouldn't survive anyway. And she wasn't sure that she'd survive either at one stage. I thought it got easier the more you had, she had shouted at the midwife at one stage, and the midwife had agreed that that was usually the case.

But eventually, she managed to push the burden out, and lay exhausted on the bed, not even asking what the baby was.

'You've got a lovely boy, Mrs Greenwood. Look at him,' said the midwife to a disinterested Grace.

Grace glanced carelessly over the squirming bundle of baby and towel, making no attempt to hold him. Eventually, the midwife plonked the baby in Grace's arms, and Grace looked down at this latest unwanted addition to her family.

The little boy looked straight up at Grace, with wide open eyes, and stopped crying, looking at Grace as if he wanted to see who she was. Grace's heart lurched with that special overwhelming love. How could she think that she wouldn't love this baby? It was hers and Robert's flesh and blood. God forgive me for not being ready for this baby, she said quietly in her head. Who knows what blessing he will bring to us?

'We'll call him John,' Grace pronounced to the midwife proudly. The midwife was relieved that Grace seemed to have come round and was happy about the baby, which she hadn't been all through the labour.

'John? That's a nice name. Yes, it suits him.'

Robert was sent for, and was mightily relieved to see Grace suckling the baby, with all the mess disappeared, and he was also happy at the chosen name. Surely, this would be the last of their family, Robert prayed earnestly.

Chapter 22

Grace noticed that Robert was becoming a little secretive after the birth of John. He always seemed to be looking at magazines or books, and talking earnestly with James about things, but would stop when Grace came in the room. Twice, Grace caught him on the telephone, but he stopped speaking until Grace passed through the hall and went upstairs. It was all very strange. Many thoughts went through her head as to what Robert could be up to.

Her worst fears were that he had found another woman. Would her Robert do that to her, she pondered, but knew that he wasn't really the sort. And he seemed to be very thick with James at the moment. It was all very strange.

On the morning of her twenty-fifth wedding anniversary, Grace found out the reason for the secrecy. Robert had been getting more and more excited for the two weeks prior to it, but Grace still couldn't work out why he was acting differently.

'Happy Anniversary, Grace. It's our silver anniversary today, so I've bought you a special present. It's outside the door waiting,' said a happy Robert.

'Outside the door?' asked Grace, 'not an expensive piece of jewellery, then,' laughed Grace, a trifle disappointed. Jethro Tattersall had bought his wife a lovely matching necklace and earrings set for their twenty-fifth wedding anniversary.

'Oh sorry, it's not jewellery, but it's a much better present. Look!' he said proudly dragging her outside. There in front of the house, with many little boys stood ogling it, was a shiny new black motor car. 'What do you think of that? We'll be able to go for rides out in the countryside,' he said like a young boy himself, his face aglow.

'You've bought this for yourself, never mind me,' laughed Grace. 'I wondered what you were up to. I was beginning to think you'd got yourself a lady friend, with all the whisperings and funny telephone calls you were having.'

'Never. You're all I want. I wanted to do something special for our twenty-fifth anniversary.'

'Shush, keep your voice down; don't tell anyone that is why you bought the car. Just say you bought it because you wanted to. That's more the truth anyway. But don't mention how many years we've been married.'

'Why not?' said a perplexed Robert.

'Because Helen was born too soon. She'll be twenty five this Christmas.'

'Why worry about that now? It hasn't altered our love, has it? Has anyone ever commented on it? You worry too much, Grace. Now you've spoiled my surprise. And I can't even tell everyone why I bought such a big present. Honestly, I wish I'd never bothered with it,' said Robert with a grumpy voice, as he walked away.

'I'm sorry, it is a nice present, and I'm sure we'll get lots of fun out of it,' said Grace. 'I just don't like people knowing our business, that's all.' Robert hugged Grace and all was well again, but Robert insisted on taking her for a drive round before she started work. They drove up Briercliffe doing an amazing ten miles an hour on the way back down the hill. Grace hung on to her hat and the side door of the motor car with little short of a panic attack, as she pleaded with Robert to go slower, as it wasn't natural to go so fast.

Robert merely smiled; he was enjoying himself too much. He had been after a motor car ever since James Brown got one.

'Motor cars are the things of the future now. They'll get faster and faster. Why, there's even a man trying to get a motor to fly up in the air, like a bird,' said Robert.

'You won't get me up in the air in a motor; this is bad enough,' shrieked Grace, but Robert just laughed.

When they got back to the mill, James and Samuel were both waiting at the front door.

'Our turn now, dad,' said James, and so Robert had to take then both for a ride before they started work. Whereas Grace had pleaded with him to go slower, the boys pleaded with him to go faster.

'Can I have a go now, dad? You said I could,' reminded James. So next James had a go, and then of course, Samuel wanted a go. By the time they got back to the mill, William was just starting off for the train to go to Manchester.

'Just think, Uncle William, you'll be able to buy one of these to go to Manchester now.'

'Not me,' replied William. 'I'll stick to my horse and cart and the train.'

'You are just an old stick in the mud like mum,' laughed Samuel, 'but I suppose it would take too long to go to Manchester by motor car.'

'Precisely. And think of all the petrol you would have to buy, and would you have enough petrol to get to Manchester? And what if you couldn't find somewhere to buy petrol? No, I'll stick to my own ways, thank you,' replied William.

But the motor car did make a difference to the family, and they started to go out for little trips after work in the summer or on Saturday and Sunday afternoons at weekends.

They sometimes got as far as Blackpool during a holiday, or to the Trough of Bowland, but more frequently, they would go and visit nearby villages, or go up on the hills around Burnley and look out over the valleys. It was a time when the family could be together, away from their busy life.

The years passed quickly for the Greenwoods and Butlers. William continued with his work for the Town Council as well as the mill. He and Jane had just the one child together, a girl called Cynthia. William complained that he was overrun with women, but he loved them all dearly.

Despite his protestations that he would never marry, Samuel eventually got married in 1910 to a young girl from another mill owning family; the Coopers. Young Annie Cooper soon had Samuel smitten, with just one toss of her curly auburn ringlets. Annie was an only one, and her father often tried to poach Samuel to go and work for him, as he had no sons to pass the business on to. But he was having none of it. Samuel continued to be heavily involved with running his own family mill.

Samuel and Annie had three children in quick succession, then seemed to stop, for which Annie was rather grateful, as she had three under three years old, just like Aunty Katie had had.

Will continued in the army as a career soldier. His family had grown to four children. Two girls and two boys. Strangely enough, Helen had the same children as Will, two girls and two boys. Robert and Grace could hardly keep up with their eleven grandchildren, as well as their own children, but enjoyed them all, and complained that they didn't see enough of Will's children.

James stayed as a tackler in the mill and seemed to have a different girl on his mind each week. Grace despaired of him ever settling down, and also worried that he would bring trouble to her door, as he was still a scamp. And he still sneaked off regularly to talk to the horses that were kept in the mill yard for deliveries, just like his Uncle William had done at his age.

Isaac had remained unmarried too, so far. He had continued to show the early promise that Burnley Grammar School predicted for him. A teacher, Mr Jeffrey, took him under his wing and groomed him for university. He had just completed a degree at Trinity College, Cambridge, and come out with a First Class Honours Degree. Not for him a glittering academic career, he just wanted to come back to Burnley and live at home. He was fortunate that he managed to get a teaching post back at Burnley Grammar School, and the whole family were every proud of him: the first member of their family to have a university education.

Thomas had grown tall despite his handicap and although the family didn't want him to go into the mill, he started at the age of fourteen, like his brothers had.

Young John was a loveable boy, who was ruined with being the youngest by a long way. Helen's children often teased him by calling him uncle, even though he was younger than them.

Maud Butler had become a real beauty with the temperament to match. She had married a local solicitor at nineteen and was expecting her first baby. They lived in a large house at the top of Manchester Road.

The mill was continuing to make a good profit, even though there wasn't as much money in weaving sheds anymore; not as much as when Mary Butler had been young. Because the family were happy to live and work in the same space, many of the profits were ploughed back into the business, rather than funding expensive houses, hobbies and holidays, as some of their fellow mill owners did.

The Greenwoods and Butlers lived a fairly simple life, built around their family, the mill and the chapel. Family gatherings were frequent and noisy, as all the children and grandchildren came together on a Sunday afternoon, after chapel. The meal was a joint effort, as daughters and daughters-in-law brought their contributions, so that Grace didn't have to do all the work. Maggie always had the weekend off, as a well deserved rest.

But shadows were gathering in Europe, and things that didn't really concern the people of Burnley, were about to affect them all. The summer of 1914 was an uneasy time in the country, and many didn't believe that the country would go to war.

Inevitably, war was declared and Grace was instantly worried, knowing that Will, as a serving soldier, would be one of the first to go in to battle. Almost as if she had conjured him up, Will arrived home without his family.

'Just a quick visit, mum,' he said, with a smile of reassurance on his face, but Grace saw that the smile didn't reach to his eyes, like it usually did. 'Probably going into battle fairly soon.'

'But I thought you were teaching young soldiers now? Surely, they'll need experienced teachers for all the new recruits that will be coming along?'

'Yes, they will, but there is a shortage of good officers to lead the new recruits. I've been promoted to Captain in the Forty-Second Battalion (East Lancashire) of the Lancashire Fusiliers. It's a great promotion,' said Will with pride.

'Not if you have to go to battle, son. I'll be so worried about you. But I suppose when you are in the regular army, you don't have an option.'

‘No, we don’t. But many of the other men in England will have no option. I think that they’ll ask for volunteers first. It’s not supposed to be a long war.’

‘All war is too long. I shall pray for you constantly.’

‘Thanks mum, I appreciate that. We’ll need all the prayer we can get, but the Kaiser needs stopping.’

Grace and Robert spent as much time with Will as they could, but ensured that he also had time with his brothers and sisters and nieces and nephews. It was a sad morning when he had to go back home before embarking for overseas service. He wasn’t going immediately, but had to train up some other trainers, who could tackle the new recruits.

The subject of war was discussed widely and constantly in the streets and mills of Burnley. It was rumoured that only single men would be conscripted at first, but anyone could volunteer at any time. Grace and Robert fervently hoped that their sons and son-in-law would have to wait a long time before their call up papers came, and prayed that weaving would be classed as a reserved occupation. Surely the government would need mills to carry on weaving cotton and wool to make all the new uniforms and clothing that would be needed for these extra soldiers? Grace reasoned to herself.

As it happened, Grace and William did receive government orders for some of their woven goods, so order books remained full throughout the war. If only that was the entire effect that the war had on the family. For the first time in his life, Grace was glad that Thomas had been born crippled. At least he would never be called up into the army to fight for his country. So at least, she could now see the benefit of his bad leg and limp.

But with sons and son-in-laws in their teens and twenties, Grace knew it was only a matter of time before one of them went. What she didn’t expect was that all of them would go, except Thomas. He tried to enlist, bless him, but was refused.

James was the first to come home in uniform, only weeks after the war had started. He was ecstatic, because he had been put into the Cavalry division due to his knowledge of horses, and he was also going to be in the same battalion as his brother Will, although in a separate section. Grace was just grateful that Samuel and Jack were married and Isaac was a teacher and probably in a reserved occupation. But it didn't stop them.

Isaac and Samuel arrived home together, a few weeks later, to tell Grace that they had also volunteered. Grace tried to remonstrate with them, but to no avail.

It was the same in the mill. Many of the single men and a few of the married ones were volunteering for the army. Grace and William promised to keep their jobs open for when they came back. Some of the wives took over their husband's weaving jobs for the duration of the war, to keep the wage coming in. Jane and Helen were busier than ever as more women weavers were coming to work. In the end they had to get two more helpers in the nursery.

The following month, Helen came round in tears to tell them that Jack had volunteered too.

'What will I do, mum? I can't cope without Jack. I'm so frightened.'

'I know, Helen. It's hard for the women who are left behind. But we can only do our best, and try to keep the family and the mill going whilst they are away. We have to be strong.'

'But what if he dies? I won't be able to live. I'll die too,' wailed Helen.

'Nonsense, of course you won't die. You have your children to think about. They'll need you more than ever now their daddy's going away,' Grace said encouragingly. 'And anyway, me and your dad will help you as much as we can, and I'm sure that Jack's mum and dad will, too.'

'But Jack's their only son, oh how could he do this to us?'

'There'll be a lot of only sons going to war, Helen. Just try and be brave. It'll be no good if you fall apart in front of the children. Now promise me, you won't nag Jack before he goes, and don't let the children see you too upset. If it all gets too much, bring them round here and sit with me,' said Grace as she hugged Helen.

‘Thanks mum, I shouldn’t be whingeing to you; after all, you’ve already got four sons in the war. And what about dad? Will he have to go?’

‘I hope not, I think he’ll be too old. Don’t remind me that I’ve already got four sons there. I try not to think about it, unless I’m praying for them. We’ll just have to help each other through it. We’ll laugh about this when the war finishes next year.’

‘I hope so, most sincerely,’ added Helen, much comforted by her mother’s chat, promise of help, and most importantly, her cup of tea.

Katie’s two boys, Stephen and David both enlisted on the same day much to Katie’s distress. Emily, her eldest child, volunteered to go out with the army nurses to work as a VAD nurse, so all three of her children were in France. It was a worrying time for many mothers and wives left at home.

But the war didn’t finish next year, as a lot of people had predicted. It dragged on, and with it, the fatalities. Every time a child ran in to the mill waving a telegram, the whole workforce stood still, to see who the telegram was for, hoping against hope that it wouldn't be for them. It was a grim existence at home, but nowhere near as grim as for the soldiers in the trenches.

Chapter 23

The war dragged on into 1915. The chapel choir was becoming overbalanced as there were hardly any men left in the congregation, except for young boys and old men. The Young Men's class had disbanded, and the women's Fireside Circle was dedicated to knitting socks and packing bandages, as their part of the war effort.

Every mill in the district had been affected by the war and had their own tales to tell about how many men had been lost. Some streets in the town had several men who were lost in the war: young boys some of them, hardly men at all. Up to now, Grace had lost three of her weavers, and both James Brown and Jethro Tattersall had lost a son.

It had been a very happy day for Grace before the telegram came. They had just received a massive order from the government for fine cotton for bandaging. A letter had arrived from both Samuel and James, who were serving in separate parts of France. And Helen was coming to tea with the children.

It wasn't the usual government telegram, which they were all used to by now, but a normal telegram. At first, Grace couldn't think why she was getting a normal telegram, but then screamed when she read its contents. It was from her daughter–in-law, Rachel. Will had been killed in the Battle of Gallipoli.

Robert, hearing her cry, came to see what the matter was, but she was unable to speak. Robert took the telegram off her and read it. He took hold of her, and took her back to the house, and sat her down on his knee and cuddled her; both of them crying together.

'My firstborn son,' Grace kept crying. 'Where is Gallipoli anyway? Why didn't the army tell me? I'm his mother.'

'Because Rachel is his next of kin now, as his wife,' Robert said gently.

'Yes, but a mother needs to know as well,' groaned Grace.

'That's why Rachel has sent you the telegram herself; she knew you would want to know.'

'And where on earth is Gallipoli? Most of the soldiers are in France. Why did he have to go there?'

'They went to protect the Suez Canal or something like that,' Robert replied.

'I know Will's been in the army all his adult life, but you never think that they are going to get hurt, even so,' said Grace, and Robert nodded. At that point, Helen arrived, as someone had told her what had happened in the mill. Grace, who had begun to calm down, now started crying again, as Robert told Helen that her brother had died.

It was a sad family that gathered round the table that night. Grace insisted that everyone ate something, but nobody had much enthusiasm. All had to come to terms with their loss in their own way and in their own time. It wasn't much comfort to hear that Will had been awarded a Victoria Cross for his heroism on the day he died. He was one of six officers who all died. It became known as 'six VC's before breakfast' amongst the soldiers.

Grace and Robert had suffered greatly when their other two children had died, but somehow this was different. When Florence and Pearl had died, it was because they had contracted a disease which had overpowered them, and there was no treatment available to cure them. But this was a deliberate act to kill a healthy man and father of children, all because of war. It was such a futile death, in Grace's eyes and as previously, she and Robert dealt with their grief in different ways; Grace needing to talk about it, and Robert bottling it up.

Now Grace was glad that Robert had bought the motor car, because when things got too much for him, he would drive up on to Crown Point, high above Burnley, and sit in solitude. It didn't help that there was no grave to go to. No place of healing and final goodbyes.

This time it was a relief for Grace that Helen was an adult and mother and was able to fully understand what Grace was going through, as she was going through it herself. Helen was grieving like her mother, in that she needed to talk about the loss of her brother.

About three weeks after Will's death, Rachel and the children arrived to see the family. It was a bittersweet time for them all, although it was good to see the children, it was poignant to see Rachel in deep mourning and struggling to come to terms with being a widow with four small children.

Grace and Robert offered them a home in Burnley, but Rachel declined.

'That is so kind of you,' she replied, 'I need to go back to my own family. But I promise you that I will bring the children up every year to see you, during the summer, when they are not at school, and when the roads and weather are better. And of course, you can come and visit us anytime that you can. That would be so special.'

Rachel stayed for a few days and then returned to her own family. It helped Grace and the family to come to terms with their loss, as they saw Rachel's quiet dignity and acceptance. Having been born in a soldiering family, she was no stranger to loss and had also lost her brother in the Trenches during this terrible war. No wonder she wanted to go back to her family, thought Grace, if they have lost their own son as well.

The war continued into 1916; the telegrams still kept arriving in Burnley. Because a lot of the young men had enlisted at the same time, they were all in the same Battalion, so sometimes brothers, friends and neighbours all died at the same time.

And so it happened with the Greenwoods. Telegrams about Samuel and Isaac arrived on consecutive days. They had both died in the same battle. Grace and all the family were distraught. Only James was left of her sons at the Front. Surely God wouldn't take her last son? Surely she had given the ultimate sacrifice by having lost three of her sons.

It was only work that kept her going. That, and a visit by James. He had been allowed home on leave, following the death of his brothers. Grace was ecstatic when he arrived home unannounced, and just sauntered into the weaving shed.

Grace smothered him with kisses right there in the weaving shed, much to the workforces' amusement, and James' embarrassment.

'Get off me, mum,' he cried, but he didn't actually push her away, just led her in to his father's office, to get a little more privacy. Even Robert hugged his son, before they went to the house to be able to talk with him.

Robert tried to ask James how things were in the war, but James avoided the question. Grace noticed that his eyes were old and his face was lined. He didn't look like the young man who had gone to war so confidently. All he would say was that once they had learned that he could drive a car, he had been spending most of his time driving, so he was out of the mainstream battle area.

'Thank God for that,' said Grace, 'I'm glad you are not in the Trenches.'

'No, I deliver supplies and equipment, or ferry the top brass around on visits. Sometimes, if they are short staffed, I drive the ambulances. Quite a cushy number really,' he grinned, but the smile didn't quite reach his eyes, so Grace didn't probe further.

Often, of an evening, Robert and James would go out together for a drive. Grace supposed that they talked about the war whilst they were driving, but they never told her of their conversations. During the daytime, James would spend time driving alone, or visiting his old friends: those that were left. The rest of the time, he just slept.

Inevitably, James had to go back to France, but Grace was more relieved now that she knew that he was not in the front line, like his brothers had been.

The mill trips to Blackpool were stopped during the war and Grace and William tried to hold little events in the mill itself to cheer people up. They had quizzes and parties during the year, and made sure that everyone got a decent gift at Christmas. Production was busy trying to meet the demands of the war effort, and Grace and William tried to plough back the profits into benefits for the workforce.

The grandchildren helped life along. They were too young to understand the horrors of war. Samuel's children were used to him being away, and were too young to fully understand the concept of death anyway. Annie had gone back to live with her parents, as it was easier to get help with the children, but she brought them round for tea every Sunday. Helen brought her children too, so it was a lively time for the adults as well as all the cousins.

Helen was looking weary, trying to cope with the children and working as well, but her friendship with Annie helped them both. They would often go out together for picnics with the children on Saturday afternoons.

Grace had told all her friends that James was a lot safer now due to his new duties, so it was an even worse shock when she got a telegram in the middle of 1917 to say that James was 'missing believed killed.'

This was all too much for Grace and she took to her bed, ranting and raving at God for letting her fourth son die. Robert tried to reassure her that he was only missing, and could turn up again, but as the months slipped away, hope was diminished, even in Robert's optimistic eyes.

Eventually, Grace got the Family Bible out and recorded all the four boys' deaths in it. Doing this seemed to have a cathartic effect on her, as she went to chapel again the following Sunday. She had not been able to go to chapel since James died. It was all too much for her. But her chapel friends hadn't deserted her, and had visited regularly, bringing little posies of flowers and cakes or pies that they had baked. The minister had visited too, trying to bring solace to her, but she just felt that God had forsaken her.

After the service that Sunday, Grace felt uplifted for the first time in many years, and determined that she would do all she could to help others who were in the same position as she was. Any time she heard of a family where they had lost their son, she would go round and visit and help them as much as she could. The people of Burnley started to call her the Angel of Mercy, but Grace said that that was what she had to do, to make sense of losing her sons.

At long last, the Armistice was signed. The war was over and parties were held all over the country as great rejoicing broke out. Memorial services were being held all over the country. A special service commemorating all the war dead, especially the Unknown Soldier, was also held and many of the Victoria Cross recipients were present. Rachel was invited along to the service with her parents, and wrote a long moving letter to Grace and Robert describing it all.

Soldiers started to trickle back to the mill, but only twenty-five of the original workforce arrived back. Another man arrived back with both his legs missing, but Grace managed to give him a job in the offices, as he could read and write very well. A special sort of lift was installed so that he could get up to the third floor, but it also came in handy for moving other people and equipment.

Helen's Jack arrived home eventually, but he'd been gassed in the Trenches, and his chest wasn't good. The doctor said that if Jack was careful, he would be all right, and was glad that he wasn't working in the actual weaving shed, as that would have been too much for his chest. Fortunately, his job as an engineer was still open so he resumed his old position, and kept out of the dusty atmosphere as much as possible.

Christmas 1918 came and went, but was a sad time for the Greenwood and Butler family, missing their young men. And then in 1919, the Spanish Flu arrived in Burnley, devastating many of the townspeople. It had started in France, and some soldiers died of the Flu rather than their wounds. But instead of it affecting the usual young and elderly, it hit young healthy individuals of twenty and thirty. It was unprecedented, and killed more people than the war.

The first casualty at the mill however, didn't fit this younger category. Mary Butler was the first one to die of Flu, but eleven other younger people died too. Grace and William and the grandchildren mourned Mary greatly, but knew that she had been having problems with her heart recently, although she had dismissed it as being a lot of fuss. She was just too weak to fight off the Flu when it came. So they buried in the family vault, alongside her grandchildren. It was a sad day for all the family, as yet another member was laid to rest, but at least this time, they had a body to bury, which had not been the case with the boys.

As the days lengthened, Grace decided that they all needed cheering up so she planned a day out for the Easter weekend. She enquired about hiring special motor driven charabancs to take the entire workforce for a day trip to Blackpool. It would be costly, but it was the least she could do for her family and the loyal workforce, after what they had all been through. Suddenly, Grace had something positive to look forward to, after all the gloom.

But other events threw all her careful planning in to disarray.

Chapter 24

Grace, finally worn down by Robert's urging, was looking at the estimates for buying motor driven trucks for the business. Several of their competitors were now using them, instead of their old horses and carts, and were getting deliveries quicker than Greenwood and Butlers who relied on either trains or horses. Sometimes, if the order was a rush job, it could mean the difference between getting the order, and losing it. So it was with a heavy heart, as she loved the old horses, that she worked on the figures.

Suddenly she heard a commotion in the street in front of the mill, and went to look out of the window. It was caused by two motorised wagons being driven to a standstill outside her mill. They pulled to a halt, and a young man jumped out of the first one. Grace's heart contracted, as just for a minute, she thought that he looked like James. But she was doing that all the time now; taking second looks at men who reminded her of her dead sons. The young man was walking into the mill.

Sitting back down at her desk with a sigh, Grace picked up the estimates; trying to assess how much capital they would have to outlay. Suddenly, there was a thundering of footsteps coming up the stairs, and her office door was thrust open, even though she liked people to knock before they came in. It was Robert.

'Come quick. It's James, it's James,' he shrieked.

'James? What do you mean? James who?' Grace replied in bewilderment.

'Our James. He's back from the war. He was hiding and now he's back. Come on,' said Robert pulling Grace by the hand. He decided that he wouldn't tell her the rest of the news until she got downstairs.

Grace needed no further persuasion. With heart pounding, she bounced down the stairs after Robert and ran through the mill to where James was standing. She ran up to him and nearly squeezed the life out of him.

'Steady on mum, I haven't survived the war, to be killed by you with too big a hug,' he said grinning.

'Where have you been? Why didn't you let us know? I just can't believe that you're home, or even that you are alive' Grace said, continuing to squeeze him.

'If you let me breathe, I'll tell you,' gasped James. 'But first, I must introduce you to my wife and daughter. This is Edith, my wife, and Marie, our daughter.' James then spoke in a foreign language to his wife, and she carefully said 'Hello' to Grace and Robert.

'James, was that French you were speaking? How did you learn that? Is Edith French?' asked Grace.

'Which question do you want me to answer first?' said James laughing. 'Look, let us have a cup of tea and we'll tell you the whole saga. We've been on the road for nearly a week.'

Grace took them over to the house, whilst Robert went to the children's area to tell Helen. Once the tea was brewed, they all sat round the kitchen table and James started his amazing story.

'You knew I'd got transferred to a driving job? Well, I was on a delivery, taking hospital supplies to a first aid post that was very near the battlegrounds. I'd been driving for a few hours and was nearly at the depot when I stopped off to relieve myself, and have a walk round to stretch my legs. Whilst I was sat on a wall, I heard voices coming and they sounded to be speaking German. So I shimmied up a tree and hid from them.

'There were four of them. They all stopped when they saw my truck, and started looking round about in the fields and countryside. I can tell you, I thought I'd had it. I was praying like mad. But they never looked upwards, thank God. Then they got in and drove off in my truck, supplies and all. Cheeky things. So anyway, I was left stranded, with nothing on me except the clothes I stood up in and a few francs.'

'What happened then?' asked Grace, the colour still drained from her face.

'I ran, ran like the wind, as far away as I could from the Hun. All the time I was in France I knew that I was your last son out here and was very aware that I had to save myself, whatever happened. I went across country, going through a lot of fields and eventually saw an isolated farmhouse. I sat and watched it for a while, to see if there were any signs of German occupation or not. I waited until nightfall, and then set off in the dark to go and sleep in the barn, whilst I decided what to do. As I set off to go to the barn, I climbed over a wall, it wasn't very high, but I caught my foot, fell over and knocked myself out on a stone.

'When I came round, I was in a bed with an old white nightshirt on. An angel was leaning over and speaking to me. I thought I'd died and gone to Heaven and was dressed in my shroud. It gave me a right shock, I can tell you.'

'Where were you?' asked Helen, who had arrived in the middle of this saga.

'I was in the farmhouse where I'd decided I was going to stay in the barn. The family had burned my uniform and had hidden me up in an attic. Marie had found me the next morning, with a broken leg, drifting in and out of consciousness, and jabbering away in English. They took me in and managed to persuade a doctor to come and set my leg and treat my concussion. They were all very brave. If the Germans had caught them, they would all have been shot.'

'So how did you get away?' asked Robert.

'Well, that was the problem,' replied James. 'They couldn't move me because of my leg, so they couldn't send me back through the usual underground channels. I was stuck there for the duration. The family had found out that the truck I was driving had been bombed, so the authorities assumed that I was dead, not knowing that my lorry had been hi-jacked. Serves the Hun right for pinching my truck. Bet it was their own side that blew them up,' laughed James.

'My leg was very slow to mend and I had to stay there for many months. As I got better, I helped on the farm. And Edith and I got very friendly, and er . . well very friendly, and er . . well, she was expecting a baby,' James said looking sheepish.

'Oh James, how could you?' burst in Grace. 'What a way to treat the family who took you in. I'm ashamed of you.'

'The family weren't too pleased either at first, I can tell you. But then they hit on the idea of us getting married and passing me off as their son-in-law, who had been injured in the war and had been sent funny in the head. That would cover up if the Germans came and were suspicious about my poor French. Mind you, after a few months, my French was pretty good, compared to how it was when I first arrived in France,' he laughed. 'All I could say was oeufs and pomme de terre, y'know, egg and chips. So that was what we did. I stayed at the farmhouse until I knew the war was well and truly over, but by then, the baby was due. The Catholic wedding was a bit awesome, though.

'I went back to find somebody to tell them I was alive, but everyone had gone, so I didn't bother. I thought I'd just wait until after the baby was born and then come home.'

'Why didn't you write?' demanded Grace. 'We've put your name forward for the Burnley War Memorial. I've even put you in the Family Bible, on the deaths page.'

'Well, you'll just have to cross me out again, and put me back in the land of the living,' he laughed. 'I didn't want to just write you a letter; I thought it would be too much of a shock. Besides, I wanted you all to meet Edith and little Marie. Marie is French for Mary, you know. So we called her after my gran. Where is she by the way? I can't wait to show Marie to her, her newest great grandchild.'

The whole family became silent. Helen recovered first. 'We've just lost Gran. She got the Spanish Flu,' Helen said quietly.

'Oh, I'm so sorry. You know, when you are away from all your family, you think about them all the time. I used to think about each one of you by turn. I'm sorry about my gran. Is she in the family vault?'

'Yes,' replied Grace. 'Mam was amazing, she was born on the day that Queen Victoria came to the throne, and lived through all her long reign, and the whole reign of her son, and the beginning of her grandson's reign. Not many people live through three generations of monarchs. And she has been such a blessing to us all. She never stinted on her love or her help.'

'I'll go and visit her tomorrow. I'll take Edith and Marie too, so that she can see them,' said James sadly.

'Good,' replied Grace quietly.

'And where's our Thomas?' asked James.

'He's gone to the 'Change with your Uncle William. He's having to learn all aspects of the business now that Samuel is gone. You'll see him tonight.'

'Good, I'd like that. Poor Edith, so many people to meet,' said James, but giving her a cuddle at the same time. A beautiful smile broke out over Edith's face, and Grace was reassured of this sign of their love for each other, that had transcended language, culture and religion.

'We'll have to sort out a house for you,' said Grace, back in her practical mode. 'We haven't a spare workers' house at the moment.'

'I was hoping we could stay with you, mum.'

'Oh you can for now, but for the long term I meant. I'm sure that you will want your own home, especially Edith. No woman likes to share a kitchen.'

James was silent for a moment. Then he said 'We're not staying permanently, mum. We're just here for a visit, and then we're going back to France. Edith is the only one left out of her family, so they want me to run the farm, as it will be ours eventually.' Now it was the family's turn to be silent.

'But we've only just got you back,' said Grace in a very small voice.

'I know, but what can I do? If I'd have gone back to my unit, I'd probably have been killed, and with the baby on the way, I had to do the honourable thing. They risked their lives for me. The least I can do is go back and run the farm. Both Edith's parents are getting elderly, as she was the youngest of the family. But you'll be able to come and visit me. Why, they've even got flying machines that go to Paris regularly. You could fly over and see me,' he laughed.

'Never,' replied Grace.

'She's only just comfortable in the car,' laughed Robert, 'and I'm having terrible trouble trying to teach her to drive.'

'Mum! You're learning to drive? That's amazing,' said James. 'I taught Edith so that we could both drive over here with the trucks.'

'Yes, where did you get those trucks from?' asked Robert.

'They're old ambulances. They were for sale so I bought three. One for the farm and two for you, so that you can get modernised.'

'That's so ironic,' said Grace. 'I was doing the costings for some sort of mechanised transport when you arrived home.'

'They're pretty solid trucks. You can kit them out how you want them. You can even put rows of seats in for when you go out on your trips from the mill.'

'Perfect. That's what I was planning as well. Now we can go on the trip without hiring as many charabancs.'

The back door opened. 'Mum, what's those trucks doing outside the mill? Have you bought some after all, after all dad's nagging?' asked an excited John, who then stared at the people who were in the room.

'Hello John,' said James. 'I'm back from France. Sorry if it's a shock.' For once John was speechless. 'This is my wife Edith and my baby daughter Marie.'

John nodded shyly to both of them.

'We've bought the trucks as a present for you, for the mill,' explained James.

'Good. I'll take a look under the bonnet at them after my tea,' John said proudly.

'John has left school and is now working in a haulage firm that have got motorised vans, so he is learning to be a mechanic, too,' explained Grace.

'That's brilliant. He can look after the trucks I brought you. Save you some money.'

'Yes, he takes after you and father, does John. Contraptions, contraptions, all the time,' laughed Helen. 'He's got my little boy as mad as him as well. Now my Robert wants to be a mechanic, even though he's not sure what one is.'

There was a lot of hilarity round the table that night as the family filled James in with all that had happened during his long absence. Grace couldn't get over the fact that she had her son back, but also a French grandchild.

They stayed for two weeks, and then said that they would have to be going home again. The neighbours at the farm in France were helping out, but they didn't want to stay away too long.

It was with very mixed feelings that Grace said goodbye to James and his new family. Knowing he was safe was good, but to have him so far away, and not see her grandchild grow up was agony. James promised that he would come and visit every summer and would write regularly from now on.

Robert drove them down to the train station so that they could get to the ferry and make their way back to France. To cheer herself up, Grace crossed out James' name on the deaths page of the Family Bible, giving thanks to God once again that her son had been restored.

Next day, it was back to work as normal for all the family, even though they had worked some of the time whilst James and his family were at home. James' return had been the highlight of the month, with many old friends and neighbours coming round to see him. Even the Burnley Express came and did an article about his escapades. Grace cut it out carefully and put it in the pocket at the back of the Bible, where she kept all her families birth certificates.

It was the perfect ending to an otherwise miserable five years, Grace thought to herself, and gave her hope for the future. The people in the government were saying that the war had been a war to end all wars and Grace was glad of that. She never wanted to go through that experience again, ever.

Chapter 25

As the nineteen twenties dawned, Robert surprised Grace with a present that she didn't expect. When their golden wedding anniversary was looming, Grace reflected back to their silver wedding anniversary, and how cross she had been that Robert had bought them a car. But she was mainly cross that people might remember that she was already expecting when she got married.

This time she didn't bother. Helen was denying she was nearly fifty anyway, and in Grace's opinion, dressed far too young for her age; dressing more like one of the Flappers, with shorter skirts that were hardly decent.

The surprise present from Robert was a gold locket. Grace was most excited; not only that he had thought of buying her something that she had always wanted, but that he'd had it engraved specially with her initial. But he knew that Grace had always admired the locket that Helen had received from Mr Haynes' will.

'Robert, that's beautiful,' she said as she hung it round her neck. 'It's perfect. Just what I wanted.'

'Really?' said Robert, pleased with her reaction.

'Really, I love it. Are there any pictures inside it?'

'No, I didn't know who you would want to put inside so I left it for you to choose.'

'I'd like to have put my baby girls, Florence and Pearl inside, but then that wouldn't be fair to the boys we have lost too, or little Eliza,' said Grace mournfully. 'So many children lost,' she added.

'But so many other children that we still have. Children, and grandchildren. We have been very lucky. Some families lost all their sons and had no one to carry on the name.'

'I suppose so, but I can't put any of my existing children or grandchildren in the locket, as it isn't fair to the others,' replied Grace.

'You could rotate the pictures every month, and give them all a turn,' suggested Robert, laughing.

'No, I know what I'm going to do,' decided Grace. 'I'm going to put you and me in it. That will prevent any arguments. Could we get some small pictures to put in?'

'I suppose so,' replied Robert. 'They can do lots of things nowadays.

'I haven't bought you anything, Robert,' said Grace, suddenly feeling guilty.

'It doesn't matter. I've still got you, after fifty years, you're still the best present I could ever have.'

'Ah, Robert, you are an old softy at times. We've been good together, haven't we? Not fallen out too many times?'

'No, and the making up has always been such fun,' grinned Robert, giving Grace a cuddle and laughing that he was still able to make her blush.

'Quiet Robert, people might hear you. What will they think at our age.'

'They can think what they like; I'm only cuddling my wife. It's legal isn't it?'

'Yes, but not very respectable in public.'

'Good job we're not in public then,' he laughed, squeezing her even more.

'Go on with you, I've got work to do now,' said Grace, but she was secretly pleased with the gift, and went to the mill to show her present to Helen, whom she suspected had something to do with the gift anyway.

Shortly afterwards, it was Grace's birthday. Helen's present to Grace had been a new outfit; several inches shorter than she had ever worn before. Grace was shocked at the new length, but Helen insisted that she would look wonderful in it.

'All the ladies have shortened their skirts now,' pleaded Helen.

'Yes, and some of them look right Jezebels,' retorted Grace.

'Oh mum. Get into the twentieth century. Everybody is wearing shorter skirts now. You look like old Queen Victoria all the time. Look at chapel. Even old Mrs Wilkinson has shortened her skirts. Go and try it on, go on, just for me.'

Grace tried the shorter skirt on, and was quite pleased with how she looked. Helen hadn't gone mad, it was only about four inches shorter, so still was around the mid calf. It came down to the top of her boots, so she wasn't showing any stockinged leg, which would have been too far for Grace.

'Let's see you do a twirl then mum,' encouraged Helen, but Grace just walked up and down the room. Although she didn't admit it, Grace felt much better in the shorter skirt; it gave her more freedom as she walked. Just at that point, Helen's daughter Mary came in.

'Oh Granny, I like your new look. You look lovely. You suit that lovely purple shade. And here's a present from me. I've knitted it all myself.'

Mary handed over a lilac cardigan, which exactly blended with the skirt.

'And here's your present from Aunty Jane and Uncle William,' she added, giving Grace another parcel. It contained a white high-necked blouse, which had small sprigs of lilac flowers on.

'Why do I think that there has been some collusion with all these presents,' she laughed happily. 'I might just go out and get myself a new purple hat for chapel.'

'Oh, I'll come with you,' said Mary quickly. 'I could do with a new hat myself.'

'Especially if Granny is buying it,' Grace said teasingly.

'Would you? That would be so kind of you, Granny,' said Mary with all innocence, until Helen protested.

'Granny has better things to do than go shopping with you, Mary.'

'Why not? It's my birthday, so I'll go shopping if I want to. Come on Mary. Anyone else coming?' said Grace, but they didn't wait for an answer, and set off to the market.

But the first time Grace wore her new clothes outside, she was very conscious that everyone must be staring at her. And when no one did, then she was cross because no one noticed her new clothes. Eventually, she daringly shortened most of her old skirts a little. And she even bought some thinner stockings and got shoes to wear instead of boots: albeit sensible ones.

Helen sighed with relief. It had taken years for her to persuade her mum to become more fashionable. Why hadn't she thought of getting the family to cooperate before for her birthday? Never mind, it was accomplished now. Grace would no longer embarrass them with her old-fashioned clothes.

In 1922, Robert and Grace had serious words about the mill.

'Don't you think it's about time you retired?' asked Robert.

'Retire? Me? Whatever for? I'm only sixty. Why would I retire?'

'Because that's the age you can retire, now there is an old age pension.'

'Are you saying I'm too old to work?'

'No, of course not, but you should think about slowing down a little.'

'Are you going to retire, then?'

'Yes, as soon as I'm sixty-five. I want to be free to do things that I want to do, while I'm still able.'

'What do you mean, still able?' asked Grace.

'Well, I've worked since I was twelve; so I think it's time I had some relaxation. Go out on drives and have proper holidays. We both could if you gave up work too.'

'But I don't want to. I've only worked since 1900. I love the mill. We've managed to keep going as a family firm, both in the management and in the workers as well. We have children of our original weavers working for us now, like a family. And anyway, we had a proper holiday last year. We had two weeks in Blackpool, at the Norbreck Hotel.'

'We always go to Blackpool. I meant somewhere a bit more adventurous.'

'Such as?' asked an astounded Grace. What had got in to Robert? She couldn't understand him.

'I think it's time we went to see our grandchildren that don't live in Burnley for a change.'

'Oh, you mean Will's children? Yes, I suppose we could go and see them, although they always come up to see us once a year.'

'No,' said Robert quietly, 'I want to see James' children too. He's finding it harder and harder to get time to come over here, now Edith's mother has had a stroke. He's lived in France for four years and we've never seen his house. Besides, I'd like to go and see the war cemeteries; see where our boys died.'

Grace was stunned. Robert had hardly talked about the boys since the war; it was just his way of coping, and Grace talked to Helen or Katie or Jane when she needed comfort.

'You want to go to France? But who will run the mill?' asked Grace.

'Who do you think? Your William, Thomas and John. They can manage perfectly without you for a couple of weeks. Especially if we go in July when the mill shuts down. We can motor down to Dover and sail across to Calais, then motor up to the farm. After that, we can go to the cemeteries.'

'You've got this all worked out, haven't you? I'm surprised you don't want to go in one of those awful flying machines as well,' said an exasperated Grace.

'I'd love to, but I know that you wouldn't,' chuckled Robert, who was still fascinated with contraptions.

'Well, I'll think about it,' conceded Grace. 'The ferry and motor car I mean, not the flying machine,' she added quickly. 'If God had intended us to fly, he'd have given us wings,' she added, not for the first time. But Robert gave her no peace and eventually, she gave in and let him book the holiday with Altham's travel agents in town. They were to go in July.

On the first leg of the journey, they stopped off at Rachel's house and met up with their grandchildren. How they'd grown! Henry had followed his father into an army career and was in his old regiment. Rachel was very proud of him. Sarah was engaged to be married and an invitation to the wedding was given to the proud grandparents.

'That'll save us the price of a stamp,' quipped Sarah to her grandmother.

'I hope you can get married when the mill shuts down in July, otherwise we might not be able to come,' commented Grace, but was met by a storm of protest, loudly led by Robert.

'Of course we are coming, try stopping us,' promised Robert, 'whenever the wedding is.'

Young Matthew was still at school and was hoping to go to university eventually to study History, which surprised both Grace and Robert, as nobody in the family liked history particularly, but it seemed that Rachel's father was very keen on military history, so perhaps it came from there. Young Louise was just happy all day long, and loved school and life in general. Little Doris however, was a taciturn child, and rarely strayed from her mother's side, and was quite shy with her grandparents. After two days of catching up, Grace and Robert set off to Dover and sailed to France.

End of July 2012

In the attics one day looking for furniture, Carrie found an old box, which was full of documents. She took them downstairs.

'GreatGramps, what are these documents that I've found? They look like the deeds to houses.'

Jake looked at the contents of the box and looked surprised.

'These are . . .deeds to mill houses.'

'What mill houses?'

'When mill opened . . . had row of houses . . . in front of mill,' Jake gasped.

'Who owned then?'

'Us. Came with mill buildings.'

'Where are they now?'

'Gone. Compulsory purchase.'

'Why?' asked Carrie, 'if they belonged to the mill?'

'Back to back houses.'

'Were they in poor condition?'

'No, but council getting rid . . . of all back-to-back houses,' said Jake slowly.

'When was that?' asked Carrie.

'1950's sometime. Can't remember exactly,' replied Jake.

'Is that when the mill finished?'

'No. Managed to carry on 'til1975. Once 'Change closed down in 1968, hardly any work,' Jake gasped.

'Did it just close down?'

'No. Sold it to big textile firm,' said Jake.

'Did they carry on running it?'

'No, took business. Then sold buildings to council.'

'Did the council want the buildings?'

Jake nodded. 'Redevelopment starting. Round Burnley Centre.'

'So is that when they built the new Sion Chapel?'

'No, 1962. New chapel nearer to home for us,' Jake laughed, but it turned into a cough. Carrie waited until the cough had abated and then got Jake a drink of water.

Jake continued, 'Only got to go across car park now.'

'That's right,' said Carrie, 'the new building is the only chapel I've known. When I was a little girl, I remember calling here after chapel and staying for Sunday lunch sometimes.'

'Yes. When Sheila still here.'

'I'm glad I knew her. She was very special, wasn't she?' Jake nodded his reply, and started to look tearful, so Carrie changed the subject quickly.

'And I remember going to Girl's Brigade and being in the pantomime,' continued Carrie. 'They're still doing the pantomimes, aren't they?' Jake nodded again.

'So why didn't they sell this big house with the others.'

'Granny Grace awkward. Wouldn't sell this.'

'Really? She sounds such a character. But what about after she died?'

'My dad got it.' Jake paused for breath. 'Then I got it. Wouldn't sell. Just as stubborn.'

'You can say that again,' laughed Carrie. 'Well, I can see you take after your grandma Grace. You can be a stubborn old so-and–so yourself sometimes.'

Jake laughed, but then said, 'Takes one to know one.'

'Are you calling me stubborn?' asked an indignant Carrie, but Jake's laugh had turned into another coughing bout, so Carrie waited and supported him until it stopped.

'Why have you still got the deeds, then, for the houses?'

'Don't know.'

'Perhaps they didn't need them if the houses were on Compulsory Purchase.'

'Could be.'

'Or is it that no one in this family ever throws anything away?' asked Carrie with a cheeky grin.

'Probably,' replied Jake, 'now let me rest. Worn out,' he added.

'OK, GreatGramps. I'll go back up the attics and see what else I can find.'

'Good,' said Jake, as he closed his eyes wearily.

Chapter 26

Grace was absolutely petrified when she got on the ferry and Robert had his work cut out, reassuring her and keeping her mind occupied. Eventually, to Grace's relief, they landed safely on dry land in Calais. They were just sorting out getting the motor car off the ferry, when they heard a voice in English.

'Mum, dad, over here.' It was James, waving wildly at them.

'James, we didn't expect you to come and meet us,' said Grace, enveloping him in a big hug.

'I thought it would be easier. Dad might not be too good at driving on the wrong side of the road at first,' he laughed. 'I got a train down, so you can give me a lift back. I see you didn't persuade her to come in an airplane then, dad?'

'You must be joking. It was all I could do to get her to come on the ferry. But sometime, I'll come on my own and fly. Now, do you want to drive or shall I? On second thoughts, I'll let you drive, James. I must admit, it's been quite tiring has this journey.'

'Well, you and mum settle down in the car, and I'll soon have you at the farm,' replied James. He got in the driving seat and speaking to the ferry official in French, set off out of the port. Grace was soon fast asleep, but Robert watched carefully as James drove: knowing that he would have to do the return journey shortly. It seemed all right until they got to roundabouts, and then Robert felt that they were going the wrong way, but he guessed that he'd soon get used to it.

On arrival at the farm, all three of James' children came running out to meet the car, followed by Edith.

'Bonjour, grandmère et grandpère,' said the eldest, Marie.

'Parle en Anglais, Marie,' replied her father.

'Mais oui, er hello grandmother and grandfather,' Marie said in perfect English, but perhaps with a Lancashire accent.

Grace and Robert repeated her greeting, in English, and then said hello to the two younger boys, Francois and Michel, who were only toddlers, but managed to say hello in English.

'How old are you all now?' asked Grace.

'I'm four,' said Marie, 'and Francois and Michel are three. Because they are twins,' she said proudly.

'You are very good at speaking English,' said Robert as Marie pulled a face.

'It is because our father says we have to,' Marie said, and all the adults laughed.

'Come on inside,' said James. 'Come and meet Edith's mum and dad.'

James led them into the house. There was a large hallway, which had doors either side. James took them through to a large room, which had been made into a bed sitting room, with two single beds in. Edith's mother, Sylvie, was laying in bed, the left side of her face completely twisted and her left arm pulled up towards her shoulder.

Grace and Robert said hello, but Sylvie only managed a grunt.

'The stroke took her speech as well,' explained James sadly. 'And here is my father-in-law, Jean-Pierre.' The adults all shook hands and then Edith announced that a cup of tea was ready.

Edith took Grace and Robert into the large farmhouse kitchen and told them haltingly in English what had happened because of the stroke. Now, Edith had to nurse her mother and look after the children, whilst the men did the farm work, although she did have help from the village every day.

After a large meal, Grace and Robert decided that they wanted to go to bed early: tired out after their journey. They could catch up tomorrow they said, as they went upstairs to the guest bedroom.

The next morning, James took Robert round the farm whilst Grace talked to Edith, and helped with the chores and entertained the grandchildren.

Grace admired her daughter-in-law, who selflessly worked hard all day, as did the young girl from the village that came to help her. An older lady also came in and did the cleaning, so that the other two could get on with the nursing and caring for the children.

Robert came back enthusing about the farm and also about some extra buildings that were almost finished.

'James and his father have built some cottages – three of them. They're going to be for any of our family who comes to stay, and when they're empty, then they will rent them out to strangers for extra money. Isn't that great? We'll be able to stay there instead of in the house next time we come, so that there will be less work for Edith,' Robert enthused.

'Yes,' said James with a laugh, 'they're by the wall where I fell over and broke my leg. That was the luckiest accident I ever had,' he grinned, looking at Edith. 'So tell all the family that they can come for their holidays now.'

'We will,' said Robert, but Grace looked less sure.

'I don't think the others will want to come gallivanting across the sea for a holiday,' said Grace.

'Oh? Is that so? Well, why have I just got a letter from Helen and her gang to say they are coming for Christmas?'

'Christmas? They can't!' shouted Grace, 'we always have Christmas at our house together.'

'Sorry mum, not this year. Helen and Jack and the children are coming out for a week. That's if Helen's mean boss will let them have such a long time off at Christmas,' James teased.

'Mean boss? You cheeky scamp. I see you haven't improved living in France. I'm not a mean boss, and never have been,' replied Grace, distinctly ruffled.

'I'm teasing, mum. I didn't mean to tell you like that, not until Helen had got chance to ask you about it, but I was so excited when I got the letter this morning. Why don't you come too?'

'Not this year. I couldn't cope with it again. Perhaps next year. I'll think about coming for Christmas next year, but no promises, mind,' Grace added.

'I won't hold my breath, then,' added James, and Robert nodded his agreement.

During the second week, James took his parents to the war cemeteries. He had already checked the records to see where they were buried. But Grace wasn't prepared for the size of the cemeteries. There were acres and acres of fields, all with white headstones. Row after row after row. The more stones Grace saw, the more tearful she became.

'All these boys. All with mothers or wives or sweethearts or children,' Grace cried.

'Do you not want to go any further?' asked James sensitively, seeing how distressed she was.

'Of course I do. I can't come here and not see my sons' names. It's just the sheer size of the place. Are we nearly there, James?'

'Yes, just about six rows further up.' James led them to the graves where Isaac and Samuel were buried; near to each other in death as they had been in life and in war. Grace broke down all together when she saw their names. Robert maintained a silent stand by her: unable to reach her or console her.

'What about Will?' Grace asked after a while.

'Will's not here,' James said quietly, 'he died in Gallipoli.' Grace nodded and so James took them to the memorial of the men who had fallen in the war in France. After reading their names, suddenly Grace turned and said she'd had enough and wanted to go home.

'Back to the farmhouse?' asked James.

'Yes, no,' she contradicted herself. 'Yes, back to the farmhouse first, but I need to go home: to my home. I want to see my own house and my other children and grandchildren, and hold them to me. The war has changed our family life so much. I want to forget it now and move on. I don't want to come here again.'

'What? Never come to see me again?' asked James.

'I'll come to see you, but I don't want to come to the cemeteries again. It's too painful. Now let's go,' Grace replied, as she walked briskly back out of the cemeteries.

It was a quiet journey home as they were all taken up with their own thoughts. But on return to the farm, Grace started preparations for going home. It was a tearful goodbye but Grace was glad to be getting ready to go home.

By this time, Robert felt more confident about driving on the wrong side of the road, so he drove them back to Calais so that

James didn't have to take another day off from working on the farm.

As soon as Grace was home, she went straight round to Helen's to tell her that she knew about Christmas, and it was all right. Helen looked sheepish about it, but was glad that they could go as the children were looking forward to it already.

The following year, Grace and Robert didn't make it to France as John got married in the July holidays. Grace had noticed that since a certain new young weaver had started at the mill, John had found that he needed to go downstairs into the weaving shed far more than he used to do. Although he was primarily a mechanic, looking after the fleet of motor vans, he had started working in the offices of the mill as well, with his uncle and brother.

Margaret, the object of his attentions, seemed to reciprocate his feelings and after a short period of walking out, they married at Sion Baptist Chapel. Margaret was a tiny girl, in comparison to John's height, and he always seemed to be bending over in a solicitous manner.

As the houses were all full, Grace offered that they could live in the house with her and Robert, but John declined and came up with a good idea. They asked if they could make over the top floor of the mill, which hadn't been used for many years. At one time, they had made it into a dormitory for single male weavers, but nowadays it was rarely used.

William and Grace agreed, and the two lovebirds made a cosy flat on the top floor, moving in right after their wedding and honeymoon in the Lake District. Their joy was complete, when in 1923 Margaret found out that she was expecting a baby. But their joy was short-lived as she miscarried that baby, and the one after it. Eventually, she carried the third baby almost to full term. Grace was excited at the birth of this new grandchild and was busily knitting and sewing little garments for the baby. Her labour started in early July, just as the mill was closing for the holidays. Although she was having strong pains, and had been for nearly two days, the midwife didn't feel that she was making any progress, so sent for the doctor.

The doctor looked grim after he had examined Margaret. He talked quietly to the midwife and Grace could hear bits of the conversation. From it, she gathered that the baby was too big to go through the birth canal. He recommended that she was taken to the hospital, as they might have to operate.

Turning to Grace the doctor confirmed what she had heard, and asked for John to be brought out of the mill. He explained the situation to John, and then he rang for an ambulance cart to take Margaret to the hospital. Only John was allowed to go in the ambulance, so Grace had to stay at home. All she could do was pray for them all.

Several hours later, John returned alone, looking weary and shocked. Grace jumped up when she saw him come in but knew instantly that it was not good news.

'She's gone,' he simply said.

'Who's gone?' asked Grace not comprehending.

'Margaret. They operated but she didn't pull through.'

'Oh John,' said Grace as she enveloped him in her arms. 'I am so sorry. And the baby too?' Grace asked fearfully.

'No, the baby survived, but he's quite shocked, so they're keeping him in for a few days.'

'He? A little boy?'

'Yes, a boy,' John confirmed.

'When can we see him?'

'Not yet; you'll have to wait until he comes home.'

'Have you given him a name yet?'

'Yes, he's to be called Jake, after Margaret's father. He died in the war, you know.'

'How are you going to manage with a small baby on your own?'

'Don't know, mum. I haven't thought that far yet. I'll sort something out.'

A few days later, little Jake was allowed home. He was feeding well, and didn't seem to have got any bad effects from his birth. Grace had organised a wet nurse from one of the weavers, who was always complaining that she had too much milk. Grace offered to pay her the same wage as a weaver to look after Jake as well as her own child. She readily agreed. John was popular amongst the mill workers and they all felt sorry for him.

When Jake was put into Grace's arms she fell instantly in love with him, just like she had with all her own children. It gave her a brilliant idea.

'John, why don't you move back in with me and your dad, so that we can help you care for Jake? It'd make life a lot easier for all of us.' John thought about it for a while, and then agreed.

'For the time being then,' he said, 'until I get sorted.' Grace was ecstatic. It was like having her own baby again, but without the inconvenience of having to carry it and give birth. She felt a very special relationship with little Jake, more than her other grandchildren, as he was always around with her.

It even had the desired effect on her not doing as much in the mill. Where Robert's pleading had failed, Jake was making her take longer periods away from her office, and letting John and Thomas get on with things. John was taking over going on the 'Change from his uncle William, as he too was getting older and was happy to do more of the day to day running of the mill, instead of trailing to Manchester every day. For John, it was a new lease of life as he got used to dealing with this new part of his job, as he met new people on the train each day.

And when Jake was two years old, Grace and Robert got more momentous news. Their first great grandchild, Peter William, was born to Sarah, Will's daughter. It seemed to start an avalanche of great grandchildren, as Helen's Mary Grace had a little boy called Dennis, followed by a boy from Helen's Joseph's wife, called David.

And Samuel's children weren't to be left out as they all produced a great grandchild during the next ten years, starting with Elsie's son, Derek. Grace was in danger of forgetting how many great grandchildren she had, she said laughingly to Katie. But Katie agreed, as she had several of her own now.

'It seems to be all weddings and dedication services, nowadays,' Grace laughed. But these good events in their lives weren't reflected in the nation. Following the austerity of the war years, many of the soldiers had returned home to no jobs, with their health shattered. Unemployment was rising as the economy took a downturn.

The orders at the mill were reduced, but Grace and William managed to keep going and didn't have to reduce their weavers' wages, as was happening in many mills and other industries. Mine owners did however cut wages and eventually this led to the General Strike of 1926. Fortunately, it didn't greatly affect 'GreenButs'. But Grace and William did their bit by making sure that free meals were available in the canteen for anyone who was on strike.

August 2012

Jake sat in his chair, pondering about his life, and the life of his family. He was enjoying writing down the family facts for Carrie, but it was quite tiring. There did seem to have been rather a lot of hurried weddings, or babies born too soon. But it didn't matter. They had all been loved.

His chest was feeling a little better today, after a course of strong antibiotics and high doses of steroids. He'd told the doctor that he had to be in peak condition to give his great granddaughter away later in the month. The doctor had smiled and said she would do her best to keep him as healthy as possible, as long as he carried on taking his oxygen, tablets and resting. Not much option to do anything else, haven't the energy to misbehave, Jake had quipped back, and the doctor had laughed.

Marc had been right. He and Jake had sat and watched a lot of football as the women in both families got wedding fever. Marc had had his instructions from Carrie.

'Just turn up at the Men's Room on Manchester Road. They know what I want you to wear and will sort you out,' Carrie had told him. And being a wise bridegroom-to-be, he did as he was told.

Running in to the room at great speed as usual, Carrie nearly squashed Jake as she leaned to kiss him, before she had put all her parcels down.

'Got enough shopping?' Jake laughed.

'She's nearly bought out the Arndale Centre single-handedly,' said Marc, who was carrying another pile of packages.

'We've been for our wedding rings today. Do you want to see them?' Carrie asked. Jake nodded. Carrie brought out the matching rings that they had chosen the week before which had been altered to the correct finger sizes.

'Didn't have wedding ring. Thought soppy in forties,' said Jake. 'Had signet ring instead,' added Jake, lifting his finger in the air, to show his ring. 'Want Marc to have it when I'm gone.'

'No, that's too kind of you, GreatGramps,' said Marc. 'Surely there is some other member of your family who is more worthy.'

Jake shook his head. 'Want you to have it,' he said pointing at Marc.

'Well, thank you. I'll treasure it always, but I hope I don't get it for a long time,' replied Marc.

'Certainly not 'til after August 18th,' added Carrie laughing, but in truth she was trying to lighten the atmosphere and fight back her own tears.

Sensing the charged atmosphere, Jake asked Carrie how she was getting on with the family tree.

'Oh, it's amazing. There is a pocket at the back of the Bible, which holds all the birth, marriage and death certificates in it, although Grace's wedding certificate seems to be missing. And all the telegrams that told Grace that her sons were dead. That must have been awful, losing most of her sons like that. It was a bit like the film 'Saving Private Ryan', but no one tried to save them, did they? And one of the sons was written in as dead and then it is crossed out with a date in 1919. What was all that about?'

'Reported missing, believed killed. Was on farm in France. Broken leg. Got daughter of farmer pregnant. Turned up four months after war finished. Wife and baby in tow,' Jake gasped, unused to such long conversations, but needing to explain the story.

'Not another one getting married with a baby on the way! What a family. Anyway, I've tired you out now, so we'll go and put my shopping away. Have a sleep and I'll bring you a drink and something to eat later. And thanks again for the promise of your ring to Marc.'

'Have you got something old yet?'

'You mean, something old, something new, something borrowed, something blue?'

Jake nodded.

'I've got ideas but nothing definite yet. I've got a blue garter from Catriona, but that's all. Except for my dress, that's new of course,' Grace laughed.

'Would you like to wear . . . Grace's locket . . . something old?'

'Would I? That would be brilliant. Oh thanks GreatGramps. Is it in your bedroom?'

'In dressing table drawer.' Carrie rushed off upstairs and went into the unused bedroom; Jake preferred to sleep downstairs nowadays, in his recliner chair. Carrie came downstairs wearing the locket.

'Whatd'y'think, GreatGramps? Does it look all right?' Carrie was stroking the locket; very aware of whom it had belonged to. Inside were small pictures of Grace and Robert, now faded with time, but you could still make out whom they were.

Jake simply nodded and looked like he was falling asleep; either that or he wasn't wanting to let his emotions show, so Carrie and Marc left him to it. Within seconds, Jake was fast asleep.

The wedding day soon came round and Carrie was a radiant bride, in her designer dress and veil that she had bought at The Men's Rooms, and her satin shoes with killer heels. Grace's locket looked perfect on Carrie, resting just above the neckline of her dress. With her hair swept up in curls, it seemed to emphasise the locket even more.

Her Great Grandfather proudly gave her away, albeit sitting in his wheelchair. Carrie had trimmed up the wheelchair and oxygen cylinder with tinsel and satin ribbons to match the bridesmaid's dresses; the bridesmaids being of course, Eleanor, Catriona and Amanda. All the mothers and grandmothers cried and said it was the loveliest wedding they had ever been to – like they did at every wedding.

Rosehill House Hotel did them proud for the reception. When they arrived at the venue, Jake told them about his friend who had lived there when it was still a private house. They'd been on the Chamber of Commerce together. And they sang Happy Birthday to Aunty Gillian too. As if she'd let them forget!

Jake slept through most of the reception, but it didn't matter. He'd made it. He'd seen Carrie married and knew there was to be another baby to follow his line and even have his name.

He was a happy man.

Chapter 27

Helen was ecstatic when all women over the age of twenty-one got the vote in 1928. She was first at the polling station, with her daughters and daughters-in-law. Even Grace was happy for them, although as a female property owner, she had had the vote since 1918.

America was affected by the Depression and eventually, by 1931; there were also over three million unemployed in England. Grace and William carried on running the mill, but as they got older, more of the responsibility was taken over by John and Thomas.

In 1935, William was made an Alderman of Burnley, in recognition of his services to the town council. He had already been Town Mayor twice before this. It was a proud day for all of them, as they attended his investiture at the Town Hall in Manchester Road. After this honour, he decided that as he was now seventy, he would retire from the mill, but Grace was adamant that she wasn't going to retire; she'd put too much effort into the mill to let it go, she complained, even though she was seventy-four.

But most days, she just walked through the mill, chatting to the weavers, and checking that everything was running smoothly. And as always, young Jake was trotting behind her, taking in all that was being said. After William retired, Thomas tried his best to get his mother to retire, to no avail, so he gave her simpler jobs within the mill, so that she still felt useful.

Her role was to liase with all the departments and office workers, as well as being responsible for ordering food for the kitchens and supplies for the mill, but the main work of the mill was shared by Thomas, John, and Helen's Joseph.

Grace was getting more and more grumpy and Robert, who had long retired, started spending longer periods in France with James and his family. He was even quite fluent in French nowadays, which Grace had never learned. He always went by airplane too; which Grace would never contemplate.

When King Edward abdicated in 1936, Grace took it as a personal affront and would tell anyone who would listen that the King had no right to give up his position, forcing his poor younger brother on to the throne, even though he did have two nice daughters.

Jake loved being in the mill and wanted to go into the business as soon as he could leave school, so they promised him that when he was fourteen, he could go to Alston's Business College which was in Burnley, to learn the ropes of business practice, whilst continuing his education. He too, seemed to have inherited the family gene for being quick at maths, and John predicted that Jake would take over from him as the Manchester Man, as soon as he was old enough.

But before this could happen, the shadow of war seemed to loom large over Europe. It seemed to throw Grace into a sort of depression. She couldn't bear the thought of her grandchildren and great grandchildren having to go to war. Hadn't she lost enough in the First World War?

Slowly but inexorably, despite lots of negotiations, Britain had to declare war on Germany and for the third time in her long life, Grace was forced to face war. She counted up all the grandsons and great grandsons that would be eligible to go to war and shuddered at the final total. She went through all the potential conscripts in her mind. It wasn't easy for her to recall them all sometimes, especially those who she didn't see very often, like James' and Will's children and grandchildren. And what would happen to them? she reflected. Would France be in the war again? It certainly looked like they would. Grace kept trying to count them in her head, but it was getting harder, and she kept losing count, so she decided to write them all down.

Her first worry was that any of her sons might be involved. Thomas was over forty and still walked with a limp so he should be all right, she mused, but John was only thirty-five. Would he be expected to go? Or would he be in a reserved occupation, like some mill workers were in the last war? James was probably safe as well, although knowing him; he'd probably be involved in some underground work like he had in the last war.

There was Will's oldest, Henry, who was a soldier anyway, so he'd definitely be going. And Will's Matthew. And Helen's Joseph and young Robert, who they called Robby. And Sam's George and Richard. And Maud's Arthur.

Thank goodness Jake was too young to go, thought Grace. She couldn't bear it if he left her home. He was too precious to her now, as he was great company, especially when Robert was off in France. And what about her French grandchildren? Would they have to fight as well? They were too young at present, but if the war dragged on like the last one did, they both might have to fight. Even Jake for that matter. Grace shuddered to herself.

And as if that wasn't bad enough, there were all the people who worked in the mill: many of them who had worked for them for generations, the same people who first worked at GreenButs, bringing their children, then their grandchildren to work, just as she and Robert had done.

And what about chapel? There were so many young men within the chapel, who were all personal friends of her family. All told, there were too many. This is no good she chided herself. My thoughts are too morbid. Getting up slowly because her left hip was giving her a lot of pain, she set off to make a cup of tea, deciding to have a piece of cake to cheer herself up. Not that she should do; her waistline seemed to have disappeared in the last few years and she was looking distinctly plump. But what was the use of having a nice thin body when you have such a face full of lines? she asked herself. No, I'm definitely not the woman I was, Grace thought.

Never mind, Robert still loved her; she consoled herself as she ate a second piece of cake. But if ever Mr Hitler came to Burnley, she'd give him a piece of her mind, that she would, she decided viciously.

But then her thoughts took another turn. What about the girls? Those figures that she had just counted up were without the girls. Some of them would probably go into war work too, she reflected. Some may even be in the forces, as girls were now joining up. Even shy Doris, Will's youngest, was driving the army bigwigs around everywhere. Who'd have thought it? And

Maud's Pearl was a Land Girl, working in Ormskirk. Thoroughly disgruntled, Grace went round the mill to talk to some of the older weavers, but they were all thinking along the same lines. It was a weary business for all of them.

When her grandchildren and great grandchildren came to see her before they went to war, Grace kept a brave face; promising them all that she would pray for them whilst they were away. Matthew followed his brother into the army, and Arthur, Robby and George all joined the army, but Richard had other ideas and joined the RAF. Robert said that it was because his love of flying had been passed down to him, but Grace wasn't amused by that comment.

The first casualty of the war from the mill was Jed Hanson's grandson, closely followed by two boys from chapel. Grace fretted about her own grandchildren and at first, none of them were affected. As each telegram was received at the mill, Grace heaved a sigh of relief that it wasn't for her family, even though she felt sorry for those who were affected.

But in 1941 came news that Matthew had been killed in France, leaving a widow and two small daughters, Jenny and Kathleen. During the First World War, whole towns had joined up together and had been killed together at the same time, so now brothers were often put into different regiments, and sometimes sent to different countries. This happened to Mathew and Henry. Whilst Matthew died in France, Henry was fighting in Africa. Grace bemoaned the fact that her grandchild had died before her. It was not right, she said. The natural order of things was unbalanced. Children and grandchildren should outlive their parents and grandparents. She even prayed to God that He would take her, rather than any more of her family.

But in 1942, Grace got a shock that took her a long time to recover from. On his eighteenth birthday, Jake came home in army uniform. Grace pleaded with him to change his mind, but he wouldn't listen to her, and went out with a smile on his face, to join his unit for basic training.

The following week, a letter came from James, to say that both the boys, Francois and Michel had run away and joined up, even though farming was a reserved occupation.

As if that wasn't bad enough, Grace lost both her best friends that year. Katie had a sudden and severe stroke and was dead within the week, leaving Grace devastated. But then shortly afterwards, Jane, her friend and sister-in-law developed a tumour in her stomach and died within the year. Grace was bereft, and losing both friends contributed to her bad feelings about the war generally.

William was alone again and Grace and Robert suggested that he come and live with them in the big house, but he declined. He said he preferred to go on living in his back-to-back house, and when he was too old to manage on his own; he would go and live with Maud and her family.

The war dragged on and unfortunately, the great grandchildren became old enough to join up. In 1943, Sarah's Peter joined the army and Mary's Dennis joined the RAF, followed by Joseph's Derek in 1944. Unfortunately Sarah's Peter was sent to Burma and ended up in a prisoner of war camp and nothing was heard from him for quite a while.

And then in 1944, within two weeks of each other, both Dennis and Derek were killed in flying raids over Germany. Grace became more and more quiet following this and even Robert couldn't cheer her up. Also, she had started having slight pains in her chest but refused to go to the doctors. Eventually, Helen dragged her to the doctors, who prescribed her some tablets that would slow her heart down. He also told her to give up work, but Grace told him that she couldn't do that, even though she was seventy-three. There was a war on wasn't there? she asked him.

But inevitably, her increasing pain in both hips slowed Grace down and her visits to the mill got less frequent. But she didn't let John and Thomas off the hook. She still reminded them that she was in charge, even though they did all the real work nowadays.

At long last, 1945 and the end of the war came. All the surviving grandsons and great grandsons came home, although Peter didn't arrive home until much later and took several months of hospitalisation to recover. Even then, Grace and Robert thought that he looked like a walking skeleton when he came to visit them, but he assured them that he was much better.

Jake stayed in the army and was seriously considering that he would make it his career, but then he started talking about a girl called Sheila in his letters. Slowly the tone of his letters changed, and Grace and Robert suspected that he would be coming home after all.

Eventually in 1946, Jake wrote that he was bringing Sheila to meet them all. What he had forgotten to tell them was that he and Sheila had already got married in the army chapel at his base.

Grace got her cleaner to scour the house from top to bottom and prepare two rooms for Jake and Sheila, not knowing that they were already married. Grace became very impatient for their arrival, but Robert encouraged her to rest as much as she could.

At long last, the day arrived, and Jake walked into the house with Sheila. She was a pretty, slim girl with long blond hair and Grace could see why Jake had been attracted to her. Jake said that Sheila was an only one and came from London and both her parents had been killed in the blitz. During the war, she had worked in the NAAFI canteen, which was where Jake had met her. With having no ties, Jake was easily able to persuade her to come and live in Burnley, with his family.

'Will you go back and work in the mill?' asked Grace.

'Yes, if you'll have me,' replied Jake. 'I never thought I'd miss the sounds of the clacking looms, but I do.'

'I think your Uncle Thomas and your dad will be glad to have you back,' replied Robert. 'Especially if it stops your Granny going to the mill everyday,' he laughed.

'You don't Granny, do you?' said Jake.

'Not a lot anymore. That stupid doctor says I've got to rest.'

'But she doesn't,' cut in Robert.

'Never mind that, let me get you a cup of tea and something to eat,' said Grace.

'No, let us do it,' replied Sheila. 'Jake can show me round the kitchen.'

'No lass, not on your first visit. I have a young girl who comes in every day and looks after both of us. I'll give her a shout. Susan? Are you there?'

'Yes Mrs Greenwood, what can I get you?'

'We'll have tea now, please,' replied Grace, just like a grand lady.

After they had eaten tea, Grace asked what their plans were about where they would live. Jake looked sheepish.

'Could we live here, Granny? I love this house and I'd like my baby to be born here.'

'Baby? What baby?'

'Sheila is expecting a baby, she's due early next year.'

'What? You can't tell yet,' said Grace a little sharply.

'No, but it's definite. That's why we got married in a rush, I'm afraid. We won't be the first and we won't be the last, I suppose.' Grace pursed her lips and said nothing.

'Well, it will be welcome,' said Robert.

'Thanks,' said Sheila shyly. It was obvious that she didn't feel that Jake had handled the announcement of the baby very well.

'And we have a lovely baby cot that's been used by most of the Greenwood babies for many years. You'll be able to use that, won't they Grace?' Robert said, turning to Grace for confirmation. Grace nodded her agreement. And so the arrangement worked. Jake and Sheila moved in with Grace, Robert and John. Sheila was able to spend time with Grace and tried to encourage her to rest as much as possible, but it was a losing battle.

Jake soon got back in to the workings of the mill, and as John predicted, he soon took up being the Manchester Man in place of Thomas, who was keen to retire.

As Sheila got bigger, so Grace seemed to slow down too, and often had blue tinged lips after exertion, but Robert would get an earful if he said anything, so he learnt to keep quiet, and simply watch.

By the beginning of April, Grace was hardly getting out of bed and beginning to get confused. The doctor was called and said that there was little that he could do. She just seemed to be hanging on, her heart fluttering at an alarming rate.

On the eighth of April, Sheila went into labour. The midwife was called, and even though Grace was weak, she insisted on being kept informed of all that was going on.

Next morning, in the early hours of the ninth of April, Sheila gave birth to a little boy, who they called Martin. Grace demanded that the baby was brought up to see her as soon as possible. Jake held little Martin in his arms, as his granny was too weak to hold the baby herself. Robert watched them both sadly.

'What is it?' Grace said softly, every breath giving her pain, but managing to touch the baby's head.

'It's a little boy. We're going to call him Martin John. He's your twenty-third great grandchild, Granny.'

Grace nodded. 'Nice,' she said and closed her eyes. Jake took the baby back to Sheila, and left Robert sitting by Grace's bedside. She was asleep, but he still held her hand. After Jake had gone, Robert laid his own head on the bed, and closed his eyes for a while.

Some time later, Jake went back up to see his granny. At first, he thought she was asleep, but as he got nearer the bed, he realised that her chest was still and her lips were even darker blue than usual.

'Granny?' he said softly, whilst feeling for a pulse, but there was no reply.

'Grandpa, wake up,' Jake said, gently touching Robert. He looked up slowly and straightaway realised what had happened. Grace had slipped away, while he was sleeping. Robert leaned over, and cradling Grace in his arms, he wept. He was so upset that Jake got worried, that he too was going to collapse.

Jake shouted for his father. As soon as John walked in the room, he realised what had happened, and sat on the side of the bed. John stayed with his mother and father, trying to comfort his father in the best way he could. Jake left them to it, and came downstairs to see Sheila and let her know what had happened.

'As one comes into the world, another goes,' said Sheila softly, 'my own granny always said that.' Jake nodded.

'How was your grandpa?'

'Not good. I thought he was going to collapse. We'll have to keep a close eye on him now. They were so devoted.'

'We will,' said Sheila, 'as soon as I can, I'll be out of my bed and help you all. Aren't you glad that you came home when you did?'

'Yes, it's as if it was meant to be,' said Jake.

'God moves in mysterious ways,' said Sheila quietly, before starting to feed Martin.

The chapel was packed for Grace's funeral; she had been such a favourite with lots of people, and the minister sang her praises. Even James Brown attended, though he was almost ninety now. Robert was silent throughout the service, but shook hands gratefully with all the mourners, asking them back to the mill for some refreshments. The chapel had been half full with all the family, and they were all in attendance, even those from France.

Despite Sheila and Jake's care of Robert, he never recovered from losing Grace, and six months later, he followed her to the grave; the family vault in Haggate. It was the end of an era.

September 2012

Carrie came home from her first day at school and rushed in to tell Jake all about it: Marc being on late shift.

'I'm teaching Year One and they're great. It's a good age to teach. They've got over the shock of starting school and are already becoming readers and writers. They are such characters. You can almost see the adults they are going to become. It sounds so funny being called Mrs Spencer. I keep forgetting they mean me! I was so used to all the children calling me Miss Greenwood when I was on teaching practice.

'And I'm to be the school science coordinator, so I'm teaching Year Six about textiles and telling them about the cotton mills of Lancashire. So my background has come in handy, after all.

'And guess what? I've found a secret compartment in the back of the Family Bible. It just looked like the inside lining of the back cover, but I noticed that it was coming away from the back. I carefully peeled it away and found Grace and Robert's marriage certificate hidden away in the secret pocket. Fancy doing that? She was really screwed up about being pregnant when she got married, wasn't she?

'Wasn't happy when it happened to Sheila and me, either. Hypocrite! Never mentioned it had happened to her too.'

'Happened to you?' screeched Carrie. 'You old rogue. I never knew that.' Jake just grinned.

'And Philip and Lindsay too.'

'You mean my mum and dad? Oh, I know about that,' laughed Carrie. 'At least we can say we are a consistent family. Anyway how are you?'

'Not good. Doctor been today. More antibiotics and steroids again.'

'Have you got them from the chemist?'

'Yes, Marc, before work,' Jake gasped.

'Oh good. I'm glad I've got him trained. Not bad in three weeks,' laughed Carrie. 'Have you taken them?'

'Yes, mother,' teased Jake.

'Well, someone has to watch over you and make you do as you're told. I'll make your tea.'

'Not hungry.'

'No, you never are when you're on antibiotics. Shall I warm up some soup for you?' Jake nodded. Carrie went into the kitchen and prepared him a small bowl of soup, then sat with him whilst he slowly ate it, having to have rests between each mouthful.

They sat in silence for a while, and then Carrie went to the kitchen to prepare her own tea. Marc would have his at work, so she just made a sandwich and had a bag of crisps. She was sound asleep when Marc came in so he left her sleeping, waiting to hear about her first day until the morning. And she was full of it; telling him all the stories that she had told her Great Grandfather. Eventually she went to school, leaving Marc in bed.

On arriving home that night, Carrie skipped into the sitting room and saw that Jake was asleep. She stood watching him for a few seconds, thinking that the sleep would be doing him good. Then she realised that the room was very quiet. No sterterous breathing or painful gasps. Carrie walked slowly over to the chair and noticed that Jake's lips were blue and his chest still. Carrie touched him gently to try and rouse him, but he was cold to the touch. His hands fell apart as she touched him, and there in his hands, was the picture of 'Little Jake'; the scan picture that they had given him. He must have been looking at the picture when he died.

Carrie leaned over and kissed him gently on the forehead, then turned off the oxygen cylinder and removed the mask. He was at peace now, but it didn't stop the tears falling. After a short time, Carrie got her mobile out and rang the doctor. Then she rang her mum; the first of many phone calls.

The following Saturday, they laid Jake to rest in the Greenwood family vault at Haggate Chapel with all the rest of the family who had gone before him. He was the last of Grace's grandchildren. His was the last space; the vault was full: the end of an era. Carrie reverently wrote the date of Jake's death in the Family Bible: a powerful reminder of her amazing heritage.

A meal was held after the funeral at Rosehill House; the same venue where Carrie and Marc had had their wedding reception.

'Didn't expect to be back here again so soon,' said many of the family to each other.

Like an old-fashioned film, the solicitor attended the funeral meal to read the will afterwards. He read all the usual fancy phrases at the beginning and then told the family what they really wanted to know. Jake's money had been shared out between all the remaining family but the house had been left to Carrie. There was also a letter and a package for her, and a ring box with the signet ring in for Marc.

The package contained a notebook. In the notebook, Jake had written all the details of the family as far back as he could remember in great detail. It must have taken him ages to write, Carrie reflected. Now she would know all that had happened to her ancestors. She couldn't wait to read it, but knew she would want to savour it on her own, at home.

Prompted by the family, she then turned her attention to the letter.

My dear Carrie

If you're reading this, I'm no longer here. I hope you approve of what I've done. I know you probably won't want to stay in the house but you will get a good price for it from the shops whose car park the house sits on. They've wanted to buy it for ages! Then you'll be able to buy a more suitable house somewhere, to start your family. I'd decided to leave you the house before you even came to live with me. I've really enjoyed having you living with me in my house. Be happy.

GreatGramps x x

'He said to be happy,' Carrie said to all her family, who didn't seem to care that Jake had left the house to her. 'We will be happy, me and Marc and little Jake. Carrying on the family. Weaving it through with love. Grace started this family, and it's

continued through the years down to me, and then my baby. Separated by centuries, but held together by love, and the legacy of weaving, not to mention the Family Bible.'

And just to remind them all that he was there, Little Jake fluttered round in his mum's tummy, leaving her holding her hands over her little bump protectively.

'As long as I don't have as many children as Great Great Great Grandma Grace did, we'll be all right,' Carrie said, causing great laughter amongst all the family. It was what you needed after a funeral.

A donation from the sale of this book will be given to Derian House Children's Hospice and Ribble Valley/White Rose Ladies Club, who raise money for children's cancer research in the north of England.

Praise for other books by Linda Sawley

Everyone Else's Children

'I just wanted you to know how much I enjoyed reading your book. It was compulsive reading. There were parts that had me laughing out loud like a mad woman! And others that brought a lump to my throat. It was truly an enjoyable read. Looking forward to the next one!!!'
Mel.

A Ring in Time

'Absolutely brilliant! When I got to page 49, I read it straight through at one go.'
Marian

The Key

'Blissfully romantic, a tragic and uplifting adventure of a girl in a man's world'
Santa Montefiore

Changes

'Changes is an addictive read. I have just finished the story which has taken me through the highs and lows of life, love, emotion and business. Although set in a time when society was organised differently, and being a woman in a predominantly man's world was a difficult, if not oppressive situation, there are similarities with modern day life of being mother, partner, wage earner and women. This was an easy flowing story and I look forward to passing copies to my family members in their Christmas stockings.' *Sandra*

The Survivor

'You've excelled yourself this time, Linda. Excellent!'
Eddie

Anna

'Linda Sawley never disappoints and her latest novel – Anna - is one of those novels that you cannot put down. The characters are strong, believable and fascinating and their story moves at a non-stop pace.'

Richard Bell - Writers News

Joshua and the Horrible History Project

'A bold and exciting plot. I am your number one fan.'

Gretchen

About the author

Linda Sawley is a retired senior lecturer in children's nursing, having worked with children for all her career. After having to re-write a 40,000-word dissertation for a Master of Philosophy degree, Linda decided to try non-academic writing. She set up her own publishing company in 1998. A committed Christian, Linda is a member of the Association of Christian Writers and an Associate member of NAWG (National Association of Writer's Groups.) Linda loves knitting, classical music, reading, talking, singing, eating out and buying shoes – not necessarily in that order! She is also learning to play the flute – much to her husband Jim's chagrin!

www.linricpublishing.com